Skipper's Revenge

Skipper's Revenge

Julie Teahan

iUniverse, Inc.
New York Lincoln Shanghai

Skipper's Revenge

Copyright © 2006, 2007 by Julie Teahan

All rights reserved. No part of this book may be used or reproduced by any means, graphic, electronic, or mechanical, including photocopying, recording, taping or by any information storage retrieval system without the written permission of the publisher except in the case of brief quotations embodied in critical articles and reviews.

iUniverse books may be ordered through booksellers or by contacting:

iUniverse
2021 Pine Lake Road, Suite 100
Lincoln, NE 68512
www.iuniverse.com
1-800-Authors (1-800-288-4677)

This is a work of fiction. All of the characters, names, incidents, organizations, and dialogue in this novel are either the products of the author's imagination or are used fictitiously.

Cover design by Katie Roland

ISBN: 978-0-595-36937-9 (pbk)
ISBN: 978-0-595-81347-6 (ebk)

Printed in the United States of America

For my father, John Michael Teahan, who always believed.

Acknowledgments

Many thanks to my team of editors: my brother, John; my sister, Mimi; Rebecca, and the Hermanator, proofreader extraordinaire. To my friend, Kate, your humor and support have been a true blessing. Special thanks to my husband, A.J., who is my best friend and biggest fan. And of course to my mother, for her love and encouragement.

Prologue

My quest to become the perfect girl began when I was nine years old. My father, John Sheehan, PhD, had been granted a sabbatical to document the history and legends of New England seaboard towns. This opportunity and modest stipend transported our family of five to Martha's Vineyard for the summer. The breezy ocean climate, rows of boutique shops, and preppy passersby were a drastic change for my brother, sister, and me, since our typical dog days were spent swinging from tree vines near our creek-side home in West Virginia.

On our second day in the Bay State's picturesque cottage town, we stopped at Larsen's Market to pick up some groceries. I was curiously peering into the lobster tank when I noticed, out of the corner of my eye, a girl pointing at me. She was about my age and dressed in a bright white terrycloth Izod ensemble. I was wearing my brother Wally's hand-me-downs: Evel Knievel pants stylishly coupled with a Mean Joe Greene Steelers tee. A college professor's salary did not provide the luxury of a new, trendy wardrobe each season. Make that *any* season. As the youngest of three, I wore the most hand-me-downs out of all of us.

An hour later, I saw the girl again when we stopped for ice cream. She muttered something to the woman standing behind her, who was busy perusing the list of flavors at the counter. Her mother covered the girl's finger, pushed her arm down to her side, and whispered, "Taylor, it's rude to stare. Leave the boy alone; he's obviously poor." I looked at my reflection in the glass case enclosing the tubs of ice cream. I could not deny that my hair was just a shade longer than my brother's (after all, we shared the same stylist—Mrs. Weitzman, our seventy-year-old neighbor). As for my clothes ... well, they *were* my brother's.

My mother, Mags, suddenly appeared in front of the woman and ordered two cones: one for my sister and one for my brother who she directed, "was to share with Paige."

"But I want a cone," I pleaded to deaf ears. Intent on maximizing my father's stipend, my mother then changed the order to two sherbet cones, because the 2-for-1 Sherbet Special sign had suddenly come to her attention.

Behind me, I heard Izod say to her mother, "I'm glad we're not poor."

While Wally and I were sharing our sherbet outside, Izod's mother appeared in front of me, holding a large dipped chocolate cone. She directed her comment to my mother, who was reviewing the receipt: "They gave me an extra by mistake, and I thought your little man here might want it." Mrs. Izod thrust the cone into my hand. My mother didn't even bother to correct the woman's erroneous assumption regarding my gender.

"Oh, that's very kind," my mother exclaimed. "Thank you."

Little Miss Izod joined her mother and, I assume, thought our poverty had never afforded me such a special treat before.

"It's ice cream," she informed me slowly.

They watched me, apparently waiting for a celebratory dance of joy upon receiving this charitable gift. My mother nodded to me. "What do you say, Paige?"

"Thank you," I muttered.

My courtesy appeared to satisfy them, although I believe they were expecting more of a response. The Izods then crossed Main Street. Before they were out of earshot, I yelled after them, "I have a pink canopy bed at home!"

This declaration wasn't even true. I slept on what had been one half of a set of bunk beds that my father had separated with a saw. The Izods both turned to look in the direction of my rambling then quickly returned to their stroll. I plopped down on the bench beside my mother, causing a crack in the hard, chocolate coating of the ice cream.

"She thought I was a boy," I said discouraged. "I don't want this." I promptly offered the ice cream to my brother, who happily traded his sherbet.

My father sat across from me. "Martha's Vineyard has seventy-five thousand residents during the summer, but only ten thousand in winter," he said, taking a bite of ice cream from my mother's cone.

Ignoring my father's statistic, my mother replied to my complaint, "Oh, don't be silly. She was wearing dark sunglasses."

It was possible that Mother Izod's Foster Grant sunglasses had interfered with her ability to distinguish a girl from a boy, but as I wiped the orange sherbet dripping down Mean Joe Greene's forehead, I knew it wasn't likely. I didn't mind the comments about my apparent poverty, but having my gender questioned really set me off. True, I wasn't necessarily into frills and lace. I had only worn dresses and Goody barrettes for school pictures, and I preferred climbing trees to playing dress-up. I had spent many years being a tomboy. However, these preferences did not negate the fact that I was definitely and undeniably a girl—and happy to be one.

That day outside Larsen's, I vowed to overhaul my image and embrace my femininity. I would grow out my pageboy haircut, pierce my ears, and—most importantly—explore the world of the girliest girl ever created. I would learn what having XX chromosomes was all about from the ideal woman: Barbie.

Upon returning home to Fairville, West Virginia, I requested a Barbie doll. Mags simply replied, "No." When I pressed her, she responded, "If you want to play with a doll, play with a baby doll." She thought Barbies were too bodacious for little girls. She wasn't a hard core feminist; she merely thought it obscene for a young girl to play with a doll whose breasts made up fifty percent of her body mass. My older sister, Vicki, advised me, "Don't bother. She won't get you one. I've tried."

I explained to my mother that girls my age were too old for baby dolls. I needed a doll that I could dress up and style. This prompted my mother's suggestion of Mr. Potato Head.

"He even has a monocle," she pointed out, "All those disguises … he can completely change his look. What fun! I don't know why you would want a Barbie."

I despised this common practice of my mother. When Mags wanted me to select something different, she would become overly enthusiastic about the item. Her objective was so transparent.

"Broccoli is so good, isn't it? I just love it. It's like eating little trees!"

My luck changed the first week of school, when I befriended the new girl, Marcy Roberts. She was wearing a yellow dress with a white butterfly collar, and knee socks with ruffles around the top. She had cornflower blue eyes and white-blond hair tied up in two pigtails, each punctuated with a pink bow. Mags had bought me a new corduroy jumper for school, and even though it featured spiffy ladybug buttons, it paled in comparison to Marcy's attire. I knew with certainty that this was the type of girl who owned a Barbie.

My prediction was confirmed during lunch, when she extracted her toasted PB&J sandwich from a pink, metal lunch box featuring the bejeweled head of my new inspiration. We quickly became friends. Truthfully, proximity was the foundation of our relationship. She had moved into a house just two blocks away from me, on Harrison Street—and, of course, she knew no one else. Because she was an only child, her parents seemed happy to host an additional child at their home, and Mags was equally happy to have one less child at hers.

More importantly, Marcy had Barbies galore. Unbeknownst to my mother, I was not having tea parties at Marcy's, as I had implied. I had gone underground for my Barbie fixes.

Technically I should say that I was aboveground. Marcy's garage was detached from her house, and on top of it was a finished room. It was like having a luxury tree house, since the rules of the main house did not apply. Furniture was expendable, the noise restrictions were lifted, and cleaning up after a day's play was not required. Beanbag chairs in vibrant colors were in every corner, and in the middle of the room sat a giant blue velvet recliner for two. Most importantly, though: lining every inch of the walls was Barbie paraphernalia—Dream Houses, cars, clothes, furniture, shoes, lunch boxes, hair accessories. It was as if Mattel had exploded right in the middle of Marcy's playroom.

For the next three years, Marcy and I were inseparable. Almost every day of our summers, we would meet at the halfway point between our houses and return to the room above the garage to play. Marcy owned every Barbie one could imagine: Malibu Barbie, Nurse Barbie, Glamour Barbie, Roller Skating Barbie, Tennis Barbie, and the crème de la crème, Disco Barbie. In the seventies, there was no upwardly mobile Barbie—or, God forbid, a proportionately correct one. The only jobs Marcy's Barbies had were looking beautiful and trying to decide whether to wear the electric blue hot pants or the sequined evening gown to go driving.

Despite an excess of Barbie dolls, Marcy had a rule that no two could be played with at the same time. This meant that I, as her guest, had to be one of two supporting characters: Barbie's adoring companion Ken or her little sister, Skipper. Since the family's Scottish Terrier had chewed Ken's right leg to an indistinguishable mess, there was really only one choice. Over three summers, I played Skipper, except for a few days one July when Marcy suddenly became fixated on Cowgirl Barbie. During that time, I assumed the role of Montana, the horse.

Mattel introduced Skipper in the mid-sixties as Barbie's kid sister. She was cute, but in comparison with Barbie … well, there was no comparison. It was obvious which girl Ken would select to take a spin in his dream car or saddle up for a horseback ride. Back when I played her, Skipper was supposed to be about fourteen years old, and her slightly concave chest and lack of curves indicated that she was a late bloomer. Her clothes left a lot to be desired; while Barbie's clothes looked as if Bob Mackie was her personal designer, Skipper's wardrobe appeared as if she had won a shopping spree at Goodwill. Marcy did not put much of her allowance toward Skipper's wardrobe. In fact, Skipper had only two choices: daywear that consisted of gaucho pants and a flowered T-shirt, and an evening ensemble that consisted of a yellow cotton nightgown with an airbrushed image of the moon wearing a nightcap.

By the second summer, I had stopped asking if I could play Barbie. I resigned myself to my continuing role as Skipper and truly embraced the identity. Barbie was the center of the Mattelian universe; the lesser characters orbited around her like second-rate moons. Her life revolved around her possessions, stunning good looks, and fashionable attire. Skipper had no empire and was forced to distinguish herself in other ways. And unlike Barbie, Skipper was often faced with challenges. In the years between 1980 and 1983 Barbie experienced only one bad day. Marcy used a curling iron on Fitness Barbie's synthetic hair, matting it together and burning a huge hole in her plastic head. It was a dark day, but Fitness Barbie was quickly replaced with one that boasted "more accessories, including two neon-colored leotards."

Skipper's life was one bad day after the next. Because she had no furnishings or incidentals, she became very resourceful and would retrofit, rehab, and ultimately, create a stockpile of accoutrements. Skipper drove a Tonka truck stolen from my brother Wally's collection. Her wardrobe was supplemented by my father's blue cotton wristband, which could be worn as a skirt, but also doubled as a tube dress when secured by masking tape. In addition, Skipper sported some ill-fitting hats from my discarded Strawberry Shortcake dolls.

One day I offered to make a pair of paperclip earrings for Parisian Barbie, similar to a pair that I had fashioned for Skipper. Marcy quickly refused my offer, stating, "She has her own earrings."

"But these are kind of fun and silly."

Marcy replied simply, "Barbie doesn't want to be silly."

Skipper and I, however, continued to live outside the box. When a raft for the pool was needed, a rubber coaster that I had found beside the velvet recliner was used. Shortly thereafter, I discovered a similar plastic circle in the top drawer of my mother's dresser, along with some KY jelly and an instruction booklet titled *How to Use Your Diaphragm*. We had learned about the diaphragm earlier in my fifth-grade year during a Science Corner report on what caused hiccups. I could not understand why Mags needed instructions on how to use her diaphragm. The report claimed it was an involuntary muscle that could not be controlled. I assumed my mother had a secret hiccup condition and wondered why the rubber coaster was hidden beneath all her silky nightclothes.

Two weeks before the start of fifth grade, Marcy and I took Barbie and Skipper to her backyard, where Mr. Roberts filled up a small, inflatable swimming pool. Marcy dressed Barbie in a striking pink and green dotted bikini. Skipper wore a bathing suit I had crafted from some medical gauze. Barbie was sunning herself on her Barbie raft, and Skipper was trying her best to soak up the rays while staying afloat on the SS *Diaphragm*, until Mr. Roberts saw it and took it away. Before we were called in for dinner, without any solicitation, Marcy said, "Maybe for a change, I'll be Skipper, and you can be Barbie tomorrow." I was stunned, shocked, thrilled, and anxious.

I relished staying over for dinner at Marcy's, since they often served tater tots and Swanson TV dinners. As I peeled off the tinfoil from my Salisbury steak, Mrs. Roberts inquired about Barbie's activities that day. I eagerly recounted our day poolside.

"But Skipper didn't have a raft," I volunteered, "so she had to use the rubber coaster. But it doesn't float too well."

Mr. Roberts looked up at me from his dinner, then at his wife. She didn't seem to notice his concern.

"Oh, well, I hope Skipper didn't get too wet," Mrs. Roberts replied. "Sounds like we're going to have to buy another raft for Skipper." Mrs. Roberts poked at her apple-crumb dessert and smiled at me.

"It's OK. The rubber coaster works fine for Skipper," Marcy said. "But Daddy took it away, 'cause he said it was dirty."

Concerned that her mother would think we took something that we weren't supposed to, Marcy added, "Paige found it on the floor by the blue recliner, and it was kind of slimy."

Mrs. Roberts looked puzzled, until I cleared things up by saying, "I have a clean one at home. My mom's got one in her underwear drawer for her diaphragm muscle."

Mrs. Roberts put her fork down and dropped her head in her hands. A look of complete disgust crossed her face. She pushed herself away from the table, cried, "Cheating bastard!" and stormed out of the kitchen.

She reappeared moments later, looking crazed and waving yet another rubber coaster in our faces.

"Marcy, is this what you found in the playroom?" she questioned. Marcy looked at me. We didn't know what was happening, but we knew it wasn't good.

"Is this what you found?" Mrs. Roberts demanded. "Apparently, Daddy uses your playroom too," she cried. Figuring the cat had Marcy's tongue, I answered, "No, no, that's not it. The one we found was pink."

A sobbing Mrs. Roberts ushered me out of the house and onto my banana-seat bike. I was never invited back to Marcy's to play. I never got my chance to be Barbie. My fate as a Skipper was forever sealed.

CHAPTER 1

Mattel's Barbie has never been a bridesmaid. This fact swirled in my head as I taped posters advertising the Washington D.C. Bridesmaid Ball between the elevators on each floor of the office. The poster featured the silhouette of a woman holding a rather ill-shaped dress in front of her on its hanger. The tagline read, "And you never thought you'd wear it again." The Bridesmaid Ball urged women to dig to the depths of their closets to extract their one or many once-worn bridesmaid dresses. For the price of the $150 ticket, you could, as the tagline predicted, defy the notion that there would never be another occasion to wear the turquoise taffeta gown from cousin Edie's 1993 wedding.

According to statistics, 2.5 Barbie dolls are purchased every second worldwide, resulting in two billion dollars in sales annually. For over thirty years, little girls and big girls alike have viewed her as the ideal woman. Perhaps the reason much of the world sees her as ideal is the fact that she has never been a bridesmaid—never forced to wear an overpriced puffy-sleeved satin creation, never made to eat phallus-shaped confections at the bachelorette party, and never paired with a groomsman who could have been mistaken as the ring bearer. After all, never having to do these things would be ... ideal.

However, I knew the world's obsession with Barbie went beyond her never-a-bridesmaid status. I had studied her and the women she represented since my childhood, realizing I was not one of them. Over the years, I had developed a theory that most women could be slotted into one of two categories: Barbie or Skipper. There were distinct differences between the two. "Barbies" come readily stocked with beauty and accessories galore. They, like their namesake, appear to drift through life unaware and unconcerned with anything outside of their Mattelian universe.

"Skippers" are the younger sisters, impatient to grow up from their awkward adolescence and fill the high-heeled shoes of their glamorous sibling. Their identities are not well-defined, and as such, they are eternally stuck in the process of becoming.

It is kind of like being born into significant wealth. Technically, you never have to learn to do anything or to be anyone. Being rich becomes your primary and sometimes sole identity. This one trait can be maximized and manipulated. People will react time and time again to it, reinforcing the adage, "money talks."

Being a Barbie is similar. You don't necessarily need to be anything more. There are exceptions to this theory, but my observations had shown this to be more the rule than the exception. Skippers are neither rich nor beautiful, and thus were destined to form their own identities—and of course serve as bridesmaids in a fair share of weddings. I, for example, had eight bridesmaid credits, including two as maid of honor. It was crystal clear to which category I belonged.

All proceeds of the Bridesmaid Ball went to whatever charity the annual committee had chosen to sponsor that year. The committee, made up of socialites and local business leaders had been accused in the *Washington Post* of being "trendy" with their annual sponsorship. The newspaper cited several cases to illustrate that point, including the year a portion of the proceeds were donated to cover the cost of a hip replacement for ZoZo, the German Shepherd. ZoZo had been the primary search-and-rescue dog used at the Pentagon after the 9/11 attack. Afterward he became a bit of a celebrity. When news hit that ZoZo was scheduled to be euthanized, because his owner could not afford the $17,000 operation, the Bridesmaid Ball committee came to his rescue. The *Post* wrote a story headlined "Search and Rescue Dog Saved by Satin." A firestorm of criticism followed. In response to the bad publicity, this year's committee selected a tried-and-true cause: the environment, specifically the donation of two hundred trees for Arbor Day. Naturally, my firm, Houston, Haffner, and O'Donnell—or, as many called it, H2O—was asked to be one of the corporate sponsors.

With over five hundred attorneys and two hundred paralegals, H2O was the largest environmental-law firm in the country, if not the world. Many historic environmental bills had been developed and approved through the assistance of H2O. Its biggest success to date was the emissions bill mandating the testing of car emissions in forty-seven states.

Although H2O was an environmental law firm, its employees were a far cry from the earthy, crunchy types one expected to work there. Most preferred

Brooks Brothers to Birkenstocks, and I personally was appalled that they did not recycle.

Had Mattel allowed Skipper to be more than Barbie's little sister and given her a career, she would have been well-suited for my job at H2O. As their employee relations specialist, I worked behind the scenes—advising and counseling employees, resolving conflicts, and reinforcing corporate policies such as diversity and Equal Opportunity. It wasn't always easy, but I enjoyed my work. While the Barbies of this world were all about material comfort, the Skippers liked to cushion people's emotions. Quite frankly, we enjoyed making things better. And in making them better, we found great satisfaction and realized our roles in the angst-ridden world.

Mr. Houston, the founding partner of the firm, had asked that I be the community service liaison for the firm, managing anything and everything related to charity work. Hence I was volunteered to coordinate H2O activities for the Bridesmaid Ball. I didn't mind the task since the costly ticket price had dissuaded me from attending the ball in the years past. In appreciation of all my service coordination time, Mr. Houston instructed me to expense the cost of my ticket.

I was taping up the last two copies of the posters when Owen Holden stepped off the twelfth-floor elevator. I ignored him and focused my attention on smoothing the edge of a piece of tape that had rumpled.

"Bridesmaid Ball," he said, reading from the sheet as he peered over my shoulder.

"Wow. You *can* read," I replied sarcastically.

He scoffed, "Are the partners going?"

"I think they have to. We're the corporate sponsor this year," I responded without turning around.

"Need some help with that tape?" he inquired in a condescending tone.

I turned on my heels. "No, thanks. I got it."

He returned to reading the poster. "Saturday, the nineteenth. RSVP to Paige Sheehan."

"Again with the reading. Impressive."

"Consider this my RSVP," he replied.

"Will you be bringing a guest?" I asked.

"Will you?" he responded.

"Not that it's your business, but yes, I'm bringing my boyfriend."

"Great. I look forward to meeting him." He walked toward the glass doors that led to the twelfth-floor offices. I called after him. "I need to know if you're bringing a guest or not, because I'm in charge of tables."

He swung the glass door open gallantly and hung from the handle, reminiscent of Gene Kelly swinging from the lamppost in *Singing in the Rain*. "Yes, I'll bring a guest."

Owen was the firm's poster boy. Women loved him because he was charming and beautiful, and men loved him because he was charming and beautiful. He had been the star quarterback at UCLA and had played professionally for his native team, the Cowboys, for three winning seasons; until he was sacked so hard his helmet came flying off. He sustained a concussion and fractured his collarbone, nose, and tailbone. This blow occurred just as he threw an eighty-seven-yard touchdown pass that won the NFC Championship. For ten painstaking minutes, the world watched as doctors and paramedics rushed to the field. Owen Holden lay there, motionless. The Dallas fans refrained from celebration and sat in silence. The medics carefully moved his limp body to a stretcher, and the wide receiver that scored the touchdown placed the football on the side of the cart as paramedics strapped him down. The stadium was deathly silent. Then, suddenly, Owen Holden's right arm raised the ball into the air. He kept it raised as they wheeled him off the field. The stadium roared. The image was plastered on every newspaper, sports magazine, and news program in the country.

Outside his hospital room, women held signs that read, O- Yes and Give Me the Big O. At the press conference after his release from the hospital, Golden Holden announced that he would not return to football because of his injuries, and that he planned to enter the field of law, following in his father's footsteps. For the next two years, his image was everywhere. He had done both television and print ads for a variety of products and secured a deal with Ziploc. Every time I turned on the television, Owen Holden was there saying, "I'm not a big fan of the sack, but that all changed when I found Ziploc's snack sack."

He had graduated from Stanford Law School and worked at the H2O office in San Francisco before transferring to D.C. It had been five years since his celebrity had peaked, but people at the firm still treated him as if he were some type of superhero. I knew better. My contact with Owen overall had been limited to three experiences. First, I had conducted his employee orientation, during which he rudely snickered throughout. Second, he had been selected by one of the partners to submit questions for a workplace satisfaction survey I was developing, and one of them was, "Do you like green eggs and ham?" I had skimmed the questions before submitting them to Mr. Houston, but had failed to strike Owen's contribution. After his review, Mr. Houston emailed me to say that he didn't appreciate my hubris.

My only other experience with Owen was in the building parking lot. While I was getting into my car, I dropped my keys. My door was positioned over a drainage grate, and the keys slipped down into the abyss. I was on my hands and knees peering into the black hole when Owen burst through the glass doors into the parking lot. I waved at him and yelled, "Owen? Owen? Sorry to bother you, but I need a little help." He didn't even look at me and made a beeline for his car, saying, "I don't have the time right now. You'll have to find someone else."

In addition, having access to his personnel file provided me with information that indicated the golden boy's shine was more than a bit tarnished.

Chapter 2

▼

My boyfriend, Ken, and I had been dating for a little over two years. I met him while going to night school at Georgetown to obtain my master's degree in organizational development. As soon as he spoke his first name, my heart sank since I believed the Skipper Syndrome that plagued me would never allow for any relationship between us. At the time, I was in a dead-end job at the American Medical School Alliance (AMSA), a nonprofit organization that monitored medical-school applications. My primary job was to investigate fraudulent applications, which was a somewhat heart wrenching task. There were students who had written their own referral letters, altered their transcripts, and even cheated on their MCAT, all in the hope of becoming a doctor.

My favorite case was that of a twenty-one-year-old from Idaho who attempted to fake the seal on a counterfeit transcript. Unless embossed with the school's seal, AMSA did not deem transcripts official. A counselor at Camp Walahatha, this aspiring doctor tried to pass off the camp's seal as that of Case Western's. The beaver head within the design alerted the AMSA processor to the scheme, and after further investigation, the applicant was forced to withdraw from all the medical schools to which he had applied.

Other wannabe doctors tried to strengthen their applications by enrolling in offshore medical programs, such as the ever-popular Doc Zobie's Medical Academy in the Bahamas. Their transcripts featured a picture of who I assumed was Doc Zobie wearing a straw surgical hat and holding a syringe in the air. He was missing several teeth and had what looked like a walleye. Needless to say, this additional documentation did not improve anyone's chances.

During my time at AMSA, I was also responsible for maintaining the DAF—the Disillusioned Applicant Folder. About once a month, we would receive an application from a mentally ill individual. Most of the applications were from the same woman, who claimed she should be admitted to medical school, as she had discovered a cure for cancer. She outlined her cure and provided illustrations. The treatment involved covering the patient's head with dental floss that had been soaked in Pepsi-Cola. The patient was then to sit under a salon-style hair dryer, preferably at Vidal Sassoon. The DAF consisted of over a thousand applications and was maintained for security reasons. On days when I felt particularly Skipper-like, I would rifle through the file to remind myself that at least I was better off than someone who believed that radioactive laser beams were emitted from Vidal Sassoon styling tools.

I had noticed Ken my first semester at Georgetown and thought he was an undergrad student, because of his youthful appearance. He was, as my father would say, "easy on the eyes," sporting a head of brown, curly hair, dimples, and small, round, wire glasses that hid the longest lashes I had ever seen on a man. When he waltzed into class, the female population in the room swooned and sized up one another knowingly. He did not look like a professor. My father looked like a professor—somewhat Einsteinesque, with crazy eyebrows, uncut nails, pen stains on his ten-year-old corduroy pants, and blazers with suede elbow pads. Professor Kenneth Marxen looked like a Chippendale's dancer. According to the contact information provided on the syllabus, he worked for Norton, Totton, and Dinnhaupt in downtown D.C. I knew the name of the law firm well. It was the largest criminal-defense firm in town and represented politicians, celebrities, and big white-collar criminals. Most recently the firm had represented a senator who had been accused of soliciting a male prostitute dressed as a dominatrix.

On the second night of class, Professor Marxen walked into the classroom with a boom box and pressed Play. The voice of Barry White rang out.

Been makin' love for hours
And, baby, with you goin' strong
Girl, this night is ours
And, ooh, I swear I feel it comin' on, yeah
Oh, I know when we get through
Girl, I won't be able to move
I don't know just what you got
I just don't want you to stop
Givin' me, all of me

All the women in the class leaned forward, including me, and waited. I think most of us were expecting him to throw his glasses into the air, ditch the professor act he had going, and launch into a gyrating strip routine. Much to our disappointment, this did not occur. Instead he pressed Stop and asked the class, "Does this offend you?" He walked around the podium and sat casually at the edge of the desk with his hands clasped loosely together. "Do the lyrics bother you? If a colleague of the opposite sex played this type of music in his office, would it bother you?"

A girl in the front row answered, "Does he look like you?" Professor Marxen laughed. A few others clapped. He continued.

"In 1988, Nancy Whitman filed a lawsuit against her employer, Fakelmann Glass. She had repeatedly informed her manager that her co-worker's music made her feel uncomfortable. The music was that of Mr. Barry White, the sexy walrus of love." He motioned to the boom box. "The employee accused cited his employee handbook, which stated that listening to personal tapes was acceptable. Was the plaintiff being sexually harassed?" He searched the room, making eye contact, and his eyes landed upon me. "What are your thoughts, Ms.... uh ..." He looked at his roster.

"Sheehan," I said.

He repeated the name. "Sheehan, sorry. It'll take me awhile to get all the names." I swatted my hand in the air to let him know it wasn't a problem.

"It depends on how you define sexual harassment."

"Well, thank you for the segue," he said, then read from a book. "The law defines it as unwelcome sexual advances, requests for sexual favors, and other verbal or physical conduct of a sexual nature when submission to or rejection of this conduct explicitly or implicitly affects an individual's employment, unreasonably interferes with an individual's work performance, or creates an intimidating, hostile, or offensive work environment."

It was precisely when he looked up from the book with his dimples working overtime and said, "Whew, say all that three times fast," that my crush officially began.

On one occasion, during a class discussion on the definition of a hostile environment, he had held my gaze for what I thought was a moment too long. Aside from this exchange, he was extremely professional and never showed the slightest interest toward anyone—until the last night of class. I was purchasing one of my favorite vending-machine dinners for the trip home, a Payday bar. Unfortunately, it got stuck in the machine. I thought tapping delicately on the Plexiglas would free it from its imprisonment between some Fritos and M&Ms. After a few taps, I resorted to banging frantically on the glass, and then to using my shoulder as a battering ram. In the midst of flinging my body into the machine, as would a hockey player going in for an aggressive check, I saw Professor Marxen out of the corner of my eye.

"I've never had a Payday, but perhaps I should. They must be delicious. Personally, I wouldn't go to such lengths unless it was for Reese's Cups."

I stopped and rubbed my shoulder. The professor began jingling some change in his hand, separating the coins between his fingers as if he were mining for gold. He sifted out two quarters and a dime, placed them in his other hand, and returned the rest of the change to his pants pocket.

"I didn't eat lunch today, so I'm a little crazy," I lied. The truth was that I was a woman, and there was a candy bar with my name on it. He moved past me.

"You're going about this all wrong. Money over muscle." He took the change in his hand, slipped it into the machine, and pressed B9. Tumbling down came another Payday bar, knocking mine to the metal receiving bin.

"Double your pleasure," he commented, touching my hand slightly as he delivered the two bars.

"Here, let me at least give you your money back," I said, digging into my purse.

"No need," he said, smiling. "Happy to help a damsel in distress."

"Thanks," I replied. "I guess I'll see you around next semester."

"I hope so." He grinned.

Ten days later, my final paper came in the mail. Professor Marxen had asked the entire class to self-address manila envelopes, so he could mail out our graded papers. A single note from a yellow legal pad was attached with a paperclip.

Paige,

Delightful read. You have shown a true interest and understanding of the subject. I may know of a job opportunity for you. Please call my office if you're interested.

The word "please" was underlined three times. I consulted my sister, Vicki, who advised me *not* to call. I had learned over time *not* to follow Vicki's advice. The first such lesson had occurred on my tenth birthday—when, at the wise age of fifteen, she told me that my new banana-seat bike could indeed fit through the hula hoop Wally was holding above the bike ramp he had built. I made the jump, and my bike stopped at the hula-hoop ... but I kept going and received thirty-two stitches: ten on my head and twelve on my knee. My respect for Vicki's opinion was forever changed. Thus, if Vicki advised not to call, that would indicate that I should call, which I did the next evening while at her apartment, which was located only a block from my condo. Vicki and I discussed living together when I first moved to the city. However, when she informed me that no televisions, cell phones, or microwave ovens would be permitted in *her* home, living by myself sounded like a good option.

Sitting on Vicki's couch the next day, I dialed the number. I had expected Ken's office to be closed. I wanted to leave a message on voice mail, but his secretary answered.

"Norton, Totton, and Dinnhaupt. Kenneth Marxen's office."

"Hi, may I speak with Kenneth, please?"

"He's in a deposition right now. Is this Katherine?" she asked sweetly.

"Uh, no," I replied. "I'll just call back later."

"Would you like me to transfer you to his voice mail?" she chirped.

"Yes, please." I mouthed the words "voice mail" to Vicki. She gave the thumbs-up. Now I could hit the ball directly into his court, and there would not be any question whose move it was next.

"Ma'am," his secretary said, "you'll hear a click and then the beep. It takes a second."

I whispered to Vicki, "His secretary asked me if this was Katherine. It's probably his wife ... or even worse, his mistress ... the bastard. He's probably got a whore in every court." I snickered at my own play on words and returned my ear to the phone. I heard an automated message: "If you'd like to review your message, press 1. If you'd like to send your message, press 3. If you would like to hear your options again, press star."

"Shit!" I exclaimed. "It just recorded that message."

"What message?" Vicki asked.

"My conversation with you. Hold on. Dammit." I flipped the phone around and pressed 1. I listened again for the prompts, but there was silence. I pressed it again.

"What are you doing?" she asked.

"I'm trying to listen to this message, but I don't hear anything. It says to press 1 to rerecord. I keep pressing 1, but I'm not getting anything."

"Oh, yeah. My 1 doesn't work," Vicki announced casually.

"*What?*" I shot back.

"The number 1, it doesn't work. I've been meaning to get another phone, but then the guinea pig got ear mites and the vet bill was $160. Plus, it's a money saver, because I can't call anyone long distance, and I also can't call Pizza Hut, because their number is 534-1111."

"What should I do?"

"Just hang up," Vicki said. "If you have to press a button to send it, it probably won't register. Just hang up." Ignoring my tried-and-true rule of not following Vicki's advice, I pressed End.

Thirty minutes later the phone rang while I gently held her guinea pig, Mr. Fatboy, so Vicki could administer his ear ointment. Vicki answered.

"Yes, this is Ms. Sheehan. Oh, wait, hold on. I believe you want my sister." She grimaced and made the type of sleesh sound that one makes when hydrogen peroxide makes contact with an open wound.

"I think it's him."

"*What?*"

"It's him. It's him," she whispered, pushing the phone into my hands.

I took the phone, exhaled, and brought it to my ear. "Hello?"

"This is Ken Marxen," he began. "I apologize; I got this number from my secretary's caller ID. I recognized your voice and just wanted to let you know that I'm not married, nor do I have a mistress. I, by definition, am not a bastard, as my mother and father were in fact married when I was born ... and most important, I do not have a whore in every court."

"I am so sorry," I replied. I searched for something to say, but there was nothing. Ken came to my rescue again.

"I did find your message entertaining," he laughed. "I was hoping you would call."

"You were?" I sat down on Vicki's couch, where Mr. Fatboy sat eating a mound of romaine lettuce, his reward for being a good patient.

"Yes, I was. How about dinner sometime?"

"Dinner?" I asked, as if it were a novel concept.

"You do eat dinner, don't you? Or would it be better if I offered to take you out for a Payday bar?"

"No, I eat dinner." Mr. Fatboy squealed beside me, vocalizing the emotion I felt inside.

"Great," he said. "How's Saturday?"

"Is this about the job?" I asked.

"What if it's not about the job?"

"W-Well, uh …" I stammered. "That's fine?" My answer sounded as if it were a question.

Ken and I went to dinner that Saturday, and then the weekend after, and so on and so on. It wasn't about the job, although through Ken's connections, I was offered my position at H2O.

For the first year of our relationship, I dated in disbelief and constant angst. He embodied what the Ken doll represented—handsome and magnetic and certainly deserving of a Barbie … someone like Marcy Roberts. Her parents had gotten divorced the summer before we started high school, the same summer I discovered the truth about the rubber coaster. I had put all the pieces together, as in a game of Clue. Mr. Roberts, in the playroom, with the diaphragm. When I fully understood what had occurred that fateful day at Marcy's home, I wondered if she somehow blamed me for her parents' divorce.

The years leading up to high school had been good to Marcy. She had grown up to be a living Barbie, standing over five feet seven with long, blonde hair that cascaded beautifully down her back. She had lips that glistened and could not be imitated, no matter how much Bonnie Bell Watermelon lip gloss I applied. There seemed to be many girls like Marcy in high school. In hindsight, I attribute this reality to the fact that my town in West Virginia boasted seven cosmetology schools. Beauty was a priority obtained through extreme discipline, a blessed gene pool, and an attitude. Three requirements … of which I had none.

I had blossomed after college and in the years since, but I was no great beauty. I recognized that I had assets and appreciated them. My hair was a shade of auburn that no box of hair color could reproduce. Women stopped me often to inquire about what product I used, but it was God-given. My breasts were small, but proportionate to my small, slender body. I had close-set eyes, but straight teeth and a full mouth, which my father said smiled even when I slept. A family of freckles dotted the bridge of my nose—as well as a lone freckle, which positioned itself underneath my left eye. I didn't necessarily resemble the Skipper of my youth but felt a great kinship with her, and had since my childhood. I had been referred to as cute, but was no match for a Barbie.

Following the anniversary of our first date, I overcame the feeling that I was unworthy of Ken. He needed a Skipper—low maintenance, accommodating, and unselfish. Dating me was simple and uncomplicated … or so I thought.

Chapter 3

▼

"How's the crouton holding up?" my father questioned me on the phone that weekend, as I attempted to make sense of the H2O table arrangements.

"The what?"

"Is it comfortable? Dr. Samuels from economics has one in his office and uses it as both a couch and a bed when his wife throws him out."

"You mean the futon, Dad. It's fine."

"Futon. Yes. Leave it to the Japanese. You know, they also created Worcestershire sauce."

"Can I talk to Mom?" I asked. "I need to ask her an etiquette question." I loved my father dearly, but he was an odd man. Many described him as eccentric, but I believed that was because calling him eccentric was far more polite than calling him odd. I liked to describe him as your typical absentminded professor, but that was also polite. Vicki would later describe him as "not of this world," which is the most accurate description. He was a true scholar and did not care much for anything except filling his head with facts and figures and words. They would spout from his mouth at any time for no particular reason.

I first noticed this habit when I was about five. "Jefferson's house in Monticello took seven years to build. The brick used was actually made of mud, not clay," he announced one day as Wally and I watched cartoons. What was so interesting about this tendency was that he wouldn't be talking to you, necessarily. He often was talking to no one. Thoughts would simply bubble in his head, and the froth boiled over. If you did have a conversation with him, it would present itself in bits and pieces and could transcend time. I once talked to him on a Tuesday afternoon about the building of the Brooklyn Bridge. That conversation had ended with his account of the many world records the bridge had broken when it was built in 1883. On the following afternoon, I came home from school to find him sitting at the kitchen table, grading papers.

"There was a huge opening ceremony," he said.

"What?"

"For the unveiling … it was an invitation-only ceremony."

"Dad, what are you talking about?"

"The bridge! The bridge!" he answered, as if my question bordered on the ridiculous. It was as if no time had elapsed; he just picked up the conversation from where it had last ended. Over time, I grew to love, enjoy and expect this idiosyncrasy.

"Hold on, I'll get your mother." My father screamed my mother's name. "Mags! Paige is on the phone."

Several minutes went by. I could hear the television in the background. Dan Rather was talking about the FDA's proposal to regulate herbal supplements. It was a bit like listening to the courtesy music you get when you are put on hold. The only difference was that I was not on hold.

"Dad!" I screamed loudly into the receiver, "Daaaad? Anyone there?"

The volume on the television decreased. "I'm watching the news. I'll help you in a minute," he mumbled.

"Dad? It's Paige," I bellowed. "I'm still on the phone!"

He picked up the receiver. "Hello?" he asked, surprised.

"Yes, hello?" I replied.

"Can I help you?" he asked.

"Hi, yeah, Dad. It's still Paige. Mags never picked up."

"Oh, sorry about that, Paigebug. I'll get her."

I was learning all about the liver damage caused by herbal remedies when Mags finally picked up breathlessly. "Hi, honey. Sorry. I didn't hear your father. I was downstairs folding laundry." Vicki had begun calling our mother by her first name, Margaret, when she was ten. At the time, my parents had thought it was a phase. Wally and I followed suit. The phase had now lasted twenty-five years and I couldn't recall when her children had referred to her as anything but versions of Margaret, including Maggie, Meg, and my personal favorite, Mags.

"I have an etiquette question for Mags Sheehan. I'm in charge of doing the place cards for this company function next weekend. Is it better to write Mrs. Paul Houston … or Mrs. Sally Houston … or just Mrs. Houston?"

"Hmmmm. That's a tough one, but I think Miss Manners would say that you should use her husband's name … Mrs. Paul Houston."

"Really?" I asked skeptically. "I don't think it's fashionable anymore to go by your husband's name."

"Do you want my advice or not?" she replied teasingly.

My mother prided herself on etiquette, formalities, and her fashion sense. But if forced to choose between fashion and practicality, she always chose the latter. I experienced this partiality my senior year in high school. Marcy had unexpectedly invited me back into her house because she needed help deciding which dress she should wear to the homecoming coronation. She, of course, had been voted queen.

Two dresses were splayed on her bed, along with several bags overflowing with new clothes. After pointing to my pick—a black velvet Jessica McClintock—I focused my attention on a pair of jeans that sat atop a department-store shopping bag. When she saw me looking at them, Marcy said, "Yeah, aren't they rad? My mom got them from a store in Pittsburgh. They're Jordache."

"Pretty awesome," I replied. "Are they expensive?"

Marcy shrugged. Since her parents' divorce, Marcy never wanted for anything; her parents gave and gave.

"They have zippers at the bottom," she said smugly, as if she had sewn them there herself.

I was in shock. Zippers at the bottom! At the time, I believed this to be a stroke of fashion genius.

That night I begged and pleaded with Mags to buy me a pair of the zippered Jordache jeans. I knew she had an upcoming business trip to Greensburg, a town located on the outskirts of Pittsburgh. Mags had gotten a job writing advertising copy for a regional carpet company. It was an ideal assignment, because she had long perfected her marketing skills on her children. She had sold us on baths, glasses of milk, flossing, church, and, for many years, Mrs. Weitzman's haircuts. I had no doubt that Mags would be able to make shag carpet sound like a must-have.

I offered to spend the entire weekend cleaning the garage in exchange for a pair of the jeans. To my surprise, she agreed. That Saturday, I cleaned out eight years' worth of crap from the garage. I worked from seven in the morning to seven that night. The following Thursday evening, when my mother came home from her business trip, she carried a bag—but from Hartley's Discount Outlet. At seventeen, I was old enough to know that a discount outlet would not carry designer Jordache zippered jeans. Maybe a discount store, and maybe an outlet store, but not a discount outlet. My mother prefaced the unveiling by saying, "I know they're not *exactly* Jordache jeans, but those jeans cost $90, which is insane! I found these at Hartley's, and if you ask me, they are practically identical."

I carefully opened the bag to reveal a pair of Joe-Dash jeans. I went to inspect the zippered, tapered leg but found snaps instead, like those found on a country-western shirt. I looked up at my mother to complain, but she was gleaming.

"Not bad, huh! Sometimes Mom pulls through." She nudged me in the side. I forced a smile and hugged her.

"They're great, Mom. Can't wait to wear them."

Recalling Mags' questionable sense for what was fashionable, I carefully penned *Mrs. Sally Houston, Table 1* onto the silver-trimmed place card.

"Have you heard from Wally?" I asked my mother, moving the freshly inked place card to the completed pile. My brother had entered the Peace Corps a year earlier and had recently committed to another two-year stint teaching in Tanzania.

"We got a letter last week. It sounds just dreadful. He wrote that one of the boys in his class had bugs crawling out of his pants ... some type of worm. Can you imagine?"

Before I could reply, my father picked up one of the phone extensions. "Origami. The Japanese also created origami ... probably why they can get the crouton to fold up so many different ways."

"Futon!" my mother and I corrected him in unison.

Chapter 4

"Where are the trees going to be planted?" Vicki asked while she repeatedly cut minuscule pieces off the coffee cake that sat on my kitchen counter.

"Just cut a real piece. Collectively you end up eating a full piece anyway," I observed.

"True, but if I do it this way, I think I'm eating less. So, where are the trees going?"

"I don't know. I guess some park or something. I'm just in charge of registering H2O people and getting the rules out," I replied, taking the knife from her hands and dramatically cutting one thick slice for myself.

"There are rules?" she inquired.

"Well, more like guidelines about the prizes."

I had never been to the Bridesmaid Ball, but based on the award categories (Dress from Hell, What Were They Thinking?, Best Retro Tux, and Most Outrageous Gown), it appeared that attendees would be rewarded for donning the most irksome wedding-attendant attire ever constructed. I explained the concept to Vicki, and her eyes widened with excitement.

"Oh my God! You should wear my bridesmaid dress from Calla's wedding. You'd be sure to win."

I had planned to wear one of the synthetic, pastel nightmares from one of the four weddings in which I had dutifully served as a bridesmaid. However, I could not argue that the dress Vicki referenced was indeed one of the most hideous items ever created.

Vicki had gone a little batty while in law school, becoming involved with Quinn, an aspiring playwright who always wore black sweatpants and a turtleneck. And I'm not using the adverb, "always" lightly; he arrived at her law-school graduation wearing them. Personally, I love sweatpants. They look fabulous on gym teachers, the track team, and Richard Simmons. However, they should not be worn out of the gym, especially if you are a man, and they are three sizes too small, which seemed to be Quinn's problem. His sweats were so form fitting that his genitalia seemed to be doing their own performance art. No matter how hard you tried not to look, you just couldn't ignore it. Wally argued that one could perhaps understand the need to wear such tight pants if the wearer in question was exceptionally endowed. Yet, based on several sideways glances, this did not seem to be the case for Quinn. As a result, the entire family referred to him as Baryshnikov behind Vicki's back. Luckily, they broke up a month after her graduation, before he completely brainwashed her. She escaped with only a mild case of vegetarianism and newfound respect for living simply and serving the vagrants of society as a public defender.

Shortly thereafter Vicki developed a great affinity for guinea pigs, after one of her clients, accused of stealing an unmarked police car, brought one to trial, unbeknownst to the court. Vicki failed to get the charges dropped, and he was convicted. The police department, who were filing his personal effects, found his guinea pig, Mr. Fatboy, in a coat pocket. The bailiff called Vicki from the precinct, asking what he should do. She drove down to the jail, and it was love at first sight. At the time of his adoption, Mr. Fatboy hardly lived up to his name. His skeleton could be easily seen under his fur, but luckily Vicki's vegetarian-friendly fridge contained nothing but vegetables, fruit, and cheese—a veritable guinea-pig smorgasbord. Soon Mr. Fatboy was … well, fat.

Vicki met Calla, an organic farmer from Leesburg, Virginia, on her first day volunteering with the Greater Metro Guinea Pig Rescue Association. At adoption days, they wore T-shirts emblazoned with the words I'm a Pig Lover in hot pink, ironed-on letters. They quickly forged a friendship, and when Calla got engaged a year later, she asked Vicki to be in her wedding, which was later featured in *Organic Life* magazine.

According to the article, most wedding and bridesmaid dresses are constructed of synthetic fabrics that are petroleum-based and made from nonrenewable fossil fuels. It stated that even conventional fabrics such as cotton and wool should not be used, because of the numerous chemicals applied to them during the manufacturing process. Thus, to obey organic etiquette, Calla's bridesmaids wore gowns made of hemp that had been dyed using pomegranate juice, and instead of flowers, they carried bouquets of mixed herbs. Their jewelry included tiaras molded of 100 percent beeswax. Just remembering the dress from the time Vicki tried it on for me made me feel itchy.

"I thought I read in the article that all the bridesmaid dresses were going to be recycled into a wedding quilt."

"Calla doesn't know this, but it got too complicated for me. The place that recycles them requires you to return the dress in a certain type of paper mailer that is sealed with beeswax ... yadda, yadda, yadda. I just kept it."

"Sounds perfect. I'll take it."

Vicki promised to drop it off at my apartment the next day. She lived only a few blocks from me. I saw her often, sometimes too often. Had we not been related, we would not have been friends. She was often exhausting to be with, always looking for an opportunity to debate a cause or take an opposing position. An innocent mention that the Potomac River looked particularly picturesque would inevitably give way to Vicki's monologue about how polluted the waterways around D.C. and Maryland had become. Over the years, I had learned to choose my words carefully and not provide her with these segues. However, one topic was constantly a topic for debate: my relationship with Ken.

Chapter 5

Working at H2O presented one problem. And it was a big problem: my boss. Cliché, I know, but I truly could not stand him. He was an idiot. And I was not alone in this thinking. The entire staff thought he was an idiot. Thankfully, I had a "commiserator," Carlita, who handled all the benefits and compensation for the firm. Carlita and I were from completely opposite ends of the spectrum. I hailed from a small town. She had survived a childhood in the "hood." She clawed her way through college and graduate school and had risen above what I surmised to be a difficult life. She was brilliant, genuinely brilliant. However, she had not completely escaped the hood, as evidenced by her frequent exclamations of "Girl!" and "Oh, no, I don't think so," along with her "mmmhumphs." Carlita was a master at communicating through a sound or a look, and I adored her.

Despite our differences, we became instant friends. When I was arguing with my parents on the phone about borrowing $3,000 from them to help with a down payment on a condo, Carlita grabbed the phone and said, "Dr. and Mrs. Sheehan. Hi. Listen, your baby girl is no spring chicken, and it's time she settled down in her own space. You've got her beat down. She's your baby; you gotta do her right." I think my parents lent me the money because they were unsure of how to respond to such a plea.

Carlita was not much older than me, but she was years wiser, which I attributed to where she grew up. She never recounted tales of her youth. All I knew was that her father was in jail, and her mother was dead. Despite what I imagined was a wretched childhood, she was the most warm and positive individual that I had ever known. Her one quirk was that she talked about sex incessantly—the sex she'd had, the sex she hadn't had, the sex she was going to have, the sex she wanted to have. This type of conversation was not shared with anyone but me, which I viewed as a compliment, as well as a constant source of entertainment. I would frequently lecture her on the impropriety of her comments, citing the sexual harassment section of our employee handbook. Her response always remained, "You're just jealous, cause you ain't getting it good from the professor."

Carlita was always "watching my back," but mostly she was watching Blair Davis. Blair was one of the most successful lobbyists for the firm, and Carlita despised her. I admit that I didn't love the woman—she was, after all, a Barbie—but I didn't associate with her much, so it really wasn't a problem. I did see her often, though, as HR resided on tenth floor east and the lobbyists' offices resided on tenth floor west. Blair had ruffles of raven hair that framed a face worthy of any fashion-magazine cover. Carlita didn't like her, because Blair called her frequently, peppering her with questions about 401K plans and whether her benefits covered facials and such. Blair never could figure out the forms and would ask questions such as, "Why is it a mutual fund if I'm unmarried?"

"I am going to 401Kick her little ass if she calls me one more time," Carlita said one afternoon after a particularly busy day educating Blair. She pumped some mist from a small canister and wafted it toward herself.

"What are you doing?" I inquired.

"It's aromatherapy from Franklin Covey. It's supposed to keep me serene." Carlita closed her eyes and inhaled deeply. I believed Carlita was single-handedly keeping Franklin Covey in business. She possessed what seemed like every item of their Successories line.

"Is it working?"

Carlita exhaled slowly. "I cannot let that girl get to me."

It was clear that Carlita's spray was not keeping her serene, since she practically tackled me at the office holiday party to alert me that Blair was talking to Ken.

"Paige, girl, I don't trust her as far as I can throw her. Noooo nooo nooo. You better get on out there. I'm sure she'd be more than happy to stuff her stocking with him."

"I'm not worried. Not a bit." I shrugged it off without another thought. Ken was a true intellectual, and when I did interrupt their interlude, the first words out of his mouth were "Please do not leave me alone again with these people. Your firm seems to love fruitcakes, and I'm not talking about what's on the buffet table."

My department *was* fruity. For starters, there was Kulfeen, our compensation specialist. She was from the Ukraine and had come to the States when she was nineteen, at which time she married someone twenty years her senior. Carlita suspected that Kulfeen had been a mail-order bride; the details surrounding her betrothal were fuzzy.

Kulfeen had what seemed to be some kind of a supernatural knowledge of spreadsheet applications, but she was a bit of an odd duck. I often wondered about the extent of her deprivation growing up in the Ukraine. She would hoard things—trivial items like boxes of pens and legal pads. She became practically orgasmic at events like our annual benefits fair, when the HMO providers gave out stuff like stress balls and letter openers. Her appreciation for handouts also extended to compensation. I believe she saw herself as a kind of a Salary Santa Claus, handing out big fat compensation packages to all the boys and girls. Unfortunately, she was frequently reprimanded by our boss for being too generous with recommendations.

I found Kulfeen fascinating and was constantly trying to determine if her foreign behavior was because she was strange, or simply foreign. It was a never-ending question. For Christmas, Kulfeen presented the entire office with tiny picture frames in the shape of a cow. Inside was a glamour photo of her wearing a gold lamé turban. It was without question the most bizarre gift I had ever received. Carlita and I weren't certain if it was meant to be a joke, so we erred on the side of caution and formally thanked her. Carlita later told me that she placed the picture along with all her family photographs at home. When people inquired about it, she explained that Kulfeen was an African queen. Surprisingly, very few questioned her about it.

Fruitcake #2 was our payroll administrator, Brian, who loved loved *loved* his job at everyone else's expense. He was a real type A. Once I borrowed his three-hole punch and forgot to return it. He wrote me a long email about the importance of being respectful of other people's possessions. Shortly thereafter he brought in a label maker and put his name on every supply in his office. His stapler, his tape—even his trash can was labeled.

Brian was tolerable but also had an annoying penchant for abbreviating names. It was quite remarkable actually. Even if you thought your name could not be abbreviated, he would find a way. Carlita was Car, of course. Kulfeen was Feen. And although it seemed impractical to abbreviate my monosyllabic name, he did. For months he referred to me as P. Eventually, this somehow evolved into PIP, which also stood for our internal probation process, the Performance Improvement Plan. The only plus to working with him was that he was a die-hard gardener on the side and frequently brought us fruits and veggies from his garden. It was like having a personal farmer's market.

Mike Hanley, Fruitcake #3, was our recruiter. He was madly in love with Blair Davis since the day he recommended that the firm hire her. If he wasn't in his office, you could always walk down the hallway and find him loitering just inside her door. If you questioned him about it, he would make up some lame-ass excuse about needing her expertise on a lobbyist-related job description. The word was that Mike was married to a witch of a woman who called a hundred times a day. He always seemed completely stressed and nervous, and would often work late—even when H2O was not hiring. Carlita and I suspected that he just didn't want to go home. Overall he was a good guy with questionable taste in women.

Last and least, there was Perry, our boss, the King of Fruitcakes, director of HR and Doctorate of Philosophy in Human Factors. Carlita researched human factors on the Web and discovered it was related to psychology and product design. Ergonomics was a subfield, which explained why Perry equipped the office with $100 mouse pads and futuristic chairs that forced good posture.

I prided myself on getting along with my co-workers, but Perry and I were often at odds with one another. He was completely tactless and frequently made inappropriate comments. Unlike Carlita, Perry's comments were not meant to entertain.

The staff and I discovered it was his connections, and not his qualifications, that had gotten him the job. One of the founding partners, Paul Houston, had been a childhood friend of Perry's back in Oklahoma. When Mr. Houston's brother went to Vietnam, he served in Perry's platoon, and Perry saved his life. The rescue was not from enemy fire, but from an orange slice. Mr. Houston's brother was choking on it, and Perry administered the Heimlich maneuver. I learned this background info the hard way. I had gone to Mr. Houston questioning Perry's ability to run the department and was served the entire story. Mr. Houston had ended the discussion with, "Perry is a great man. A little unorthodox, but a great man." I wanted to argue that a great man does not always translate into a great HR director, but I knew the point was moot. Of course news of my tattling wound its way back to Perry, and our relationship had been strained ever since.

I returned from getting my midday snack to find a yellow sticky note from Perry. My primary issue with Perry was that he could not seem to communicate through any other means besides the yellow Post-it note. Occasionally he would switch to neon green, but he never changed the cryptic, gruff-sounding messages:

"Need to talk to you ASAP," or "Problem!" or my personal favorite, "Must talk." The one decorating my computer screen that day simply read, "Important!!!"

Wow, I thought. *Three exclamation points.* In the beginning, Perry's urgent messages would send me into a panic. Over time I realized that his definition of urgent and important issues usually meant that a ream of paper was missing, or one of the attorneys had gone to a prohibited Web site. In the three years I had worked for Perry, I had become extremely adept at waiting until the very last possible moment to respond to him. Eventually I would make the long walk down our hallway to his office. It always felt as if I were being called to the blackboard when I didn't know the answer.

"Perry, you wanted to see me?" I chirped.

Perry shuffled some papers around his cluttered desk and under a pile of folders found his dry-erase marker.

"Voila!" he shouted as he held the marker up to show his discovery. "Shut the door, Paige."

I quietly closed the door, sat down, and prepared myself for the day's critical, heart-stopping issue.

"We've got ourselves a problem on the sixth floor ... a paralegal," he began. "Some Russian guy named Klavic. His co-workers say that he has severe BO."

"As in body odor?" I asked.

"Yeah, you know. Those Slavs take showers like once a month."

"Well, I don't think we should make generalizations, Perry. And he's Russian, not Slavic."

Perry gave me the warning finger, the "don't mess with me" finger. He then quickly brought out his small whiteboard and scribbled the plan of action like a coach during half-time. Perry loved his dear whiteboard. Hence the excitement after finding his long-lost dry-erase marker. Personally, I have a three-person minimum before breaking out the whiteboard. But Perry would frequently whiteboard just for me. It was as if he thought I could not grasp anything without visuals. With his green marker, he wrote,

<u>Euro's BO</u>
Talk with his manager.
Notify employee.
Follow up in two weeks with co-workers.

Then at the very bottom, Mr. Post-it wrote his tagline:

Communication is the key.

"Who's his manager?" I asked, pulling the cap off my pen as I prepared to write.

"Holden," he answered, leaning back in his chair and revealing a small triangle of skin above his belt, which his shirt strained to cover.

I rolled my eyes. *Just my luck*, I thought. "I'll talk to him first thing on Monday."

Chapter 6

Eighty-five H2Oers had RSVP'd to the event. Technically we only had eight tables of ten, but Mr. Houston suggested I accept all of the registrations anyway. "You always lose a few people at the last minute," he advised me.

I told Ken to meet me at the event, as I needed to arrive an hour early to ensure the place cards and table assignments submitted were correct. I was also setting up the booth that H2O was providing for the silent auction. All the fruitcakes in HR had volunteered to man the booth for one hour each during the night.

The ball was being held at the National Museum of Women in the Arts, on the corner of New York Avenue. The museum was the only museum in the world dedicated exclusively to recognizing the contributions of female artists. Their collection comprised more than three thousand works from the sixteenth century to the present. Paintings, photographs, and sculptures adorned every wall and corner.

I had not anticipated the ball decorations would be so extravagant and elegant. Chairs draped in white gossamer surrounded small cocktail tables, accentuated by two calla lilies in a streamlined, silver vase. A light show basked the room in alternating pastel hues, and billowing sheers of silver and white hung from the ceiling. The food stations appeared to be floating on clouds of snow below gleaming ice sculptures in the shape of evergreens. As the corporate sponsor, H2O had given $25,000, and it appeared that the decoration committee had used every cent of it. The room was breathtaking.

I had taken advantage of my responsibility for table assignments and strategically placed Ken and me at the partners' table. I figured any face time with the

H2O honchos was time well spent. After ensuring that everything was in its place, I headed for the ladies' room and unwrapped my dress from the opposing plastic garment bag in which it had been contained. I had glanced at it when Vicki dropped it off, but did not try it on, as my figure was almost the mirror image of my sister's. For years she and I had swapped clothes, although it was rarely to my benefit. Vicki was not the best about wardrobe maintenance. The aftermath of her sweatpants-wearing boyfriend included general disdain for material objects, especially other people's material objects. Several times she had borrowed skirts from me that had been returned with stapled-in hems.

As soon as I unleashed the organic gown from the confines of its polyurethane cover, it seemed to breathe and expel what I can only describe as the smell of earth. I carefully slipped into the berry-stained dress and laughed. I would definitely be bringing home an award. The dress resembled what a peasant would wear during Renaissance times. The top featured an off-the-shoulder, long-sleeved blouse with ruffled edges along the neck and wrists. A full, sweeping skirt draped from an empire waist that resulted in amazing cleavage for my B-cup breasts. This benefit was the dress's only blessing. I swept my hair up at the sides and affixed the beeswax accessories. It was two minutes to eight, the official start time of the event and my scheduled time to man the silent auction. I laughed aloud again and smiled, anxious to see the display of unique wedding-attendant attire.

Upon exiting the bathroom, the first woman I passed was garbed in a stunning, black, strapless gown. I thought how unfortunate it was that some people refused to get in the spirit. People were gradually entering the grand hall as I positioned myself in the booth opposite the entrance, and the nervousness in the pit of my stomach grew with each dress I saw. With the exception of one woman, who carried a parasol and wore a peach-colored hoopskirt, all of the women wore dresses that were, to my dismay, lovely. I sat down at my post and prayed that the early crowd was not representative of the ball population.

An hour later, Ken waltzed through the door and stopped in his tracks when he saw me. He glanced around the room and then continued toward me slowly, as if he were afraid.

"Don't," I began, and managed a smile.

"What do you have on?"

"The announcement implies that you should wear a bridesmaid dress gone wrong," I said angrily.

"Where did you even get that?"

"Vicki wore it in a friend's wedding."

"Enough said," he replied, but looked unnerved. "Do you want something to drink?"

"Yes, please ... and do me a favor. See if you can switch our place card and put us at another table. I don't want to sit next to Mr. Houston wearing this."

Ken nodded, but shook his head in a disapproving manner that confirmed that I looked as ridiculous as I felt. He reappeared and delivered my wine. "We're at Table 7 now," he announced. "I switched with Bill and Patty Petersen."

I grimaced. "Ugggh, that's Holden's table."

"Most of the place cards had already been picked up," he explained.

"Oh, well, that's fine. I'll deal."

At 9 PM Kulfeen came to relieve me of my silent-auction duty. With Ken in tow, I sheepishly made my way to Table 7, which comprised Mike Hanley and his wife, "witchypoo," Brian and his partner, and Owen and his guest—who, to my surprise, was Blair. After introductions I announced, "I'm intent on winning one of the awards," thinking my remark would preempt any inquiries about the dress ... but no such luck. Everyone stared with an intense curiosity, as if they were trying to dissect each section of the dress in order to understand the sum of its parts.

Owen leaned across Blair, who sat between Ken and me. "Is that hemp?"

"Yes, it's hemp. It was a bridesmaid dress in the wedding of an organic farmer, a friend of my sister's. I thought it was appropriate given the environmental theme."

"It's fabulous," Owen remarked mockingly.

I retorted, "I find it interesting that you were so quick to identify the material. Does H2O need to start up its random drug tests again?," referring to the fact that hemp was made from the stem of the cannabis plant.

"Is she always so biting?" Owen directed his question to Ken.

"Only when she smells like mud and looks like Mother Nature." The table roared with laughter. This prompted a cycle of comments about me and the dress. I realized that their fun was not meant to be malicious, but after an hour of nonstop banter about how down-to-earth and recyclable I was, I politely excused myself claiming the booth needed to be checked. I wanted Ken to come after me. It should have been obvious to him that I was upset. After two years together, I thought he should be able to read my gracious half smiles and reticence. A quiet corner behind one of the ceiling drapes provided me with some reprieve. Fifteen minutes passed as I hopefully waited for Ken to seek me out.

Sophisticated and elegantly garbed partygoers scampered across the floor, and I pondered why I was always on the sidelines. Like Skipper, I seemed to be forever on the cusp. The parallel between the character I played as a youngster and the woman I had become was telling. My thoughts drifted to my time serving as the high-school mascot. Unable to make the cheerleading squad, I settled for the role of the Fairville Patriot. My uniform consisted of a shiny, metallic blue revelry jacket, knickers, a ruffled shirt, white knee socks, and some witch's shoes. The shoes that had come with the uniform were too small for my feet. Mags found some shoes that were part of a witch's costume at an after-Halloween liquidation. They weren't exactly right for the costume since they had a black cat and cauldron on the top of the lip. Mags assured me that from afar, you couldn't really see it. Dad said that I looked like a young George Washington, adding that "it was often thought by scholars that he was gay." I wasn't exactly sure where he was going with this comment, but I think he thought it was a compliment. I was certain that the boys would take notice of me as the Fairville Patriot. My naïveté prevented me from seeing that a patriot shaking her musket paled in comparison to a cheerleader shaking her pom-poms and other body parts.

A commanding voice brought me back to the present.

"You better get close to the stage," directed someone from behind the wave of fabric. I stepped forward to find Owen looking rather cautious and sympathetic. I did not reply. He added, "They're about to name the finalists."

"I prefer to sit this one out. It's not fair to the other contestants. The hoopskirt and parasol can't even compete with this," I replied, gesturing across my body.

He moved closer and batted at the sheer decoration that swayed in between us. "I'm sorry we gave you such a hard time back there. I personally think it's great that you came decked out like this."

"Right. I'm sure you wish Blair had worn this and not the low-cut, short, slinky, satin number that prevented Mike Hanley from blinking for fear he might waste one second of seeing all that skin."

"Believe it or not, Ms. Sheehan, I searched high and low for a powder-blue tuxedo. If I had found one, I too would have joined in on all the fun. I love this stuff."

A drum roll interrupted our exchange and hushed the crowd in preparation for the awards. Owen moved beside me to watch the festivities. I casually glanced up at him and smiled, a subtle show of my appreciation at his successful attempt to make me feel better.

The announcer beckoned the winning ladies to come to the stage and asked the audience to assist with identifying the finalists based on the judge's descriptions. The top three finalists in the Dress from Hell category were, "in no particular order," the young lady with the peach parasol, the woman wearing what appeared to be an old afghan, and the tie-dyed renaissance wench.

"I think that's me," I sighed and reluctantly began my ascent to the stage.

Owen called after me, "Good luck, wench!"

We seemed to be on stage for an eternity. The spotlight drilled down upon each of us as we answered a series of questions about our dresses—a history of how they came to be.

After sharing the tale of Calla's organic wedding, I decided to go for the gold, presenting the dress as if it were being shown on a runway in Milan. Taking the microphone from the master of ceremonies, I began my sell.

"This one-of-a-kind, environmentally friendly gown was inspired by sixteenth-century peasants. Trimmed in generous ruffles and able to enhance the most modest-breasted woman, this recyclable piece is handmade of 100 percent unprocessed hemp, which gives it that rough and uncomfortable look. Triple-dyed in pomegranate juice to achieve the uneven and blotchy coloring, this frock will definitely turn heads. Coupled with the biodegradable tiara and matching jewelry, molded from pure beeswax, it is certain to seal your fate as always a bridesmaid and never a bride."

I ended my spiel with a catwalk turn and a curtsy, and the crowd cheered. My monologue was rewarded with dinner for two at L'Auberge Chez Francois, one of the top restaurants in the area.

Table 7 politely applauded for me when I returned to my seat.

I passed my trophy, a silver-plated miniature bouquet, to Ken. Unimpressed, he tossed it to Blair as if he were playing a game of hot potato. Blair, in turn, plopped it onto the table as if it were a basket of rolls.

"Careful, folks. That's the Super Bowl trophy of fundraising events," Owen advised.

Ken glared at Owen and responded in a biting manner. "Perhaps they'll also award her with the Bridesmaid Ball equivalent of a gaudy Super Bowl ring. I see you are sporting yours tonight. Ah, the glory days."

I shot Ken a look, confused by his sudden attack.

"I only wear it for special occasions," Owen retorted, "or when I'm preparing to rumble. It packs quite a punch with some force behind it." After a few awkward seconds, Owen's face broke into a grin, relieving the brief and bizarre tension.

On the way home, I apologized to Ken for leaving him alone with the fruitcakes. Enduring an evening listening to Brian's account of winning second place at the Montgomery County Farmer's Fair for his strawberry-shortcake recipe most certainly fueled Ken's agitation.

"It was fine," he replied.

"Did you have a miserable time?" I asked.

"No, it was fine," he sighed. "So what were you and Golden Boy talking about?"

"Owen? Nothing really. He just came to check on me." I turned my face to the window and bit my lip to keep from grinning, realizing that Ken's outburst was due to jealousy. "You know, I would have appreciated a little support from you when the table ganged up on me."

"C'mon, we were just having fun," he droned.

"I know, but it was a little extreme. Mike revising the lyrics of Carole King's "Natural Woman" song and then *you* chiming in with the remark about the one time I forgot to shave one of my underarms."

"Paige, lighten up. You bring this stuff on yourself anyway. If you weren't such an easy target ..."

"What does that mean?'

"Nothing," he replied curtly. We sat in silence for a bit longer.

"At least I wasn't the only one who was embarrassed," I said. "How can Blair, an environmental lobbyist, not know who Ralph Nader is?"

Ken did not respond to my rhetorical question and pulled into the semicircle driveway in front of my condominium building.

"You're not coming up?" I asked.

"I'm tired and need to go into the office tomorrow for a few hours." He kissed me tenderly. "If I'm going to take next weekend off, then I have to put some extra time in this weekend."

"OK. Call me tomorrow."

Once inside I stripped off the dress to reveal patches of irritated skin. I was thankful that Ken had opted to go home so not to bear witness to the leprotic-looking lesions on my arms and torso. Note to self: hemp is not for those with sensitive skin.

As I took the clips out of my hair, I noticed that my hair remained stationary. I leaned into the mirror to inspect it more closely to discover that the beeswax tiara had melted. After a painstaking hour of trying to separate the clumps with repeated shampooing, I surrendered and laid the congealed mass of hair upon my pillow.

Chapter 7

▼

It was not the first time that I had gotten a haircut for reasons other than split ends or a sudden urge to duplicate a celebrity style.

A month before the start of high school, I noticed significant hair loss when I showered. At first I ignored it, but the problem persisted.

"I think my hair's falling out," I told my mother.

"It's not falling out. It's just your imagination. It's just getting long, and it looks a little straggly. We'll go into the Hairhouse on Saturday."

The Best Little Hairhouse in Fairville was our local beauty parlor. I'd been getting my hair cut there since I was ten—when Vicki, then fifteen, had demanded that a professional cut her hair instead of Mrs. Weitzman. Over the course of my five-year patronage at the Hairhouse, Bobbi, my stylist, had gotten married, had a baby, gotten divorced, and married a new man, named Spitz. I was never sure whether this was his first name, last name or nickname. I idolized Bobbi, which concerned my mother. "I don't think she's a very wise girl," my mother shared when I waxed poetic about Bobbi one day after a haircut. I didn't really care. She was always kind to me, and her hair encircled her head like a lion's mane. It was magnificent.

"I think my hair's falling out," I told her when I settled into the chair.

"People lose over seven hundred hairs a day," Bobbi replied. She pumped the metal lever underneath my seat and popped her gum in perfect synchrony. "We also have a shedding period, like dogs. For me, I shed in the summer, but you might shed in the fall. It's different for everyone."

"I don't know. It seems like a lot is coming out." I was not convinced.

Bobbi shampooed my hair and then began combing it straight. I watched her in the mirror. Suddenly she stopped and started weeding through my scalp like a monkey looking for bugs to eat. She beckoned one of the other stylists, who joined her exploration. The other stylist pointed to something on my head, and Bobbi nodded.

"Paige, sweetie, you do have a teeny, tiny bald spot back there, so somepin' must be going on. Have you switched shampoos or been using anything different on your hair?"

"No, nothing. I've been doing the same thing I always do."

Bobbi twisted her mouth sideways and made the snick sound with her cheek that often precedes someone telling a horse to giddy up.

"Well, sweetie, I'd go see your doctor just in case, but not to worry. I'm going to give you a really cute cut. We'll just layer right over that sucker, tease it up, and with some hairspray, you won't even be able to see it."

Dr. Seth Knoll was the only dermatologist serving the tri-county area. My mother called to get an appointment, but the only available slot was three months away, due to what his receptionist said was an unusually high number of psoriasis patients. I panicked. Although the spiky haircut Bobbi had given me did indeed make my hair look thicker, Mags cried when she saw it, saying, "You look like that crazy lesbian fitness instructor on TV." Her remark was not meant to be malicious, but it unleashed a flood of angst inside me, which I wore on my face. She quickly retreated and softened, putting her hand on my shoulder, "We're going to get this taken care of," she assured me. "Don't you worry, Mom is on the case."

Mags began a full-scale, phone-tree assault, contacting every person she knew in hope of discovering some connection to the dermatologist. After about ten calls, she found one. Wally's former Boy Scout troop leader's wife was on the Women's League along with the dermatologist's mother. It was a long shot but a shot nonetheless. Mags called Mrs. Knoll and tried to appeal to her as one loving mother to another. The conversation lasted about three minutes. I sat at the bottom of my mother's bed as she spoke on the phone, lightly bouncing my hand against the gelled spikes sprouting from my head. They were as hard as glass, and I wondered whether I could spear someone by running headfirst into them.

"Oh, thank you, Mrs. Knoll. You don't know how much we appreciate it."

My mother hung up the phone and bowed her head as if in prayer. "Oh, thank God. What a lovely woman. She said not to worry. She's going to get us an appointment first thing on Monday."

Dr. Knoll's mother must have reprimanded him severely. He met us bright and early on Monday and apologized profusely that his office assistant had not realized the importance of the matter when Mags had originally called. My appointment began with a battery of tests to identify the cause of my hair loss. Part of this series included a stress test that indicated I had a high level of anxiety.

"You seem extremely stressed for a girl your age," Dr. Knoll began after the nurse had tallied my scores. "Is something bothering you?"

"Well, yeah. I'm fourteen and going bald," I replied, to which the dear doctor merely nodded.

The typical treatment, Dr. Knoll advised, involved the administration of a steroid that promoted follicle growth. He had Mags review and sign some consent forms, and I was led to another examination room for the procedure. Mags went to sit in the waiting room, claiming that she didn't think she could watch. A hefty nurse appeared, wearing a button that read, "Beauty is only skin deep, but skin is all you see!" She prepared five syringes on a tray, along with a bundle of cotton balls. Her West Virginia twang was so thick, it made me squint when she talked.

"Paige, this is gonna hurt a bit, 'cause we gotta shoot it right into the scalp, and the skin ain't that tough, and you got a lot of nerve endings on your noggin." I nodded. "Did Dr. Knoll tell you 'bout the side effects?" she asked, tapping the bottom of the first needle.

"Well, I know that steroids make people moody."

"That's normally for anabolic steroids, which ain't what we're using. These are hormonal. The side effects are a little different, but I know Dr. Knoll talked to your momma, and she signed the consent form, so I'm sure she feels the rewards outweigh the risks." I nodded and sat as the nurse clipped parts of my hair down with bobby pins. She was about to administer the first shot when I leaned back.

"Um, just real quick ... what are the side effects for this type of steroid? Just so I know. My mom's in the waiting room."

"Well, not all girls get a reaction, only 'bout 70 percent, but sometimes the steroids don't know which parts they're s'pose to be fixin', so some girls get some hair growth on their faces and torso. But you can either shave them parts, or Dr. Knoll can give you a prescription that'll take it right off."

"And it doesn't grow back?"

"Oh no, it does. You'll just have to keep grooming it. OK now." She smiled and was going in for the shot when I hopped off the bench and ran into the waiting area, clutching my gown. My mother looked up, surprised.

"Did you know the steroids can cause hair growth on my face and chest?"

"What? Dr. Knoll said nothing about that!"

The nurse followed me out into the waiting room. I covered my head and moved out of reach in fear that she had followed me to get me from behind.

"It's all on the consent form, Mrs. Sheehan," the nurse said.

"Well, I didn't really read the fine print." My mother looked at me apologetically.

"I don't want a beard and a hairy chest," I protested. My mother picked up her purse and followed me into the examining room, helping me to dress.

"I have a plan B," she informed me. "Don't you worry."

Plan B involved going to a wig store downtown that, judging from its stock, appeared to only serve Dolly Parton, Tina Turner, and any woman over the age of eighty. Mags insisted that I try on a few samples, which I did, but each one proved more appalling than the last. As a result, plan C was deployed, which involved wearing a purple beret.

I sported that beret the first six months of high school. The school's dress code forbid hat-wearing but Mags wrote a note to the principal stating that my "condition" warranted an exception. Unbeknownst to me, a rumor started around school that I was suffering from cancer and undergoing chemotherapy. The following spring, my hair mysteriously began to return, although I continued to wear the beret.

As the end of the school year neared, the cheerleading moderator asked if I'd be interested in the position of the team mascot, the Fairville Patriot. She told me that she had watched my "undeniable spirit" during the year and that I served as an inspiration to others.

Now, fifteen years later, I wondered where my purple beret had gone. I feared it would need to be resurrected to mask the creative coif that would most likely result from cutting the beeswax free. A bit longer than a pixie cut and shorter than a shaggy bob, the hairstyle that resulted was manageable. Much to my relief, no beret would be required.

Chapter 8

▼

According to Golden Boy's personnel file, Owen had been placed on probation after a formal grievance was filed against him with the California Bar Association. The San Francisco office had transferred him to D.C. and indicated that during this time, he was forbidden to handle trial cases. His file further noted that he had undergone psychiatric treatment six months prior. After discovering this fact during a review of his benefits, Carlita hopefully added, "Maybe it's 'cause he's got a sexual addiction."

"Doubtful," I said. "Could be drug related."

"Or maybe it's because of a sexual addiction," she offered. I decided not to quash her hopes. It had become a running joke between us.

On Monday morning, I walked into Carlita's office which was wallpapered with inspirational quotes and posters from Successories with sayings like "You cannot see the sights unless you set sail from shore." I leaned up against her Fly High poster, which featured a hang glider hovering over a beautiful ocean.

"What's with the new hair, Miss Bridesmaid Extraordinaire?"

"Long story," I replied, not wanting to give her the details. "I've got to go see Holden about something," I said in a teasing voice.

"Nuh-uh. Hope that something is somethin' somethin'." She winked. "'Cause, girl, you need a good poke."

"A what?"

"A poke." She gestured with her index finger. "I was getting such a good poke last night I thought my toes were going to be cut off by the ceiling fan."

I rolled my eyes. "Carlita! God! You're shameless, utterly shameless. Thanks for the image, though. That one is going to stay with me for a while."

"Any time, Powdered Sugar." She whirled around in her chair, back to her computer.

"Lunch tomorrow?" I asked.

"Only if we go to the deli. I'm starting Atkins again."

"That's fine. Well, I'm off," I said, saluting her.

As I was headed toward the stairs, she yelled, "Tell him I can help him out with that *problem* of his." Carlita's cackle followed me down the hallway.

I stopped in the bathroom to freshen up before going to Owen's office. Blair was at the faucet, washing her hands. She smiled at me politely, and I smiled back. I walked into the stall and latched the door. Through the slit between the stall door, I watched her with a genuine curiosity, hoping to catch her routine. I had always assumed that she had to freshen up several times a day in order to maintain her flawless look. The fact that she had never done anything to me made my dislike for her difficult to maintain, since I had graduated with top honors in Catholic Guilt. I acknowledged that part of my disdain for her sprang from pure jealousy. A piece of me desperately wanted to be *that* girl who turned heads and maintained a chipless manicure for more than two hours, a woman who could wear an all-white outfit and, at the end of the day, not look like the "before" picture in a bleach commercial. The previous summer, I had tried to capture her look by buying a pair of starched, white cigarette pants. I had worn them for approximately fifteen minutes before the first stain in my daily repertoire appeared. I had leaned against one of Perry's whiteboards and had the faint outline of the word KEY on my behind, which read YEK backwards.

Blair finished washing her hands, looked quickly at herself in the mirror, and tucked a single piece of hair behind her ear. Much to my disappointment, there was no makeup meltdown, no food stuck in her teeth, and no stain on her clothing. If Barbie ever needed a worthy competitor, Blair could give her a run for her money.

When she left, I stood in front of the same sink and evaluated myself in the mirror. I was a far cry from flawlessness. My nose was peeling since I had forgotten my sunscreen the prior weekend at the Norton, Totton, and Dinnhaupt Annual Golf Outing. I rubbed some water onto my nose in an attempt to minimize the dryness. This measure only caused the area to peel more, and it now appeared that something other than skin hung from my nose. I dampened a paper towel, wiped the corner of my lips, and sighed. I knew I was blessed and should not feel inferior. My frustration came from my realization that I would never be perfectly pulled together. There was always a button missing or a hair of out place, and my wardrobe seemed to be as stylish as Skipper's gaucho pants. I rubbed again at the skin on my nose and finally headed to Owen's office.

Holden's Lair, as many of the women at the firm called it, was on the twelfth floor. I walked the two flights of stairs and smelled the fetid scent as soon as I opened the door. It was vile—stunning, actually. It didn't smell like normal BO. It was like an olfactory cocktail of feet, rotten eggs, and cheap, musky cologne. According to Perry, complaints had been coming in all summer, and I could not believe that these poor people had been dealing with the stench all that time. As I approached the counter, a twenty somethings who looked more like ten somethings gazed up at me. "You have to file your research request online now through the intranet."

"Oh, I'm not here to request research," I quickly responded. "I need to see Owen Holden."

"Last name and sector? And is this in reference to an open ticket?" he droned, as if he were reading from a manual.

"I'm Paige Sheehan from HR. I have a matter to speak with him about."

A look of relief registered on the boy's face.

"You here about Klavic?" he asked, without waiting for an answer. "He's making us all sick. Sometimes I can't even eat my lunch. Every time someone comes down to request research, they ask what the stink is. The guys and I actually left a bar of soap on his desk hoping he'd get the hint, but …"

I interrupted, "If you could just let Owen know I'm here." The boy disappeared around the corner, and shortly thereafter, Owen appeared, looking perfect as usual.

"Mother Nature," he began. "Why don't we go in my office." He stood with his legs shoulder-width apart and one hand on his waist, and motioned for me to follow. As I walked behind him, I couldn't help taking note of the perfect crease of his khaki pants, the shine of his brown leather belt, and how amazingly wrinkle free the back of his pink oxford shirt was. He was what Mags would call "neat as a pin."

Although it pained me to admit it, Owen was extremely sexy. I had seen pictures of him when he was younger, but at the age of thirty-six, he was even more handsome than when he played ball. He looked like Paul Newman after a fight. His features were fine and chiseled, but disrupted by a rugged, prizefighter nose. His look was unique—one that drew you to stare and marvel at its anatomy. I sat, very conscious of how I crossed my legs. I held them tightly together and at an angle, à la Katie Couric, in hope they appeared much sleeker and longer. I tucked the unruly section of my new 'do behind my ear and thought about how ultimately girly I was being. To counteract, I sidestepped the chitchat and went straight to business.

"I wanted to talk to you about one of your employees, Klavic ... um ..." I looked down to my notes to refer to the last name and coyly looked up through my mascara-laden lashes. "Klavic Gilyosavic. We've received several complaints from your department. Are you aware there is a problem?"

Golden Holden looked taken aback, as if I had said something truly shocking and surprising. He paused.

"What?" I asked.

He twirled his pen elegantly between his fingers and smiled at me. His eyes were a pale blue, and the pink of his shirt made them that much brighter.

"I just feel like I'm being cross-examined," he chuckled. "Am I being brought up on some sort of charge? You may have heard that I have some experience getting into trouble." He leaned back in his chair and put his hands behind his head. I once read that most trial lawyers learn to read the body language of jurors. The "hands behind the head" move indicates the juror has formed their decision. I wondered what decision Owen had made about me.

"Yes, I know ... uh, no, I'm sorry. It's just been a long day, and I'm just trying to get a handle on what the situation is ... if there is indeed a situation."

He straightened in his chair and leaned forward toward his desk.

"By the way, I was impressed with your stage performance on Saturday night. You're a natural. No pun intended."

"Hopefully I won't have to defend my crown next year, as it melted all over my hair. Hence, the new haircut." I pointed to my head and settled into the chair.

"It's cute. It suits you." His eyes moved from my hair to my eyes, and then to my mouth. I cleared my throat and looked down to my notes.

"About Klavic?" I asked.

"Yes, there is a problem," he responded. "Klavic's a great employee. Very bright. One of our top paralegals. He was a physicist in Russia before getting his law degree, so he understands the science behind a lot of the environmental issues. He's studying now for the D.C. bar ... but, to be blunt, he does indeed stink. I've talked to him about it already. I told him that he could use the showers here if he needed to."

"He doesn't have a shower at home?"

"Well, here's the deal. You know that block of Northwest that burned down about six months ago?"

I nodded. "The block burned down by the arsonist?"

Owen continued, "Yeah, well, he lived in that strip. He lost everything … and no renter's insurance. Nothing. For the past six months, he's been living above the deli on K Street, but since he's got no car, he rides his bike here. He's got a toilet and a sink, but no shower. He's been using the ones here in the office."

"So, what's the problem?"

"I think he's just embarrassed. Our shower is right at the end of the urinals. He's probably got an audience every morning."

"Doesn't it have a door?"

"No, it's like a locker-room shower. Bizarro, if you ask me. Not exactly what I'd expect from the firm, but technically I think it's there for emergencies … all-nighters, you know. Not for daily use."

"Hmmm, I'll see what I can do about the door. I know the women's restroom has a door on its shower, so I'm sure we can get something from facilities." I moved the Fruit Stripe gum I was hiding out from under my tongue and tried to subtly move it to the side of my mouth, but the maneuver proved to be too complicated, and the gum fell out onto my shirt. I quickly picked it up and popped it back into my mouth. I looked up from my notepad, and Owen's eyes looked at me quizzically.

He glanced down at his watch, and his eyes bulged. "Whoa. I'm late. I'm sorry, but I'm going to have to cut this short." He stood, slid into his blazer, and brushed some lint off the sleeve. "I've got a dinner meeting tonight down at D.C. Coast."

"I live right around the corner from there." I regretted the remark as soon as I had made it; I sounded as if I were searching. Owen stood and opened his desk drawer. With one smooth motion, he opened the cap from a bottle of Ralph Lauren's Tweed cologne, turned it upside down, dabbed both sides of his neck, capped it, and placed it back in his desk drawer … all with one hand. I thought briefly about how that dexterity could be used outside of the office.

Owen then motioned to the door. "Could we perhaps meet for coffee later this week? I'll be out tomorrow, and I just don't have the time to discuss it right now. I'm really sorry to bolt like this but I was supposed to be there five minutes ago."

"Sure thing," I replied, as I uncrossed my legs. I suddenly realized that my Katie Couric leg pressing had caused my right foot to fall asleep. I stalled.

"Actually, if you don't mind, I would like to talk with him. Is he here today? Perhaps you could ask him to meet with me for a few minutes. Would you mind if I used your office?"

"His officemate is out today, so let me walk you down there."

He motioned to the door. I shifted and reluctantly rose from the chair, tapping my foot subtly against the floor in an attempt to wake it from its slumber. Although originally dead set against the chitchat, I pointed to the little bobblehead in Owen's likeness at the edge of his desk.

"Nice bobble," I said.

"That's supposed to be me." Owen tapped the little bobblehead, clad in a Cowboys outfit, on the head, and it began nodding wildly.

"I figured as much, with the big head and all." It was a witty and winning remark, and I celebrated it with a proud grin.

He smirked. "Ha, ha. Yeah, it's one of the few souvenirs I have from my Dallas days." He walked out the door, and I followed. However, my right foot was still asleep, and I stumbled forward, knocking the bobblehead off his desk. It smashed on the floor, splintering into several pieces. I covered my mouth with my hand to muffle the shock. He had already exited his office, but popped his head around the door when he heard the crash.

"What the hell was ..." he stopped and bent down to his bobblehead on the floor, as if he was a child, and I had just wrecked his precious sand castle.

"Jesus, Paige. It's obvious you don't like me for some reason, but this is a bit immature, don't you think?" He picked up the pieces, and I bent down to help him.

"I am so, so sorry, Owen. I honestly ... uh ... my foot was asleep, and I didn't mean to ... really. I lost my balance and went to grab something to hold onto and must have knocked it off ..." I gave him my sincerest face, and it was genuine. Although it was true that I didn't care for Owen, I would never intentionally break something out of spite. I gathered the pieces on top of my leather portfolio. "I could try to glue it back together. It seems like most of the breaks are pretty big." I looked at him eagerly, and he shook his head and sighed.

"That's OK. I think it's beyond saving. Let's talk later and see where we are with Klavic."

Owen collected what was left of his caricaturized bobble face and tossed it into his trash can. We walked to Klavic's office in silence, and Owen was gone before Klavic and I finished our hellos. Klavic immediately sung Owen's praises and told me that Owen had even offered the use of his apartment temporarily.

"He so very nice man, very good man, what they call a good seminarian," Klavic explained. I knew what Klavic meant to say but his account of Owen's kindness conflicted with what I thought I knew. As Klavic and I discussed the shower situation, I tried my best to smell the body odor in question. As I breathed in deeply, my nose could only detect the lingering smell of Tweed.

Chapter 9

Ken and I had played phone tag for most of the week. With his day job at Norton and evenings spent teaching, he had little free time in his schedule. Since the beginning of our relationship, I had always been very understanding and accommodating. It was one of the reasons, I believed, he had been attracted to me in the first place.

On my way home from work on Thursday, I dialed Ken to ask him if hiking boots would be required for our weekend away. We had planned a romantic getaway at Blarney Brook Inn in Deep Creek, Maryland, two hours north of D.C., to celebrate the end of my three years in night school and the completion of my master's degree. However, there was speculation among my family that the weekend would be the backdrop for Ken popping the question.

I was doubtful. I questioned whether Ken truly loved me. He claimed he loved me; he wrote the words on cards. He said it at all the right times—at the end of a call, after sex, and when I brought him takeout on the nights he worked late. He respected how independent I was and valued my accommodating nature. All in all, I was low maintenance. But sometimes I did feel he took this for granted, and that I ranked about fifth on his priority list.

"Hey, sweetie. You busy?"

"Paige, I'm on a call. Let me call you back in five." Ken never called me back in five. I had challenged him about this before. It was a pet peeve of mine. You shouldn't say that you'll call in five unless you plan to call in five. Each time, I would take note of the time, then feel completely dejected when thirty minutes had passed.

I stopped by Hecht's to peruse their boot selection and was questioned extensively by the salesman about the terrain I would be climbing and my skill level. I tried on several pairs but, upon seeing the $150-and-up price tags, decided that I could do without.

On my way out of the shoe department, I passed the bridal department and saw a young woman standing atop the circular platform, adjusting the mounds of silk that surrounded her. As I watched her, I wondered if the weekend ahead would indeed involve a marriage proposal—and, if so, if I was prepared to say yes.

Vicki called me on my cell phone as I headed to the Metro. "Hey, do you have any of those plastic egg crates?"

"For what?"

"Mr. Fatboy has diabetes. I just came from the vet. I'm trying to create kind of a guinea-pig gym. I've got some hollowed-out oatmeal boxes and some perches, but I wanted to put a few egg crates around as obstacles."

"OK, that's weird. But I think I have some down in my storage locker. I'll check when I get home."

"Can you drop them off tonight?"

"Sure. I'll come by about seven."

My condominium building was one block from the Cleveland Park Metro. I went directly to my storage locker and dumped two egg crates full of books onto the floor. I picked up my Jetta from the dungeon like parking lot underneath the building and arrived at Vicki's door ten minutes later. Although her building was close by, I rarely walked the distance since she had given me her garage passkey. Vicki believed owning a car was like dining at an all-you-can-eat buffet. Because people paid a hefty ticket price, they felt the need to "pig out" and drive everywhere, rather than walk or take advantage of public transportation. Normally Vicki asked if I had hoofed it or not. Her enthusiasm over the egg crates, however, made her forget to berate me for being a gas-guzzling glutton.

"This is perfect. I owe you," she said as she positioned them amid the makeshift gym on the floor of her bedroom.

"Hey, you don't have any hiking boots, do you?" I asked, plopping down on her bed. "I need them for this weekend with Ken." She retreated to her closet and rummaged through the wreckage on her closet floor. While she burrowed, I searched for signs of Mr. Fatboy's newly inspired athleticism.

"Here," she said, handing me a pair of very official-looking boots.

"These look like the real deal! Why do you have these?"

"Quinn," she said curtly. "God, he was an odd duck." I caught a glimpse of Mr. Fatboy, who sat idle in the makeshift gymnasium, chewing on the oatmeal box. Vicki then proceeded to counsel me on Ken and our incompatibility.

"It's like he's a pair of beautiful shoes," she said, "only he's a size seven."

"What?"

"Ken. He's not your size."

"What are you talking about?" I asked.

"Have you ever bought a pair of shoes that were too small?"

"Yes."

"Why? Why did you do that?"

"Because I liked them. Because they were on sale. Because they looked good."

"Exactly. It's like all your life you've had this vision of the perfect shoes. You knew what color they were, the height of the heel, the quality of the leather. You've dreamed about them. You've searched for them every time you've stepped into a shoe store."

"I got it. I got it. My dream shoes."

"Right. Finally, you find them ... but they are a size six and a half and you are a seven. But they are perfect ... almost. And you think to yourself, 'I can wear a six and a half. They'll stretch a little, and I'll make them work.' So you buy them. After all, they are just shy of what you want."

"And they are the best buy of my life," I answer.

"Wrong!" She pointed at me. "Wrong, wrong, wrong. You wear them, and they begin to give you blisters, but you think, 'It's OK. I'll put a Band-Aid over it.' But they continue to rub you the wrong way ... and soon you curse these shoes. You can't wait to take them off at night, and you don't want to put them on in the morning. They simply don't fit you."

She bit the end of a carrot and shook it at me. "Ken doesn't fit you, but you are so afraid to go barefoot and so stubborn that you will continue to wear those shoes until you have corns and bunions and are going to the podiatrist every week."

"OK. OK, OK. Enough with the shoe analogy."

I left Vicki's and wondered if there was any truth to what she had said. Was Ken not the right fit for me? Perhaps there was a strategic reason Mattel had never developed some soap-opera-like twist pairing Ken with Barbie's sister. I envisioned a boardroom full of Mattel executives with pie charts and spreadsheets, discussing the low statistical probability and poor sales revenue that would result in this coupling.

I exploded into the foyer of my condo, dropping my lunch bag, purse, computer bag, and hiking boots. My eyes darted to the phone, where a single red light blinked—a message from Ken. There were always messages from Ken. He had a tendency to call my home phone at times when he knew I wasn't there. He always denied this, but in my heart I knew it was true.

"Paige, hey. Sorry I missed you. I've been on conference calls all day. Listen, I'm going to have to cancel this weekend. The trial has been moved up, and Granger says that we all have to work through the weekend. Anyway, I'll call you at work tomorrow."

And with that, I opened the fridge and popped open the bottle of wine I had selected for the weekend. I was feeling desperately sorry for myself and proceeded to drink all but two glasses until I fell asleep on my couch.

Chapter 10

▼

I woke the next morning feeling very harried and rushed into work. I had established a tactic for when I woke late and didn't have time to shower or do my hair: I would grab the best outfit out of my closet to negate anything disgusting or unsightly going on with my face and hair. This particular morning, I grabbed the new Dolce & Gabbana tweed pants that I had practically stolen from Nordstrom Rack. They were originally $400, but I had gotten them for a thrifty $49. They were beauts and very thinning, because they zipped in the back. The style reminded me of a pair of pantaloons that Mattel's 1982 Uptown Girl Barbie had worn in pink pleather. The zipper was a little tricky and almost certainly the cause of the grand discount, but with a little elbow grease, it worked every time.

I hoisted my computer bag over my shoulder and headed downtown to the office. When I arrived, there was another sticky note from Perry. It was a standard, "See me ASAP." I first stopped in the coffee room and fixed some tea. Blair Davis was waiting for something by the microwave.

"Hey, Blair." I smiled.

"Good morning," she said politely.

"TGIF."

"Excuse me?" she said, as if not understanding.

"I said TGIF. You know, Thank God It's Friday."

"Oh, yes. Yes. Thank God."

"Have any plans this weekend?" I asked.

"Not really." The microwave beeped, and Blair took out her mug. Her slender fingers slowly emptied one packet of sweetener into the steaming liquid. Mike crowded into the room and poured himself a cup from the stainless steel carafe.

My eyes bore into him, since I knew he had sworn off coffee after being diagnosed with an ulcer. He sheepishly averted my glance. Blair stopped to read an announcement on the bulletin board, and both Mike and I observed her. She playfully bit on the end of the plastic coffee stirrer, and it dangled from her mouth, proving that even a coffee stirrer can be sexy. After she sauntered away, Mike took a swig from his cup and declared, "God, I've missed coffee."

Blair was one of the beautiful people. We called them BPs in college. Carlita and I shared a pastime of speculating about her. It was rumored that she was dating a married congressman, but we had no evidence.

Perry's door was closed, so I loitered in the hall. Carlita stopped to chat.

"Did you see what Miss Thing was wearing today?"

"I know. Winter white again. It's depressing. I could never wear all white. She's like some sort of android."

"Well, I bet all her parts work just fine, if you know what I'm saying."

"I tried to have a conversation with her today, but she hardly said two words. I don't get it. How can you be a successful lobbyist when you can't carry on a conversation?"

Carlita stared at me. "Girl," she said. "Is anything up there in that red head of yours?"

"Ah, yes," I said. "You're implying that she's doing more than talking."

"Damn straight," Carlita answered. "I think she's cleaning up the C&O canal by letting 'em pollute hers."

"Carlita, come on."

"I don't know, girl. She seems to accomplish a lot, and I am attributing that to her big ideas, if you know what I'm saying." Carlita rounded her hands around her breasts. Just then Perry's door opened.

"Good morning, ladies."

"Morning."

"I just wanted to know how the conversation with Holden went."

"It was fine. I didn't get all the specifics, but I'm going to talk with him again next week. I have a few things to check into first."

"Good," Perry said gruffly. "Need to be responsive to this. This can't be another Seeing Eye dog thing."

Perry was referring to a case where one of the executive assistants for the Water and Waste group tried to pass her pooch off as a Seeing Eye dog. She claimed to have temporal periphery vision loss but had no documentation to support her claim. She was also driving herself to work, which made her need for a guide dog more than questionable. The dog, Tartan, was a Skye Terrier, weighed about twenty pounds, and barked incessantly. He spent his time at H2O defecating under conference tables and furiously gnawing at his makeshift harness. It was obvious to everyone that Tartan was not a certified Seeing Eye dog. Despite this no one said a word. For five months, she brought him to work with her. Only when Tartan bit one of the lawyers did the case come to the attention of HR, but our office was criticized severely for not being more responsive to such issues.

Carlita had to reschedule our lunch date, freeing up my 12 PM–1 PM timeslot. I called Ken and got his voice mail.

"Hey, it's me. Just calling to see how your case is going. Give me a buzz." I had just hung up the phone when Kulfeen popped her head into the office.

"Mike and I are going to Taj of India for lunch. Do you want to come? I have coupon," she said in stilted English.

I stood up and grabbed my purse. "Let's go."

The H2O offices were on the corner of 26th and M, a short walk into Georgetown. It was a prime location on the cusp of downtown. The only problem was that H2O was seven blocks from the closest Metro. Our building had a garage, but it cost $20 a day to park. I reserved driving into work for days when the weather made walking seven blocks miserable, or when the terrorist alert level was elevated to orange. Mags insisted on that, and even offered to pay $5 of the cost.

The three of us walked to the restaurant and ordered. I misinterpreted the *S* logo on the menu as denoting one of the restaurant's specialties and ordered something extremely spicy. My lunch ended up being one part food and five parts water.

"I feel like someone just shaved my tongue," I announced.

"Speaking of shaved ... Blair told me that she got a Brazilian." Mike drooled as he finished the sentence, which he attributed to his spicy dish.

"She told you that?" I asked. "How does something like that even come up in conversation? 'Hold the elevator. I got a Brazilian.' Please tell me."

Mike wiped his mouth to reduce the high level of drool he was producing as a result of the topic of conversation. He quickly defended her. "I noticed she was kind of walking funny and asked if she was OK, and she told me."

"In Ukraine, they melt honey candy in a pot and pour it on your legs and private areas to take out hair. It's very painful, and there are blisters afterward," Kulfeen shared in her thick Eastern European accent.

Both Mike and I grimaced at the thought of it. He added, "I want to stop at the pharmacy on the way back to pick her up some cream."

"Are you kidding me?" I inquired after gulping down another glass of water after one bite of my food.

"What?" he answered.

"Don't you have a wife at home?" Kulfeen joked.

"Yes, and she's mean as a snake."

Since Kulfeen insisted on using her "buy one get one free" lunch coupon, the processing and calculation of the check took twenty minutes, causing us to be several minutes late for our afternoon staff meeting.

For the past year, Perry had scheduled staff meetings on Fridays at 2 PM, so that people couldn't sneak out early to begin their weekends. It was a son-of-a-bitch thing to do, but it worked. The purpose of the meeting was to obtain and share status in a round-robin forum. Inevitably Brian, who loved to hear his own voice and loved his job a little too much, would talk for about fifteen minutes longer than needed. The rest of us would knowingly look at each other, then return our gazes to Brian, who was giving his monologue. We hoped the combined energy of our stares could telekinetically shut him up. In addition, Kulfeen's command of the English language sucked up time. Perry typically asked two questions for every statement she made. She would rephrase and rephrase her status until he understood. I normally went last and would provide my status update in two minutes flat. Despite my efficiency, the meeting would often last until well after 5 PM, as it also took Perry a while to capture everything on the white board.

This time, I spent the meeting contemplating my day, trying to decide what to do for the weekend now that my big plans had been canceled. By the middle of the meeting, the gallon of water I had consumed at lunch had caught up with me. I waited until the meeting was over and ran to the bathroom, only to discover that my panty hose had gotten stuck in my pants zipper. For ten minutes, I worked the zipper in the bathroom with little success. It was now becoming an emergency. I didn't care about my bargain pants any longer. I just needed to get them off. I left the bathroom in search of one of my female colleagues, but as on every Friday, everyone had left in record time. H2O was a ghost town. The only person I saw was Moman, our facilities guy from India, watering plants.

I ran back into the bathroom and clawed crazily at the top of my pants. I stood in the same spot where Blair had stood hours earlier in her perfect glory. I looked at myself in the mirror. I looked like shit. I decided that a man must have applied his definition of long-lasting to my "all-day wear" makeup, because it seemed to wear off in twenty minutes. I returned my attention to my pants. After a few more minutes of trying to rip the back of my pants apart, I realized that I was left with no choice. I left the bathroom to get Moman.

"Moman, hey!" I said sweetly. He looked up at me as he was emptying one of the wastebaskets.

"I have a bit of an emergency," I said coyly. "The zipper of my pants is stuck here, and I really, really need to go to the bathroom."

Moman waved his hands in the air and nodded and spoke very thickly. "So sorry, Ms. Paige. I married man."

"Yeah, I know. I'm not trying to make a pass at you, Moman." I turned to show him the back of my no-longer-a-bargain pants. "I'm desperate. Please."

Moman looked around.

"No one is here," I pleaded. "There is nobody else. Please."

Moman followed me into the bathroom. Since he was much smaller than my five-foot-six frame, I braced myself against the sink counter and leaned forward, so he could get a good hold.

"I very nervous, Ms. Paige," he said. "I don't think I should be doing this. My wife …"

"I really appreciate this, Moman. Rip them if you have to … I don't care. This is the last time I buy irregular pants." I could see Moman in the mirror with an intense look upon his face, as if he were examining the most complicated problem.

"The weave of pants is very good, Ms. Paige. Very good weave. Is like the weave of good Indian rug. Very strong."

I screamed, "Moman, please! If you don't get these pants off me in like two minutes …"

"Yes, Ms. Paige. I think I get something to cut with or to pick out stitching that is stopped in zipper." I nodded and raced out and retrieved the letter opener from my desk and handed it to Moman.

"Ms. Paige. I'm going to first try to pull panty out of zipper. If that do not work, I try to force it down with point of stick." Moman jerked hard and pushed the letter opener into my back.

"Owww. Careful."

"Yes, da weave is very strong."

"I know. I know. Apparently they are very good pants … if you never have to take them off."

Frustrated, I let out a long moan. "Ahhhhhhgggh. Oh my God, Moman, if you don't get these pants off me soon, we're going to have a problem."

"I go as fast as Moman can. I try."

With one final jerk, Moman pulled hard, ripping the pants and sending us both to the floor. When we landed, Blair Davis appeared in the doorway. I immediately realized how bad the scene appeared—Moman and I on the ladies'-room floor, with a portion of my pants dangling like a tail on my backside. I jumped to my feet, holding the back of my pants together. Blair did not say a word. She simply backed up and went out the door. Moman stood up. I looked at Moman sympathetically.

"Oh, no. Oh, no," he whimpered. "Moman going to get in trouble."

"Don't worry, Moman. It's fine. I'll take care of it. Thank you."

I ushered Moman out the door and swiftly entered a stall to relieve myself. As I exited the bathroom, I caught a glimpse of my backside in the mirror. I realized that I needed something to cover up the gaping hole, which revealed a pair of green-shamrock underwear.

Women normally had their good underwear and their bad underwear, but I had three categories of underwear. Category A underwear were fairly new, typically had lace, and belonged either to the thong family or the string-bikini clan. These were the panties you wore when you were expecting a "poke" or anything related. Category B underwear were generally gifts from my mother. The fabric was usually 100 percent cotton, and they resembled Underoos, since they typically featured some novel or seasonal characters (for example, shamrocks). This underwear had one purpose and one purpose only: comfort. Category C underwear were once A or B underwear but had been demoted for various reasons. This was underwear that should have been discarded but had managed to survive the quarterly drawer cleaning. They were worn when no A or B undies were clean and, of course, when it was that time of the month. The green shamrocks were undoubtedly a proud member of the C class. They had served their time. My mother had bought them for me in Ireland when she and my father went there to celebrate their thirtieth wedding anniversary.

I ran to the office coat closet. All that was hanging inside was a giant, yellow slicker. The slicker was ever present. I never saw anyone wear it and had often wondered who owned it. I began to close the door to search for other options but knew that, despite the shamrocks decorating my backside, my luck had run out. I grabbed the slicker and jogged to Blair's office. The lights were out and the door closed. There was no sign of her. I decided that damage control would need to wait until Monday.

I received several stares on the Metro, since I looked like the Gorton's fisherman on a beautiful, late August afternoon. I returned home to find a colorful bouquet of wildflowers. I loved wildflowers for two reasons: 1) they weren't cliché and 2) they lasted forever. The card read, "Wildflowers for my wild girl. Tuppence, Ken."

Tuppence was from *Mary Poppins*. We had argued for two hours on our first date about its meaning. Ken was certain it was a British word for love. I argued that it was a variant of two pence. On our second date, we rented the movie, and much to Ken's chagrin, my answer proved to be correct. I held the card and smiled as I looked at Ken's handwriting—well, typesetting, actually. He never wrote in cursive. He always wrote in caps, and all his letters were perfectly symmetrical, except for his *X*, which was always a little larger than the rest. The first time he wrote me something, it looked as if he had used one of those label makers.

I called him at 6 PM to thank him for the flowers. He called back an hour later.

"How's the case?" I asked.

"It's a nightmare, but we're getting there."

"Did you cancel Blarney Brook yet?"

"I'll do it after we hang up. Thanks for the reminder."

"The cancellation policy is forty-eight hours, so we'll lose the deposit."

"I'll bill it to the firm," Ken replied. "Get some rest. I love you."

"Me too." And I drifted off to sleep.

Chapter 11

▼

I awoke two hours later, disoriented. At first I thought I had slept through the night but then realized it was only 8 PM. I opened the fridge, ate a hunk of cheese, and searched for a movie. *On Golden Pond* was on, and I wondered if my entire weekend would consist of watching the eighties-movie marathon on TBS. I looked at my packed bag and the pile of books I had planned to read during the weekend. I picked up the Blarney Brook Inn brochure from the coffee table.

"Nestled in a woodsy glen in the heart of Deep Creek Lake, Blarney Brook offers private guest rooms furnished with period antiques and fireplaces. Retreat to the outdoor hot tub with spectacular mountain views, or simply curl up with a book in our beautifully appointed garden room. After enjoying some of our Bedtime Brownies, fall asleep to the music of the trees sashaying in the wind. After all, you deserve a little piece of heaven."

I picked up the phone, called Ken's office, and left him a message, "Hey, don't cancel on Blarney. I've decided to have a little me time."

I called Blarney Brook and asked if he'd canceled yet. He hadn't, and I wasn't surprised—Ken was terrible about the follow-through. I grabbed my bag and headed out the door.

Hours later I was hunched over the steering wheel, peering through the windshield as the wipers squeaked furiously back and forth. A heavy downpour had caused traffic to slow to a snail's pace. I had only the blur of brake lights in front of me as my guide. Normally I would have pulled over in such conditions, because my Jetta (the Silver Fox, as I called her) was a bit temperamental in the rain. However, it was almost midnight, and I was exhausted. The drive to Deep

Creek Lake normally took two hours, but the Silver Fox's dashboard was digitally reporting that I had been driving for 3.35 hours.

Finally I saw the sign for Blarney Brook and turned onto the gravel road which was surrounded by deep and desolate woods. As my car fought the bumpy terrain, I half expected a deranged lunatic to bolt out of the woods covered in blood like a scene in some horror flick. Finally, I saw the glow of a lamppost. The inn appeared around the bend. I shoved the gearshift into park and grabbed my bags, trotting through the mud to the front door. It was locked, but I could see some feet up on the counter. I tapped on the door, and the feet came down. A young Asian girl cautiously moved to the door. She had a number of piercings and a tattoo of a snake on her neck. She wore a kelly green Blarney Brook V-neck that looked incompatible with her cargo pants and Doc Martens.

"It's wicked out there," I said as I shook some of the rain off. "I apologize for dripping everywhere."

"No problem, but I'm sorry ... we don't have any vacancies. We're completely sold out, but there's a Motel 6 about ten miles up on I-68."

"Yeah, I know. I'm sorry I'm so late, but we were going to cancel, and then I decided to come. It's been one of those weeks. I called earlier. The reservation is under Marxen."

The girl looked completely dazed and went behind the small counter to look at the registration book. She stuck her tongue out and began batting the tip of her tongue against the piercing that jutted from the side of her lip. I sauntered up to the counter and read the names upside down.

"There," I said, pointing to Marxen. "That's it. It was going to be two of us, but he had to work, and I decided to come at the last minute, since we were going to lose our deposit anyway."

The girl stammered, and I was beginning to think she might have a drug problem when I saw the perfectly capped letters to the right of the reservation. *K. MARXEN, 3459 LAVIDA LANE, ARLINGTON, VA, 22201*. A drop of rain from my sopping-wet hair dropped upon the page, smearing the tail of his extra-large *X*.

"Oh my God. He's here. That's weird. I don't understand."

Unnerved, she backed away from the counter. "Are you OK?" she asked, staring at my dumbfounded face. "The Briodys, the owners, are at a wedding in Pennsylvania, but I can call them," she added anxiously.

I talked aloud, trying to make sense of it. "So, he's here ... did you check him in, Mimi?" I questioned her, reading the name of her shamrock-shaped tag. She stood motionless. I spun the book around and pointed. "Did you check him in? There are only seven rooms, right? You'd remember checking him in."

She stammered, "Y-Yeah, I might have ... I don't know."

I rubbed my face with my hand and began to get teary-eyed. I leaned over the counter. "Please answer me," I said.

"Let me call the Briodys. Just give me a second."

"Mimi," I said calmly, "it's obvious you checked him in. Just tell me if he was with a woman or a man."

Mimi pulled nervously at her eyebrow piercing. "I really don't think I should be answering these questions." But then, curiously, she asked her own question. "Are you his wife?"

I sat down in the rocking chair in the small lobby of the main house and tried my best to assess the situation and react appropriately. I rocked nervously, like Rainman. I pulled out my cell phone, but Mimi warned, "We don't get cell coverage up here."

I continued rocking and started to talk to myself. "Option 1: Go to the room and knock. But then what? Cause a scene? Or maybe he *is* working. Maybe it's just a colleague ... a female colleague. I have colleagues of the opposite sex, right? Option 2: Go to the Motel 6 and think this through some more. Option 3: Go home to D.C. Maybe he had a breakdown and just wanted to get away without me, and he didn't want to say anything. He has been pretty stressed." I stopped talking and weighed my weak-ass options.

Mimi asked nervously, "Do you want me to call someone?"

I didn't answer and instead walked out to the car and attempted to drive away—but I went nowhere. The back tires were so mired in mud from the storm that I only sunk the back end of the Fox deeper into the ground. Mimi obviously thought I was about to "go postal"; she cautiously backed away from the counter when I entered.

"Mimi, are there any other rooms? Anything at all. A sun porch I could sleep on? A couch? Anything. Please." I was on the verge of tears, and Mimi gave me a sympathetic look.

"Well, one of our new cottages is almost ready. It's still under construction. "There's a bed in there, but the bathrooms aren't finished yet. I could give you some sheets and towels."

"Fine, whatever."

Mimi strapped on some galoshes over her Doc Martens, and we trudged our way in the rain to the cottage under construction. I put my stuff down, and Mimi began the spiel.

"Breakfast is served from 7 to 10 AM. There is a library in the main house. You're welcome to take one of the books home with you. If you get hungry in the middle of the night, there are homemade, chocolate-cranberry Bedtime Brownies in the foyer. Scrabble, dominoes, Monopoly, and other board games are …"

I interrupted. "Mimi, I appreciate the lowdown here, but I don't think I'll be playing any Scrabble tonight."

"Oh … Riiiiight."

I didn't sleep at all. At 3 AM, I began running possible scenarios in my head. Perhaps Ken decided to give the weekend to one of his colleagues instead of losing the one-night deposit. No, that didn't explain Ken's handwriting on the registration book. At 4 AM, I stopped making excuses and decided to accept the most likely scenario: Ken was cheating on me. At 5 AM, I walked back to the main house and slid underneath the registration counter. I again looked at Ken's handwriting. It was unmistakable. I called Carlita collect from the phone in the main house. I whispered, "Hi, it's me."

"Why are you whispering, and what time is it?"

"It's 5 AM."

"Where are you?"

"I'm sorry. I'm having a major crisis, and I needed to talk to someone." I started to sob, spilling the whole story to Carlita. I cried into the phone for ten minutes. Then I spent five minutes vowing to kill him. Two minutes of nervous, hysterical laughter followed, and then seven minutes of desperate ranting, which concluded with another bout of tears.

"So, what should I do?"

"If I were you, I would do the goddamn windmill on his ass."

"The what?"

"The windmill. It's how girls fight in the city … you know, with arms flying every which way. It's like Kung Fu on speed, girl."

"I feel sick. I don't want him to see me. I look atrocious, and I don't have a bathroom."

"What kind of fucked-up bed-and-breakfast are you at?"

"Ironically, I'm staying in the honeymoon suite, but it's in the middle of construction. It was the only room they had open."

"Well, if it was me, I'd fuck him up, you know what I'm saying? But you're sugar, *not* spice, and I think it's best if you come back home. You're not the Jerry Springer type who would go wild on his ass at a bed-and-breakfast. Wait until Mr. High and Mighty comes on home to find that message on his machine."

It was helpful to talk to Carlita. And I decided to follow her advice. I returned to bed and fell into a restless sleep. As soon as it was light enough, I was out the door and working on my car. The mud had dried, but my car was still stuck in its resting place from the night before. I decided to gather some leaves, sticks, and gravel to create the traction needed to rock my car out of its rut. Just as I was about to get in the car to give it a try, the door of the Loon's Nest opened. I ducked so quickly that I hit my head on the car's bumper. I could taste blood. I put my fingers to my mouth, and sure enough, I was bleeding. I saw the funhouse image of myself in the chrome bumper. It appeared that I had not only bloodied my lip, but chipped my tooth.

I watched as Ken walked down the ramp toward the main house. Trailing behind him was my worst fear: a Barbie. However, this wasn't just any Barbie. It was Lobbyist Barbie. They laughed, and Blair threw her head back. Her long, brunette ponytail swung back and forth as she walked. Obviously Ken had not checked his office messages yet. I expected it would only be a matter of time, so I had to work quickly.

The car was almost out, but I needed some more branches. I went a little into the woods and found a pile of twigs and brush. As I tugged to pull one of the largest branches from the pile, I saw a furry little creature underneath. I jumped, and so did it—a cute, little squirrel with a white streak on its back. Then, much to my dismay, I realized it was not a squirrel. I stood motionless, and so did he or she. I held my breath. It was a standoff. It seemed like an eternity before the skunk turned and retreated. I breathed a sigh of relief and returned to my spot. Suddenly there was a surprise attack as a family of "squirrels" scampered out from underneath the brush. I stumbled, trying to catch my balance, but I fell forward, right into the line of fire. I had smelled skunk before when driving along country roads, but nothing compared to 100-proof skunk spray. Just at that moment, I heard the screen door of the main house open and slam shut. I turned to see Ken running out of the main house, scanning the parking lot. Then he spotted the car and me, several feet away.

"I can explain!" he called. "Paige?" He ran toward me. Behind him ran Blair.

"Blair, leave us alone for a minute," he instructed her.

It was a race to the car. I jumped in and slammed the door just as he reached it. I gunned the engine, praying that my car would free itself.

"Come on, Fox! Come on!" I begged. Ken pounded on the window.

"It's not what you think." His voice was muffled. "I needed her help on something." Noticing my bloodied lip, he said, "Paige, you're hurt. Come inside."

I would not look in his direction. I stared straight ahead. The Fox suddenly popped up and out, tires squealing, branches snapping. Ken threw his hands in the air. I could see Blair running behind him, shooing the malodorous scent that thickened the air. I now felt Klavic's pain. The acidic oil from the skunk's spray burned my lips. Once on the interstate, I pulled over and flushed my face with some bottled water.

Chapter 12

I don't recall much of the trip home. I do recall that the sky was unbelievably beautiful. The rain had left a dense fog that was lifting, and a mix of orange and pink emerged from behind the mist. I showered as soon as I arrived home but could not seem to rid myself of the stink. In addition, a peculiar rash formed on my arm. I called my doctor, who suggested I meet him in the emergency room after his rounds that afternoon. I hadn't been to an emergency room since college. I wondered why I could never have a normal emergency, like a broken arm or a sprained ankle.

I thought back to the night of my previous trip to the ER, when I was a senior in college. If Mattel had created a dorky younger brother for Ken, they could have used my college boyfriend, Neil, as their prototype. Neil sang a capella in the campus men's group, the Thanes. When they performed, they wore these very elaborate Renaissance-era outfits. Neil was enthralled by it. To help with tuition, he was a resident assistant, forced to write people up for various campus violations, like urinating out their sixth-floor window and public vomiting. I felt sorry for him. He despised confrontation, and the jocks gave him hell. It was Neil who technically deflowered me—another disastrous and less than perfect moment in my life. I was expecting it to hurt the first time. Vicki had told me that there was usually some bleeding.

"I don't feel very good," I said after it was over. Neil lay squished up beside me, panting on the dorm room issued bed.

"Jesus," he said. "You're bleeding a lot."

We inspected the bed sheets. It looked as if a violent battle had taken place upon Neil's twin bed.

"Is this normal?" I asked nervously. "I don't think this is normal."

Unfortunately, uber-Catholic Neil's sexual resume consisted of a couple of hand jobs and a subscription to *Penthouse Forum*. This meant that he could educate me on how to have a three-way with a amputee or perform oral sex while engineering a locomotive. On everyday problems, however, he was as clueless as I was.

After a short debate, Neil said that he was going to call Ronnie Turner, the Thanes' lead tenor, who lived down the hall. According to Neil, Ronnie had a lot of experience with the ladies. I discovered at our five-year reunion that Ronnie's so-called experience was on par with Neil's, since it consisted of watching a lot of XXX videos and looking at pictures in his father's medical textbooks. I hid in the bathroom as Ronnie assessed the situation.

"Fuck, man," I heard him say to Neil through the door.

"Have you ever seen this much blood?" Neil asked.

"Hell, no," Ronnie responded emphatically. "I think we should call my dad."

"No!" I yelled, panicked, from the floor of the bathroom. "It's OK. I'm fine, really."

I looked down at the new silk Maidenform undies that I had bought for our special night together. The lace was saturated with blood, and suddenly I felt slightly woozy. I called for Neil, who cracked open the bathroom door.

"Call Ronnie's dad," I said tearfully.

Dr. Turner was an ob-gyn in Massachusetts. He confirmed that profuse bleeding was "definitely abnormal," and that I should be taken to an emergency room immediately. Because Neil didn't have a car and was on RA duty that night, he called campus police, who arrived at the dorm with lights flashing and sirens blaring. As we exited the dorm, a crowd of coeds formed. Neil had to stay behind, and Ronnie volunteered to escort me to the hospital. However, I think the only reason he was so eager to assist me was that I was braless and dressed only in one of Neil's T-shirts. I was a bloody mess, but this did not prevent Ronnie from caressing my knee on the way to the hospital and wrapping his arm around my waist, which he apparently thought was chest-high. It was awkward, but I was so frightened and had such extreme cramps that I didn't care. Ronnie delivered me to an examination room, where I waited for some time. As I lay upon my back, looking up at the ceiling, silent tears gravitated to the outer corners of my face, landing on the tops of my ears. After what seemed like an eternity, a young resident drew the curtain that surrounded the hospital bed.

"Hi, I'm Dr. Goddard," he said. "Based on the nurse's preliminary, I'm going to have to do a pelvic exam."

"OK," I replied.

I had never been to a gynecologist before, so I was not sure what this entailed. Dr. Goddard guided me into the stirrups and helped me slide down until my derriere was teetering on the end of the table. I felt completely exposed, both literally and figuratively. Either in an attempt to minimize the awkwardness or to maximize it, Dr. Goddard struck up a conversation.

"So, you go to U of M?" he asked, as he stuck what looked like a barbecue utensil inside me.

"Yea ... oh," I winced. "Ow. Uh, yes."

"I hear you have a good basketball team this year. This might pinch a bit." The barbecue utensil turned.

"Uh huh," I exhaled.

"My cousin goes there, you know." Dr. Goddard withdrew the barbecue utensil and grabbed a pair of rubber hot-dog tongs, which he promptly inserted.

"Miranda Robinson. That's her name. She's a freshman. What year are you?" He seemed to be turning the dogs inside me, and I whimpered.

"Sop-ah-more," I exhaled, as I stared at the brown water leak on the ceiling. He chatted on and on for another five minutes as he probed and poked and prodded. Finally he said, "OK, we're all done here. I've cauterized the source of the bleeding. You can sit up."

I rose and pulled the large paper-towel blanket around me.

"It looks like you're having a reaction to the condom," he began.

"I'm allergic?" I asked.

He stripped off his latex gloves. "Not exactly. Do you know how long your partner had that condom?"

I knew Neil had been optimistically carrying around the same condom since his senior year in high school.

"A couple of years, I think," I answered.

"That's what I thought," he replied. "Condoms are made of a thin latex, which is a rubber. After a while, that plastic can harden in places. It's fairly uncommon but can happen with less expensive prophylactics. Did you or he put the condom on?"

I shifted uncomfortably and looked down at my dirty Keds sneakers on the floor.

"My boyfriend did. It was our first time."

"Well, in his excitement, he probably didn't notice the tip had hardened. Basically, each time he thrust inside you, it was like one of those plastic picnic knives rubbing against your vaginal wall. The cuts were small ... but voluminous, which caused the bleeding."

The doctor walked over to a cabinet, pulled out a bag, and handed it to me.

"Here are some new condoms and some info about proper usage."

"Thanks," I said weakly.

"But don't have intercourse for at least a few weeks to allow your vaginal lining to heal."

"I don't think that's going to be a problem."

When I returned from the hospital, Neil was waiting for me in his room. Once he found out that I was going to live, he recounted the events of his evening. Apparently, while I was hanging out in my stirrups, some guys from the lacrosse team had gone into Neil's room during his rounds. They had allegedly stolen his beloved, feathered minstrel cap and thrown it in their quad's toilet, then urinated on it. Neil was incensed. I was too, but they were dumb jocks, and I expected such behavior. However, I was more disappointed that Neil did not seem to recognize that my ordeal was just a tad more upsetting than having piss on a fruity, feathered hat.

"It's an injustice," Neil said. "They better watch out the next time they plan to have a keg party, because I'm going to be right there waiting with my violations pad in hand."

Because I was still under my parents' medical insurance in college, my father received a bill for my ER visit and called me to inquire about its validity. "It just says pelvic emergency," he said. "I don't remember you having any emergency."

I lied to him, claiming that I had fallen on the bar of my bike after hitting a huge pothole on campus. This seemed to satisfy him. When I informed Neil about my cover story just in case my parents mentioned it at graduation, he nodded and said, "God, that was a bad night ... those fuckers." He talked about the Thanes Cap Massacre almost every day until we graduated. Shortly thereafter we went our separate ways. Last I heard, he was married and playing a Yankee in Civil War reenactments. I only hoped the Confederates hadn't gotten hold of his hat.

At least now I had my own health insurance, and my peculiar medical troubles would need no explanation or cover. The admissions nurse at George Washington Hospital argued with me about the urgency of my condition, suggesting that I wait until Monday to consult a dermatologist. A reinforced-glass window separated us, and I knew that once the scent found its way to the small, circular pass-through, she would surrender ... which she did. The ER was crowded, but no one sat beside me. A man whose arm was bleeding profusely stood against the wall in the opposite corner rather than take the empty seat next to me. Dr. Walsh came into the waiting area personally to fetch me. I walked up to shake his hand, and he grimaced.

"I know," I said, "it's pretty bad. I don't know what to do. I've showered three times, but I can't seem to get rid of it. My sister called her vet, and they said that they advise dog owners to douse their animals with tomato juice, and that usually does the trick. I only had three cans of V8 and a jar of Prego, but that did nothing."

"Now you smell like skunk with a side of marinara," he quipped.

"I wish I could joke," I said. "The sad thing is that this isn't the worst part of my weekend."

"No?" He led me to an examination table, and I hopped onto it.

"I caught my boyfriend with someone from my office."

"Ouch!"

"And I can smell myself. That's never good."

"No," he agreed. "It's quite potent, but that's because the human nose can detect the glandular oil of a skunk at about ten parts per billion."

"I'm impressed. Looks like I came to the right guy."

"Don't be. I looked it up on the Internet after I grabbed your chart."

"Oh, well, thanks for the info. Although I don't think I'll be telling anyone the science behind my reeking."

Dr. Walsh listened intently. He had a wonderful bedside manner, and I would have spent the entire afternoon talking to him if some little girl hadn't swallowed her lollipop, stick and all. He advised me to take a bath in douche. Supposedly the same neutralizing agent used in douche to combat genital odor worked on the odors of all glandular secretions. As for the rash, he suggested I consult a dermatologist and offered to have his office fax me the referral letter.

Chapter 13

▼

I drove straight from the hospital to the CVS near my condo. I never had used a douche before. In college they had given the women a sample in our welcome packets, along with Tic Tacs, a razor, shampoo and other giveaways for the entering freshmen. But instead of using them, most of the girls had douche fights in the hallway. The CVS had quite a selection: Rose Petals, Spring Rain, Country Flowers, and Regular. I decided to go with the Regular. Unfortunately their stock was low, so I had to ask the salesgirl to check the back room.

"How much do you need?" she asked.

"Hmm. How much douche does it take to fill a bathtub?"

"Are you serious?" she asked.

"Unfortunately, yes," I answered. "I guess I'll need about a dozen or so."

She brought out a brown cardboard box with the Massengill label on the side, marked with their slogan: "Be fresh. Be clean. Be beautiful." I did not notice the person standing two people in front of me. It was Owen. I pushed the cart up to the cashier's line and waited.

"Hey, stranger," he said. He turned to the person standing in between us. "You can go ahead of me," he offered, repositioning himself in line.

"Hiiiii," I muttered painfully. "What are you doing in my neighborhood?" I leaned over my cart nonchalantly and launched several packets of Fruit Stripe gum into my cart, trying to disguise the contents as much as possible.

"I've got another meeting at D.C. Coast and needed to pick up some file folders first."

"Oh. Well, good seeing you." *Oh God, please help me.*

"Out getting your supply of ...?" He looked into my cart and saw the box. I blushed instantly.

"It's douche," I announced, stating the obvious. For whatever reason, I gave him some more specifics: "A dozen boxes. Regular scent."

"I see that."

"It's not for what you think it's for."

He waved his hand. "No need to explain. It's fine, really. I apologize for being so nosy."

I was intent on explaining. "I was sprayed by a skunk ... actually two skunks ... maybe even three. I'm not sure. It all happened very fast. Skunk oil can be detected by the human nose at ten parts per billion."

"Good to know," he said, smiling. "And my nose did detect it but I just couldn't quite put my finger on the source."

"My doctor says that the douche may help eliminate the smell. I have to take a bath in it."

He laughed heartily, which caused him to take quick and rapid breaths. "Whew. It's making my eyes water."

"I know. Sorry." I looked down and casually kicked the side of the cart.

"Didn't know the city had a skunk presence."

"They don't. I went to Deep Creek this weekend and ... well, it's a long story."

"Do you think you've got enough?" he teased, pointing to the boatload of boxes in my cart. "Maybe, if you have a little extra, you can donate some to Klavic."

"Stop it," I begged, but couldn't help laughing. Despite the circumstances, it was funny. Owen waited for me as I paid the cashier and pushed my cart out of the door to the parking lot. He then placed the box in the trunk of my car.

"Well, have fun douching," he said sarcastically, as he dug his keys out of his jeans pocket.

"Always do," I answered as I climbed into my car. I chastised myself: *Always do? What kind of answer is that?* I had backed out halfway from the parking space when he reappeared at the side of the car. I rolled down the window. He leaned on the rim.

"If you're not busy after your bath," he said, "you should pop down to the Coast. I could probably score you some free dessert. I go there all the time." His white oxford hung open as he teetered on the edge of the window. His chest was in partial view, and I checked him out. I had always scolded my male friends for being so obvious when they checked out a woman's breasts. However, my attempt at subtlety was apparently a failure; he noticed and caught my eye. The right corner of his mouth turned up slightly.

"Uh, I don't think so. I have a bunch of stuff to do today."

He stood and pulled his sunglasses down from the top of his head.

"What about tomorrow night?" he asked.

"Yeah, maybe just for a drink."

"Great. Hope to see you there around five."

I sat for an hour in my douche bath. As I toweled my hair, I finally decided to listen to the messages that were inevitably awaiting me. They were all from Ken.

"Paige, please call me." BEEP.

"Hey, I screwed up. Just hear me out." BEEP.

"Me again. Please, I'm asking you to at least call me. Five minutes, that's all I ask." BEEP.

I looked into the mirror and touched the jagged edge of my cracked front tooth, wondering if Owen had noticed my snaggletooth. I looked like one of those eighteenth-century whores from *Les Misérables*. I called the dentist. Fortunately the office had weekend hours and they could take me at 3:00 PM on Sunday. I spent the rest of the afternoon and evening making up the sleep I had lost on Friday night. Mags called at noon on Sunday, waking me from my depression-induced slumber. I let the answering machine pick up the call.

"Paigey, sweetie. It's me. We are all dying to know what happened this weekend. Aunt Judy has called twice. The whole family is buzzing. Call me when you get back into town. I need to know if I should start browsing mother-of-the-bride dresses!"

As planned, I went to the dentist at 3:00 PM. She attached some temporary bonding to the cracked tooth and fitted me for a porcelain veneer. I hadn't expected her to give me novocaine, but they had to shave down some of the tooth so the bonding material would adhere. She also prescribed two painkillers to help reduce sensitivity. I returned home, changed, picked up the prescription, took one pill, and headed around the corner to D.C. Coast. Owen was not there. I was about to leave but figured that I owed myself at least one drink at the bar.

"Un vokkah tonac," I said. My mouth felt disconnected from the rest of my body.

"Excuse me?" The bartender covered his ear, indicating that he couldn't hear me over the crowd.

"Vokah tonac."

He nodded. I sat there and surveyed the crowd. There were several Gen Yers decked out in their look-at-me clothes. The bartender came around again and said very slowly, "This is from the maaaan over there." He pointed down to the other end of the bar. Owen held up his drink and a finger, a promise that he'd be there in one minute. He was.

"Hey, glad you came."

I nodded. "I can't weally alk."

"Huh?"

"Dehtis." I pointed to my teeth.

"No wonder." Owen broke out into a huge grin and threw his head back, laughing.

"Wha?"

"The bartender thought you were ... how shall I say this ... mentally challenged."

I put my head in my hand.

"Hey, why don't I grab a table away from the bar? It's kind of tough to hear you." I nodded.

The restaurant was packed, and from what I could see outside, there were people waiting for tables. Owen strolled over to the hostess and pointed in my direction. She tilted her head, touched his arm, and grabbed two menus. He motioned for me to follow.

"Shelley, this is Paige."

"Hallah, ni ta mee you."

Shelley leaned forward and spoke slowly. "It's nice to meet you, Paige. Your dress is very pretty."

I looked to Owen strangely, and he spoke slowly to me. "It means she likes it."

We followed Shelley's backless-shirted body to the table and sat down.

"Have a nice dinner," she said.

I glared at Owen. "Wha did oo tell er?"

"That you lived at Karlton House, and that I was your brother and promised to take you out on the town tonight, because you just landed a job bagging groceries at the Kmart." Karlton House was a halfway house that prepared mentally impaired adults for the workforce.

"Owaan!"

For the next two hours, we sat talking about family, careers, and aspirations. He told me how he wanted to get out of the legal field and into broadcasting. I told him how I fell into HR and how I ultimately hoped to run the department. I felt completely at ease and wondered whether the few vodka tonics were the reason for my comfort or whether it was Owen. He excused himself to answer his cell phone, and I sat picking the dried wax drippings from the candle that rested in the middle of the table.

I leaned from the table to watch him as he stood in the hallway outside of the restrooms. Carlita was right. Owen was hot. His shirt was casually untucked, and his curly blonde hair had become somewhat unkempt. He spoke animatedly, pacing back and forth with his hand resting on his hip. He looked up and caught my eye and winked, raising his finger again to indicate that he would be detained for just another moment. Sure enough, he was back in his chair before I had time to compile all my wax pickings and hide them under my napkin. I thought he might disclose the identity of his caller. He didn't, and I realized that it wasn't my place to ask.

Then I hit what Carlita referred to as the Alc-HO-line. It's the point when you still have enough presence of mind to know that you should stop drinking. It is a crossroads: you can either enjoy your buzz and call it a night, or opt for another drink and head down the path to full-blown drunkenness and probable promiscuity. Hence the emphasis on the middle syllable: Alc-HO-line.

The waitress came by. "Can I get you anything else?"

"So, I bet you've got girls all over the place," I said, after ordering another.

He leaned forward suggestively, "How astute you are. Yes. I have hundreds of them, all over the world. It's a full-time job."

I smirked and tried to spear the lime floating in my drink with the straw.

"And what about you and Kenneth?" he inquired.

As the liquid courage surged through my veins, I slurred my way through the tale of Ken and Lobbyist Barbie, chipping my tooth, and the skunk attack. He listened intently. At some point, we moved from the table to the street, where I leaned up against a telephone pole and began to explain my fate.

"You see, Ow-en Holden boy, I'm a Sssskipper."

"You're what?"

"I'm Skip-per!"

"You're a dolphin?"

"What?"

"A dolphin. Flipper, the dolphin?"

"No, I said Ski-p-per ... from the sixties." As if this additional piece of information would close the communication gap.

"From Gilligan's Island?"

"No, the doll, the doll. You see, we are one and the same. I'm her. She's me. We are family. I've got all my sisters with me. Hey, who sang that song?"

And that's the last I remember.

Chapter 14

▼

On Monday morning, I woke up in my bed with all my clothes on. My head screamed. I stopped off at Mickey D's and ordered what I had long heralded as a no-fail hangover remedy: a Value Meal #1 with extra bacon. The thought of cramming my hungover self into a Metro car was unbearable, so I hailed a cab and rapidly consumed my breakfast. As soon as I walked into the office, I saw a note from Perry. "Please see me ASAP."

I answered some email and called facilities about getting a shower door installed for Klavic. I was just about to head down to Perry's when the front desk called. "You have a delivery, Ms. Sheehan." I took the elevator down to the first floor, and twenty-seven red roses were waiting. The card read, "One rose for every month. Please call me."

"Sign here," the man said, extending an electronic box to me.

"I don't want them. Take them back."

"I can't."

"Why not?"

"I'm supposed to deliver them."

"OK, then. I'll give you $50 to deliver them somewhere else. I just need about five minutes."

The man tucked the electronic box under his arm. "Fifty bucks. Sure, I'll wait for that."

I took the flowers up to my office and called Carlita. Moman's janitorial cart had been left in the middle of the hallway. I snatched a giant, black trash bag from the cart. Together with Carlita, we massacred the roses, cutting them into pieces and dumping the remains into the plastic bag.

"Girl, I know you're angry, but isn't this a little psycho? Maybe I should let you borrow my aromatherapy spray, because, to be honest, you need some tranquility, and you still smell like a wet dog."

I did not respond, and she knew me well enough not to push the issue. I returned to the lobby and presented the bag, Ken's work address, and a personal check for $50.

"Mind if I ask what he did?" the guy asked, taking the bag and tucking the check into his back pocket.

At that moment, Blair strolled into the lobby, wearing a camel-colored pantsuit, mirrored sunglasses, and stiletto heels. She didn't seem to notice me as she glided to the elevator. She fluffed the back of her hair and pressed the Up button.

"Her," I responded, pointing to Blair. "He did her."

I was not yet prepared to confront Blair. Forgetting all about Perry's request, I headed out for lunch. I also wanted to stop by CorpRate Living, an executive apartment service that H2O used when Congress was in session, and lawyers and lobbyists from other H2O offices were in D.C. for extended periods. I picked up a sandwich from the deli and walked the five blocks to their offices.

"Is Caroline here?" I asked the front-desk receptionist. I patiently waited as the receptionist buzzed her and announced me.

Caroline called out to me from the loft area of their modern offices.

"Come on up. Follow the blue arrows."

I did not deal with Caroline very often. I had only called upon her when problems arose with reservations, like when one of the visiting H2O lawyers from San Francisco refused to stay in one of the suites since it didn't have a water-saving feature on its toilet and showerhead. Technically it was Perry's responsibility to handle executive contracts, but he always pawned such tasks off on me. I sat across from her on a sleek red plastic chair.

"I haven't looked at our contract lately, and I'm wondering if H2O has any suites vacant right now."

Caroline's eyes narrowed, and she banged on her keyboard with such flair that she looked like a concert pianist.

"Let's see here." Her fingers followed something on the screen.

"Yes, there's a unit in the Charleston Building on Connecticut, and it doesn't look like we have it reserved for anyone until next month."

I explained Klavic's situation to Caroline. I half expected her to launch into a spiel about policy and procedures, and how placing someone not on the official executive list would be a violation. Instead she responded, "Well, it's paid for, so someone might as well use it. Right? I'll send his name in to the office manager."

I gave Caroline all the necessary information and was so pleased with the arrangement that I couldn't wait until I returned to the office to let Klavic know. I dialed the company operator from my cell phone and asked to be connected. Klavic was beyond thrilled at the news, and I was tickled pink to have helped him. I also left a message for Owen. When I returned to the office, there was another yellow sticky taped to my chair. "ASAP means now!" My message light was blinking. I checked my voice mail.

"Girl, it's Carlita. You've got to call me immediately."

I decided that I'd better see Perry first, as I had never received a double-dose of Post-Its.

"Paige Sheehan, reporting for duty," I said, as I whirled into Perry's office. Perry motioned for me to sit down at the small conference table where, to my surprise, Mr. Houston sat as well.

"Oh, I'm sorry. I didn't realize."

"Paige, please close the door." I shut the door and sat down.

I knew this was big. The last time I had a meeting with Mr. Houston and Perry was when one of the paralegals was downloading child pornography on his desktop computer.

"What's up?"

"There's been a sexual harassment complaint."

"Oh my God!" I immediately thought about Carlita. "Who?" I asked, concerned.

"It's someone in HR, which makes the situation even more complex."

"Is it Carlita?" I inquired.

"What?" Perry asked. "No, it's not Carlita."

I looked at Perry, and then at Mr. Houston, who looked back to Perry, where my gaze returned.

"Who is it?" My question was met by silence. "Is it Mike?" I searched for a response.

"It's you, Paige." Perry cleared his throat and looked at Mr. Houston as if he needed direction.

"What? That's ridiculous. Who would accuse me? I didn't do anything." I huffed and began to giggle, dismissing the very notion.

"Can you tell us what happened on Friday night after the meeting?" Perry asked.

"What? I don't understand. I ..."

Mr. Houston threw up his hands, irritated. "Don't be difficult, Ms. Sheehan. This is very serious."

"Did anything happen on Friday after work, after the staff meeting?" Perry uncapped his pen and stretched his right arm, as if to warm up for his penning exercise. I couldn't think of anything. My mind was blank. *Friday. Friday night. Drove to Deep Creek.* I glanced out the clear glass panel between Perry's door and into the hall where Moman's janitorial cart sat.

"This isn't about the thing with Moman, is it?" I asked incredulously.

"Ms. Sheehan, what was the 'thing' with Mr. Ishmahed?"

I provided a play-by-play to both Perry and Mr. Houston. When I finished, Perry leaned forward.

"And, of course, there's this." He held up a fax. It had been posted on the fax board since 5 AM that morning. He handed the piece of paper to me. In big block letters it read, "REFERRAL FOR PAIGE SHEEHAN. REASON: SEVERE PUSTULE RASH ON ANUS. PAINFUL ITCHING AND INFLAMMATION."

"You can imagine how uncomfortable this makes people, Paige."

"This is a mistake," I said. "The rash is on my arm. I can show you." In desperation I stood up and began to peel the sweater I was wearing down off my shoulder.

"Ms. Sheehan," Perry shouted. "Please, pull yourself together."

"I'm having an allergic reaction. I had to get a referral letter. I ... I ... please, this is absurd." I sat down, stunned.

Mr. Houston picked up where Perry trailed off. "We've been talking to some of the staff today, and there seem to have been other instances where your behavior was inappropriate."

"Like when?" I demanded.

"Well, for starters, you apparently gave one of the guys in accounting a bunch of cherries."

"Excuse me? What does that have to do with anything?"

"Paige, I'm sure I don't need to teach you some of the slang terms used for the female anatomy."

"Mr. Houston, I will have you know that Brian gave me those cherries from his garden. I took them, because he had practically a wheelbarrow full of them, and I didn't want to seem ungrateful. I gave them away, because cherries upset my stomach."

"Well, this individual said that you left them on his desk with a note that said 'If you'd like some more cherries, come to my office.'"

"Oh, come on." I threw up my hands. "This is totally absurd. Perry, please, you know that I ..." Through the window, I saw Blair slither past the janitorial cart. "Blair!" I erupted. "Blair can tell you this is a mistake. She came into the bathroom."

Perry wiped the corners of his mouth and grunted, "We've talked to Blair, Paige. She reported the incident with Moman."

I struggled to digest this information and repeated his statement. "*She reported the incident?*"

Mr. Houston interrupted. "As you can imagine, this is a very complicated issue, as you are technically the person who would handle such complaints or address this type of behavior. I'm afraid we are going to have to suspend you temporarily until this matter has been fully investigated."

Perry closed with, "I think the best thing for you to do is to just go home today until we've sorted this thing out. We'll be in touch."

I nodded. I returned to my office and called Carlita.

"Carlita?" I said shakily.

"Sugar, I'll be right there." Carlita appeared within seconds.

"You will not believe what just happened."

"I heard," Carlita barked. "I'm as shocked as you. And that whole thing about the slicker ... Good Lord."

"What about the slicker?" I asked.

"Oh, good God, girl, you know this rumor mill around here."

"What did you hear? Out with it." The aftereffects of too many vodka tonics did not seem to be softened by my morning breakfast, and I felt somewhat queasy. I dropped my head onto my desk and listened. According to Carlita, my episode with Moman had ground its way through the rumor mill, and the story had evolved into my attacking Moman in the ladies' room when he came into clean it. I had, according to sources, threatened him with a letter opener if he didn't have sex with me. Carlita also said that she overheard someone in the coffee room saying that during the assault I was wearing a fisherman's hat and a yellow slicker. My stomach churned.

"I think I'm going to throw up."

Carlita grabbed my arm and hustled me down the hallway toward the bathroom. I didn't make it. Instead I regurgitated all contents of the Value Meal #1 into the ficus tree outside one of the conference rooms. I could not get out of the building fast enough. I needed my best friend. I needed comfort. Ignoring my better judgment, I called Ken.

"Hi."

"Hey," he said sweetly. "I didn't think I would hear from you. I got the butchered flowers."

"Yeah, sorry about that."

"Listen, I know you don't believe me, but it's not what you think, Paige. You sound so upset. Meet me for dinner, and let's talk about this. Please."

I whimpered, "That's not why I'm upset. I mean, it is, but it isn't," I rambled. "Something happened at work ... and then you ... and just ... everything. Everything is falling apart, and I think I'm in a lot of trouble."

"You mean *trouble* trouble?"

"Not pregnancy trouble. Jesus! I'm in trouble at work. Someone has accused me of sexual harassment."

I explained the story to Ken, to which he replied, "This is disastrous! What were you thinking? You know better than that."

"I know, I know. I wasn't thinking, but honestly, it was an emergency! What should I do?"

"Let me talk to some people here. I'll call you in an hour." I returned home, changed into my flannel pajama pants and a sweatshirt, and hunkered down on the couch with some Fiddle Faddle. An hour passed, and there was a knock at the door. I expected to see Ken through the peephole, but it was Owen.

"I was in the neighborhood and thought you might need some more gum. Fruit Stripes your poison, right?" He presented me with a ten-pack.

"Yes," I clutched the packet to my chest in a guarded fashion, "How did you know where I live?"

"Remember I took you home last night after you sang a very bizarre rendition of the Sister Sledge song."

"Oh, God. Please don't make my day any worse by recounting anything I said last night."

He smiled. "Promise. I actually came to see how you are doing and to offer my help."

"I guess you heard."

I motioned for him to come inside. "I can't stay," he said. "I'm meeting someone for dinner." He leaned up against the frame of the door, and his voice softened. "I did hear. It's bordering on insane. I cannot believe that they'd believe a janitor over an HR person. Do you have counsel?"

"Why? Do you think I need it?"

"Based on what I heard, Moman is going to press formal charges."

"You're joking!"

"No, unfortunately, I'm not. I came looking for you to thank you for what you did for Klavic, but you were gone. Carlita filled me in, and I believe your story, despite the fact that I just noticed you have a giant, yellow slicker hanging on your coat rack." He looked past me, toward my foyer. "I am going to pretend I didn't see that, because I'm certain you have a very good explanation."

"I do." I smiled weakly.

Owen scratched the side of his five o'clock shadow. "Now don't freak out."

"Oh God, what?"

"From what I hear, there are two charges involved. Two misdemeanors: the harassment charge … and a reckless endangerment charge because of the weapon."

"What weapon? There wasn't a weapon."

"The letter opener."

"Oh, Jesus." I moved further into my apartment, and he followed, closing the door behind him.

"I know. Most of the time, you can't even nick a piece of paper with those things, but it is what it is."

I suddenly became aware of my frumpy outfit and adjusted my position so that the large collar of my sweatshirt would slide down to reveal my bare shoulder. A long moment passed. He adjusted his satchel behind his back and squatted like a catcher balancing himself, with one hand on the arm of my loveseat. The response to the act of concern has always fascinated me. When a child falls or bumps his head, he will look to his mother and father to gauge whether he is supposed to be hurt. If the mother looks alarmed, the child will cry. If the mother smiles, the child will merrily continue playing as if nothing has happened. Owen looked alarmed, and I responded accordingly. He moved beside me upon the loveseat and rubbed my back. Suddenly the magnitude of the situation hit me.

"Could I go to jail?"

"It's unlikely."

"But possible. Oh my God! This can't be happening."

"Listen, I'd like to represent you, unless you have an attorney."

"You can't. That would be a conflict of interest and …"

I was about to make reference to the statement forbidding trial cases in his file but stopped myself.

"I know, but I'm leaving the firm."

"For me?" I touched my chest.

"No, not for you. I've been thinking about it for some time. It's a long story I can't get into right now, but the gist is that I've got an offer from MAX TV to be a commentator for a new show about the business of football."

"Good for you. That's great."

"We're still in talks about the deal. There are a few issues I need to sort out. That's what all these meetings have been about. It looks like it's definitely going to happen. They want me to start this fall."

"That's what you wanted, right?"

"Yeah, it's just what I've been hoping for, but I'd never left a field without leaving in style, and I don't want to leave the field of law without a win. It's important to me. It's important to my father."

"I'll need to think about it. Ken is talking to some people at Norton."

"You're back with Ken?"

"No. I don't know. No, I'm not."

"OK, well, the offer stands, so let me know. Regardless, it'll be OK."

I nodded and to convince myself repeated his words: "It's going to be OK."

He squeezed my shoulder and promised to call me the next day. I ran to the window to watch him cross the street to his car. He looked up towards the window. I quickly retracted so he wouldn't see me, but he did and waved.

Chapter 15

I failed to reset my alarm clock, and as usual it blared at 6:30 AM. For a split second, I had forgotten all about Moman and the yellow slicker and started to get up for work. It was a blissful moment, but it soon passed when my memory awoke as well. I pulled the covers around me and returned to sleep. Between losing sleep on Friday night and my drunken slumber on Sunday night, I was exhausted. I slept until noon. I checked my messages expecting word from Ken, but there was nothing.

I called him at the office. "Hello? Remember me?" I was pissed. For someone who was desperate to make amends, he was doing a terrible job. We still hadn't talked about Lobbyist Barbie.

"I was just about to call you. I talked to the guy who handles prominent sexual harassment cases here, and he's willing to take your case ... but it will cost you."

"How much?"

"$300 an hour. And he needs at least a $5,000 retainer."

"Where am I going to come up with that kind of money?" I wanted him to say that he would help me. I wanted him to take care of me. I thought to myself, *This will be the true test of his love.* He failed miserably.

"You'll just have to figure something out. Let me take you to dinner tonight. We need to talk." I agreed.

I spent the rest of the day doing things I had been wanting to do for months but always found an excuse not to do. I cleaned out the closet and packed a trash bag full of all the clothes I was just five pounds away from wearing again. I also cleaned out the linen closet and threw away a hundred or so bottles of shampoo and conditioner, which I had collected over the years from hotel stays. Right after *Oprah* and the last bite of Fiddle Faddle, my mother called.

"Paige, it's Mom. Vicki said you were fired."

"How did she know?"

"So, it's true?" Mags yelled. "What did you do?"

"Does it always have to be something I did, Mom? Can you imagine for one second that it might not have been my fault?"

"Paige, don't yell at me. I just don't understand. You were doing so well there. Why don't you go back in and ask for another chance? I'm sure whatever mistake you made can be remedied."

"I can't."

"Paige, Henry Ford said those people who believe they can't are right. If you go into it with that attitude, you are sure to …"

I cut her off. "You've been listening to Dad too much. I can't! I can't, can't, can't. It's too screwed up."

"I don't believe you. Never say never!" she exclaimed.

"OK, let me give you the specifics. I'm accused of cornering our janitor in the ladies' room and threatening him with a letter opener unless he had sex with me."

The phone was silent.

"Mags? Are you still there?"

"Yes. I'm here. You have such an odd sense of humor."

"I'm not joking, Mom." The phone was silent again.

"What does Ken think? And what is the word from the weekend?"

"Well, Ken's been too busy fucking our office whore, so I don't know."

My mother gasped. "The language, Paige, please! I'm not one of your pierced, hippie friends." I had introduced her to one friend who had a nose ring and just happened to wear a head scarf; as a result, any time I said or did anything my mother deemed inappropriate, my network of "pierced, hippie friends" was referenced.

She continued, "Just explain to them that you made a terrible mistake. Issue an office memo."

"An office memo? I can't talk to you right now." Before she could say another word, I hung up.

Ken was picking me up at 8 PM. I took a bath and lay down for some quick shut-eye. At 7:45 I awoke to the doorbell ringing. For the first time, Ken was early. When I opened the door, and he saw my bird's nest of hair styled by my quick-drying turban towel and pillow, his eyes bulged.

"You're not ready?" he whined.

"Just give me a second." I dashed into the bathroom, wet my hair, and pulled it back into a low ponytail. I slid into a pink, wool turtleneck and long, black skirt, grabbed my purse, and we were on our way to The Red Sage.

We had just finished our aperitif when The Talk began.

"Paige, you're a great girl. You're attractive and fun to be around, but … I mean, your life is just continuous chaos." I reached across the table and dipped some bread into the whipped-herb spread in the middle of the table. He pointed to my sleeve. "You've got a trail of dip on you."

This was not the apology I was expecting. I bent my elbow and brushed away the creamy spot that dotted the cuff of my turtleneck.

"I like things a certain way," he continued.

"And I'm not that way?" I questioned, biting off a piece of bread. He launched into a diatribe of all the things that were wrong with me. He claimed I was disorganized, clumsy, too casual. I lacked style. He provided supporting arguments for each. He stated he needed someone who complemented him. There was not much I could say. Law school had taught him well, and he had prepared a great closing argument, anchored by my recent sexual harassment charge.

"What was the point of the roses and the card?"

He looked at me blankly and shrugged.

"So, is this it?" I asked.

"After last weekend, I thought I had made a huge mistake. I have invested a lot of time in this relationship, and I wanted to make it work, but I don't think I can handle life with you."

"What does that mean … can't handle life with me? Am I that difficult? Is being with me that awful?"

He folded his napkin and placed it across his plate. "I'm sorry, Paige."

My female curiosity was killing me. I wanted to know: Why Blair? How long? When? Where? How could he? I stopped before launching into twenty questions; I knew there wasn't a single answer that would make me feel better. We both agreed that it was futile to have dinner, so he paid the check and drove me home in silence. On the ride home, I could only surmise that his cold and quick manner resulted from his feelings of guilt and shame. Like ripping off a Band-Aid, he wanted it over as quickly as possible.

Upon returning home, I called my mother.

"John," my mother yelled into the phone, "pick up the line. It's Paige."

I heard an audible click, and then a bang, and another click. Whenever my father picked up or hung up, it sounded as if he were using the phone as some sort of percussion instrument.

"Hello?" my father's voice boomed.

"Hi, Daddy."

"Out with it. I've gotten bits and pieces from your mother. It actually reminds me of a ghost story about a seamstress whose garments cannot be removed from those who wear them."

"Dad, please," I moaned, and caught my cry before it got going.

"What is so terribly wrong?" he asked.

"Everything," I whined.

"Everything cannot be wrong."

"I was asked to take a leave of absence, and Ken and I broke up. What else do I have?"

"That's a silly question, and you know it," he answered.

"I just feel kind of lost, you know? Like I can't get a break. I try to do everything right. I always play by the rules, you know ... and what does it get me?"

"I'm sorry I overreacted earlier," my mother interjected. "I'm sure whatever you did was done for a good reason, and this is all just a big misunderstanding."

"Not exactly." I recounted the accusations, as well as my breakup with Ken. My mother did her best to remain calm but still whimpered and sighed dramatically into the phone.

"Get off the phone, Margaret," my father ordered. Mags hung up the phone. My father's voice breathed heavily as he moved. I could hear the echo of footsteps and visualized him as he headed down the wooden stairs to his office, so that he could talk to me in private.

"Now, take a deep breath," he commanded. I did, and so did he.

"Now, let's talk this through. Are you sick?"

"What?"

"Are you sick?" he asked again.

"What do you mean?"

"I mean, do you have cancer, or are you dying from some horrible disease?"

"No," I sniffled.

"I cannot stand to hear you cry. It breaks my heart. You sound so small."

"I'm sorry." I caught my breath.

"Don't be sorry, Paige. Beecham said that tears are the telescope by which men see far into heaven."

My father continued to talk, and I was surprised to find myself listening. He talked about how disappointing the world can be and how much he admired how I handled the challenges in my life and cherished the victories.

"You used to catch lightning bugs," my father blurted. I assumed this sentence was the start of one of his random tangents. "The morning after your first night catching some, you were devastated they had died. Do you remember?"

"No," I lied, hoping to end the unrelated lightning-bug tale.

He continued. "I explained the bugs couldn't live in a jar, and you should let them go shortly after you catch them."

The truth was, I did remember that summer and the many thereafter. My father would sit on our porch swing, reading with a book light clamped to the binding of some anthology. He would never turn the porch light on since the bare bulb produced a glare that would eclipse the glow of any lightning bug around. While he read, I would catch the bugs, only to release them an hour later.

"You told me that you didn't mind releasing them, because what you really liked was watching them glow in the dark."

"That's a nice story, Dad," I responded weakly.

"Do you know why I call you Paigebug?"

"No," I sniffled. "I assumed you made it up."

"I did make it up. I gave you the name that summer, because you were like one those lightning bugs ... flittering around, shining in the darkness. You have always glowed in dark times."

He ended by saying, "Let me cry the tears tonight and see far into heaven. Paigebug, you will shine again."

Chapter 16

For years I had maintained a long laundry list of activities that I would complete and hobbies I would take up if given the time. *Washingtonian* magazine had a monthly listing of exhibits, plays, and events that I would review and think, *if only I weren't so busy.* The Farren Center, a building that was only a five-minute walk from my place, also offered a variety of classes and seminars. The organization was subsidized by a grant, so the programs cost next to nothing. I had shared my wishes of taking yoga and visiting museums, and the unfortunate constraints of my schedule, to anyone who would listen. I wanted to be one of those slick, cultured city dwellers who took advantage of everything living in a big city offered. But it had been ten days since I began my suspension at H2O, and all I had managed to accomplish was the eradication of Ken-related paraphernalia and the clog in the garbage disposal. I had barely left the confines of my nine-hundred-square-foot apartment.

The investigation at H2O was ongoing, and formal charges had indeed been filed. Owen had called the 14th District Station to request a copy of the report. Ironically I had written H2O's employment policy, which mandated the suspension of any employee who had been criminally or civilly charged for an offense that occurred in the workplace. Fortunately my policy provided continued insurance coverage, as well as two-thirds of one's salary during the suspension, for up to 120 days. Bottom line: I was not going to starve, and my benefits would remain in effect.

Owen advised me to be on the lookout for the summons in the mail. I checked every afternoon after watching *Oprah*, but nothing was delivered. Owen called every night to check in on me and to inquire about the summons. He would ask me questions about my day, and I did my best to exaggerate and glamorize my daily account by applying a technique I learned during my many years in Human Resources. By simply exchanging some regular verbs for power verbs and replacing nouns with more descriptive terms, you could make anything sound interesting and challenging. It was a tactic frequently used on resumes, and as HR professionals, most of us had learned to see past the language. We knew that "catalogued financial documentation and related materials" actually meant that the person filed invoices. "Conceptualized and delivered multimedia presentations" translated into creating a PowerPoint file. When Owen called that night, I applied the technique.

"Hey, how was your day?" he inquired.

"I was engaged with multiple tasks," I replied.

"Great. You should take advantage of this time. What did you do?"

"Well, I centralized my grocery allocation at Whole Foods and procured several items: wheat products, vegetation, and animal proteins. I also acquired some unleaded energy for my transportation and assessed the reconstruction of a living room on an interior-design broadcast."

"I see," he responded. "Did the summons come?"

"I did solicit the mail carrier and evaluated all the correspondence delivered, but no legal documentation is in receipt."

"Have you been drinking?"

"Just water, which I will no longer refer to by its chemical name."

I realized after talking to Owen that he was right; I should take advantage of this sudden gift of time and actually do something constructive. The next morning, I walked to the Farren Center and enrolled in the afternoon Kripalu yoga class advertised as being taught by famed yogi master Mushtaq Paleez. Its scheduled time was 4 PM, which meant I would have to miss *Oprah*, but the other classes required a prerequisite on wave breathing, so they were out.

On the following day, I arrived five minutes before the start of class. Several people were already in the room, sitting on their rubber mats with legs crossed and eyes closed. I quietly unrolled a mat and sat down. Incense burned in the corner atop one of the sound system speakers, which emitted what I could only describe as the sound of a whale mating with a porn star. The music began with high- and low-frequency pitches that ended with the growling noise of a whale forcing air through its blowhole. In the background was the breathless lilt of a woman saying, "Love. Harmony. Yes. Body. Heat. Unity. Energy. Force. Flow. Yes."

I bit the inside of my cheek to refrain from laughing and lifted my gaze to the man sitting cross-legged beside me, who was inhaling and exhaling and circling his head to the cadence. Yogi Mushtaq arrived and positioned himself at the front of the room. He was a slight man of South Asian descent and wore a red unitard. All I will say about the unitard was that it brought back memories of Vicki's new-age ex-boyfriend, Quinn. Mushtaq's body gave me the heebie-jeebies. His skin had a rubbery quality, and when he closed his arms, an abnormally large mass of armpit hair protruded, as though he had two small dogs in a headlock. He dimmed the lights and outstretched his arms to the ceiling, muttering a word I didn't know, then politely asked everyone to position themselves on their mats. I slowly lowered my body one vertebrae at a time as directed, wondering what I was missing on *Oprah*, as he increased the volume of *Shamu Woos Shawna*.

I expected the class to involve the contortion of body parts in positions that I would not be able to achieve. I was prepared for the point in the class when the instructor made his or her way to my place in the room to quietly point out what I was doing incorrectly. The last time I had taken an aerobics class, the instructor yelled, "The girl in the purple shorts, just try to get the steps, don't try to do the arm movements." I had never been very flexible or athletic. However, for fifteen minutes, all Mushtaq asked us to do was breathe, which I did with great aplomb.

Thirty minutes into the session, I wondered if I could get my $35 registration fee back, because I could breathe back at home while watching *Oprah*. But then the yogi began speaking. He talked about the energy of breath and how it was the voice of one's soul. If my eyes had been open, I would have been rolling them, but I lay quietly and listened. He spoke about inhaling and exhaling and how it represented the ebb and flow ever present in our lives.

"You must appreciate both the inhale and the exhale," he intoned. "You must witness the give and the take, and allow the integration of all sensations and feelings as they flow through you. Listen to your soul. Breathe and hear its messages."

To my surprise, I eventually stopped thinking about *Oprah* and thought about the concept behind the spiritual gobbledygook. How my life had ebbed and flowed. For years I had been alone, with few friends and no boyfriend. Many Saturday nights had consisted of watching a movie or reading a book. I had bounced checks and counted days until payday. Then I met Ken and was hired at H2O, and had friends galore and a modest bank account—but I often missed the quiet Saturdays and the sweet relief that had come twice a month on paydays. Now I was again alone and on a budget, with time to spare. But you never want what you have.

I thought about Mags, who, as a working mother of three, rarely had time to read a newspaper and drink a cup of coffee at the kitchen table. She was always running to buy poster board for one of our school projects or working late on proofing the new ad for stain-resistant berber. She had been ragged and exhausted during much of my youth, but now, retired with an empty nest, she seemed anxious. She had spent so many years riding the waves, swimming with the current that swiftly carried her forward; now that the waters had calmed, she seemed to have forgotten how to float.

Mushtaq continued to speak and walked silently around the room. I followed his voice as I inhaled and exhaled deeply. He stopped at the foot of my head and I peeked at him through half-shut eyes.

"We all look for the next wave, don't we, students? We hold our breath and wait to exhale. We wait and wait until the next wave comes. Kripalu says that you destroy the energy of life when you do not allow for the rhythm. I would like you to exhale deeply and not take another breath until I tell you to."

A uniform "wheooooooo" was heard as the class expelled the air from their lungs. After five seconds, I struggled against the natural instinct to take another breath.

"You will feel panic flow through your body. You will feel tense. You will feel slightly asphyxiated. Now breathe." A chorus of "hauuuuuuuuuhh" rang out as we inhaled as much air as possible.

Mushtaq asked us to open our eyes and sit upright. He thanked us for a respectful class and instructed us. "You must cherish both the give and the take. The ebb gives us the energy for the flow. The flow gives us appreciation for the ebb. Breathe. Inhale and exhale, and understand the importance of both."

Chapter 17

The next day, I woke early and went for a run, paying close attention to my breathing, as Mushtaq had instructed. I hadn't run for a while, and it was just what I needed. I imagined that I was pushing down all my troubles with each step.

Fall seemed to be arriving early. It was the middle of September, but already most of the leaves had turned or fallen to the ground. I ran through a crowd of protesters undoubtedly headed for the Capitol. Cinnamon and gold trees swayed gently in the wind, and leaves fluttered along the entrance to the park. Banning Park was not much of a park, really; it was about half the size of a football field and had a few picnic tables and benches, usually occupied by homeless people. I found an empty bench and sat down to watch a beautiful German Shepherd jumping into the air to catch a Frisbee. A small mutt attempted to steal it from the Shepherd's mouth, and he growled, prompting the mutt to lie down submissively.

I didn't often feel sorry for myself, but I felt a twinge of sadness and fear well up inside me. The reality of the past few days seemed to catch up with me as I sat alone with my thoughts. Before the tears started, I stood up and began jogging again, this time toward Vicki's apartment. She had called that morning and asked me to check on Mr. Fatboy since he hadn't eaten the apple she had left in his cage the night before. She kept a key hidden in the bow of the grapevine wreath that decorated her door. I let myself in and immediately went to her kitchen to get a glass of water. I noticed a bowl of apples on her counter and was carving one when she appeared in the doorway.

"Jesus!" I jumped. "You scared the hell out of me. What are you doing here? I thought you had a big trial today." She moved toward me cautiously, her hand trailing the countertop.

"Sit down," she said. "I have some bad news." She slowly took the apple and knife from my hand and walked me over to her couch. One of the springs was sticking out through the fabric and poked at the back of my thigh. Vicki was always intense, so her brooding demeanor did not alarm me. It was when I stared into her face and saw the blotchiness of her skin and noticed a swelling in her eyes that I knew that something was truly wrong.

"What is it?" I asked.

"Mom called me today at the courthouse." She paused, almost unable to get the next sentence out. "Daddy collapsed. She tried to call you, but you must have been jogging." I stared blankly at her and waited for more words, but instead she began to cry.

"What happened?" I said breathlessly, my heart still pumping from the run as sweat slipped down the small of my back.

"He was teaching a class and just stopped talking in the middle. He went to his desk, sat, and put his head down."

"Is he dead?" I swallowed, wiping the sweat pouring down my face with my forearm.

"No, he's alive ... but they did a CAT scan, and it's a brain tumor. Malignant." She waited for me to digest that piece of information before continuing. "And they think the cancer has spread. They are still running tests, but the doctor says, just based on its size and location, it could be anywhere from three to twelve weeks."

I wanted to run out the door and down the street. I wanted to run until I passed out. I wanted to close my eyes and go to sleep and wake up to another day, a day far in the future, when this moment was just a memory. Tears poured down my face, and Vicki hugged me. For over an hour, we sat sobbing. We booked two tickets to West Virginia, then called Wally's post headquarters in Africa and left an urgent message to call home. Vicki packed up Fatboy, and I ran to my condo to pack a few things.

I was wrestling my suitcase out from the closet when my doorbell rang. Two police officers stood at the door. One asked for my name, smiling. My first thought when I saw them was that Vicki had arranged for a police escort to the airport. She had become good friends with a few of the officers while working in the public defender's office.

"Are you Paige Sheehan?"

"Yes, I am."

"I'm Officer Kroener and this is Officer Roland. We have a warrant for your arrest for failure to show up for your scheduled court date."

"What are you talking about?"

"Failure to appear is an arrestable offense, ma'am. Your court date was three days ago."

"What? I swear I didn't get it. I've been checking every day."

"Paige Sheehan, 3D Charleston Towers. Right?," He said reading off a piece of paper.

"No. This is 8D. You're on the eighth floor. It must have been mailed to the wrong address."

"I'm sorry, ma'am, but I have a warrant here for your arrest."

"But it's a mistake. My sister is Vicki Sheehan," I responded. "She's with the PD's office. Let me just call her and …" My lame attempt at name-dropping was unsuccessful. Officer Roland cuffed me, and I did not resist. In fact I said nothing and did nothing. By the time I was processed, two hours had passed. I had agreed to meet Vicki at the veterinarian's office where she was going to board her pig. The plexiglas holding cell was vile but it had the one feature I needed, a payphone. I made a collect call to the vet's office. They informed me that Vicki had waited for me for thirty minutes but then took a cab to the airport, saying, "Maybe we got our messages crossed. She may have thought I was going to meet her at the airport. If she shows, just tell her to meet me at the gate."

I hung up the phone. I attempted to make another collect call to Carlita but got her voicemail message singing, "Talk is cheap, but my cell plan isn't, so keep it short."

I looked down at my hands and picked at some of the fingerprinting ink that had gotten trapped in my nails. The digital fingerprinting machine had been on the fritz when I arrived. Officer Kroener informed me that he would have to process me "old school" as he rummaged around several cabinets to find fingerprinting cards.

Officer Roland had not uttered a word to me during the arrest or booking. He passed the cell as I examined my hands and stopped. He spoke to me through the small drilled holes. "It's not like in the movies. You get more than one call. You can keep calling until you get someone," he informed me. I stared back at him blankly. Smoothing his mustache, he asked, "Did you hear what I said?"

I nodded to indicate my understanding. I had heard him. I was merely stalling to decide whom to call. Did I swallow my pride and call Ken? Did I call my mother, who had just learned that her husband was dying? Neither of those options seemed like good options. "Do you have an attorney?" Officer Roland asked.

"Yes." I thought of Owen and moved closer to the holes. "I know someone, but don't have his number."

"We have a listing of licensed attorneys," he said. "What's his name? I'll look him up."

"Owen Holden," I replied. "He was with Houston, Haffner, and O'Donnell or was with them."

"Owen Holden from the Cowboys?"

I nodded.

"He's an attorney now? Wow. You want me to call him? I'll make the call if you want. It would be a kick."

I nodded again. I didn't want to talk to anyone. I seemed almost unable to utter a word. Part of me feared that if I tried to speak, if I tried to explain anything, I would break into heaving sobs and incoherent sentences. And I wasn't even sure what to tell Owen if I did reach him. *Hi. I'm in jail and have no one else to call.* Officer Roland winked at me and promised to return after he made the call. He promptly told one of the guards that he was about to call Owen Holden, and the guard high-fived him and followed him out, leaving me alone with a rat-haired woman, who looked completely strung out. I moved to the corner of the cell and looked through the dirty but still translucent wall.

"Put away the fucking oranges, you fucking bitch. Fuck up," my cellmate mumbled. I turned around, ready to defend myself if needed, but she remained slumped over on the bench in the corner. I watched her as if I were observing an animal at the zoo. There is something terrifying about unpredictability, about dealing with the unknown. In my opinion, I would have felt safer contained with a crocodile. I had watched many episodes of *When Sea Creatures Attack*, since it had been a regular Saturday-night feature during my arid dating period prior to working at H2O. I knew that the crocodile would go for the throat and try to pull me down in a death roll. Maybe the FOX network had produced a *When Crazy People Attack* series, but if so, I hadn't seen it. The woman whimpered a bit and rocked back and forth, mumbling, "Oh God, Oh God, please help me. Please, please, please."

I whispered the same words, looking up to the ceiling, where the paint blistered and patches of spackle seemed to be haphazardly applied. The woman moved onto her side into the fetal position, clutching her stomach. All the while, her eyes remained closed. She then appeared to fall asleep. After some time, I heard the buzz of a door, and the officer appeared, smiling.

"He's coming down. Said he'd give me an autographed hat if I got you out right now and kept you at my desk until he got here. My son is going to flip. He had every trading card of Holden's. Huge fan."

Officer Roland escorted me to his desk and poured me a cup of coffee.

"May I make another call?" I asked.

"Sure. Sure, absolutely." He turned the phone towards me and handed me the receiver.

"It's long distance," I informed him.

"Go ahead. No problem. Just dial 5 to get an outside line," he said, straightening his desk in what I could only assume was preparation for Owen's arrival.

I dialed 411 and was connected to the hospital. I left a message at the nurse's station to tell my family that I would catch a flight later that night. Owen arrived moments later.

"You OK?" he asked.

"Hi," I said shakily. "Thanks for coming." I was breathless. My heart raced.

"Are you OK? What happened?"

As predicted, tears began to form in my eyes.

"They mailed my summons to the wrong address. I never got it."

"It's OK. It's OK. I'll get it straightened out. Why are you crying? Did they hurt you? If anyone touched you, I'll file a charge against the department."

"No. I'm fine, but my father is sick, and I need to get home. He's in the hospital. I was leaving for the airport when they came, and now I've missed my flight, and I need to get home. I really need to get home …" I choked, and the heaving sobs and incoherent sentences followed.

Owen's eyes narrowed as he tried to decipher the language of this hysterical woman before him. "OK. We'll get you on a flight."

He drove me home and waited for me as I finished packing, and then he drove me to Reagan National.

Outside the Delta shuttle gate, he put the car in park and turned. "I know you don't want to deal with this, but there is going to be a preliminary hearing, and you'll need to be there to enter a plea. It's typically a day or two after the arrest, but I'll see if I can get it rescheduled."

"That would be better."

"Here's my card with all my contact info. Call me tomorrow if you can. I'm really sorry about your father. If you need anything, call." Owen carried my bags to the curb and hugged me.

"Take care," he said, and I turned and hurriedly headed for the ticket counter.

Chapter 18

I arrived at the hospital at 2 AM, directly from the airport. I was routed through Pittsburgh, then took a puddle jumper from Pittsburgh to Bridgeport, West Virginia, twenty minutes away from the hospital. In hindsight it would have been faster to drive, but I was finally there, and for the past ten hours, that had been my only goal. Because Dad was in intensive care, the hospital was very strict about visiting hours and would not allow family to visit until morning. I quietly rolled my bag through the hallway, stopping at the information desk to find out where the family waiting room was located. Vicki was alone in the room, looking uncomfortable, propped up on two chairs she had pushed together to form a makeshift bed. She was reading an information booklet entitled *Healing from Within*. Vicki had elected to stay the night at the hospital, so that Mags could return home and try to sleep. Vicki sat up, and the two chairs separated, screeching across the linoleum floor.

"Do you have a sweatshirt in there?" she said, pointing to my bag. "It's freezing in here."

I bent down and opened my bag.

"Well, what's the word?" I asked.

Vicki warned me that Dad did not recognize her when she visited him earlier: "The tumor is pressing on the part of his brain that stores memory."

I peppered Vicki with questions, but she had few answers. She had missed seeing his attending physician by an hour and had gotten little information from the staff. "And Mags seems to know nothing. It's like she doesn't want to ask any questions, because she doesn't want to know the answers."

I pulled a sweater from my bag and handed it to Vicki. She in turn gave me her keys, urging me to return home to be with Mags.

"Mrs. Weitzman's with her, but it would be better if one of us were there. Wally can't get here until next week."

"Ugggh."

"You can tell me about your prison break tomorrow." She pulled the sweater over her head and returned to reading.

I had not been a fan of Mrs. Weitzman since she had lectured me when I was ten years old on the inflated prices of my lemonade stand. Every time I saw her, she reminded me that I once tried to sell her a five-cent glass of lemonade for fifty cents. And then there were her dreadful haircuts. I later learned that she had been in the dog-grooming business in the early sixties which was her only qualification.

I left the hospital, drove back to my childhood home, and slipped quietly into my parents' bedroom. My mother was fully clothed, asleep on the bed. I backed out, closed the door, and headed to my room—but lo and behold, Mrs. Weitzman was sleeping there. I gently pulled the door to close it but she awoke and bolted upright in my twin bed.

"Who's that?" she whispered. "Maggie?"

I whispered to her through the door, "It's Paige. I just got in. Go back to sleep."

I quickly turned and retreated to Wally's room, but she appeared as I searched for the light switch. She was wearing a filmy, yellow nightgown that looked as if it came from Victoria's Secret.

Unfortunately, on Mrs. Weitzman, the garment held no secrets. Her sagging breasts looked like two oblong squash hanging off her round body, her nipples positioned like a root at the bottom of each. She hugged me tightly against the squash and released me dramatically.

"Your mother's having a terrible time. I brought over some braised beef, but she didn't even touch it. And what about you, sweetie?"

"I'm OK. I'm too tired to think or feel right now."

"You poor thing. It's such a shock. You're just never prepared." She crossed her arms across her chest and hoisted the squash forward. She looked at me and then dropped the squash and hugged me again. "So good to see you. Such a darling girl. You know, when you were little, you were always scheming. You once tried to sell me some very ill-tasting lemonade for ten times the cost."

I smiled. "I'm really tired."

She waved her hand and departed, leaving me alone in Wally's bedroom. The decor had not changed since he was eighteen—plaid wallpaper, a Larry Bird poster, a collection of boy knickknacks on the bookcase (a football, a model airplane, and a stack of *Sports Illustrated* magazines). I collapsed on the bed, said a prayer, and slept.

Vicki woke me in the morning. "Hurry up and get ready. We're all going to go up together. Mom's in the shower."

"Where's Mrs. Weitzman?"

"She went back over to her house to change."

"You should have seen the nightgown."

"I saw the nightgown and everything behind it. Not pretty. Come on. We want to get there before his attending physician arrives."

I debated whether I should shower, but given that I hadn't seen so much as a washcloth since running three miles, being jailed, and traveling for six hours, I thought it unkind to visit a hospital in my current state, covered in sweat and germs. I quickly showered, changed, and headed for the kitchen, where I could hear Vicki's insistent voice. "Mom, you need to eat something."

"I know. I will. I'll get something at the hospital."

"Just eat a piece of toast." Vicki buttered a piece of bread and placed it in front of my mother.

"Hi." I entered the room and approached my mother from behind, wrapping my arms around her neck. She patted my hands and gently pulled them away, turning to see me.

"Oh, good, we're all here. Let's get going."

I shot Vicki a glance to question Mom's formal, matter-of-fact behavior. Vicki shrugged. We rode to the hospital in silence. When we arrived, my father was sitting up in bed. Vicki and I held hands and walked in, and he smiled. Each of us went to one side of his bed.

"I have a tumor," he began, as if it were something he had picked up at the store.

"I know," I said, squeezing his hand. He stared straight ahead.

"What time does that clock say?" I looked in the direction of his gaze. There was nothing, just a plain, blank wall.

"What time do you think it says?" I asked.

"Four o'clock," he said. "Is that right?"

Vicki answered, "Yes, that's right."

"It's a good time. Good times are ahead. It's a good time," he repeated, and drifted to sleep.

They say things always happen for a reason, and my forced leave of absence did seem to have occurred at just the right time. My mother was beyond consoling and had basically checked out, not acknowledging that her husband of 35 years was dying. Her daily mantra became, "He'll pull through. He's three months from retirement."

I spoke to the grief counselor at the hospital, who claimed my mother's response was typical and understandable. I was devastated, but I could not imagine what my mother was feeling. My father was dying—but her husband, best friend, lover, father of her children, and future were at risk. Her beautiful golden years—all they had planned, all they had saved for—her entire future was dying. It seemed to be too much for her to bear. I called some contacts in Baltimore and decided to get a second opinion from an oncologist at Johns Hopkins. The hospital in West Virginia applied laser radiation to the tumor to temporarily reduce its size and impact on my father's neurological functions. After he was informed of his options, he decided to make the drive with me to Baltimore. Dr. Dapoor, the director of Hopkins Oncology Center, thought it was possible to prolong my father's life. There were some clinical trials with stage-three brain tumors that showed promise. I begged the doctor to qualify my father. He assured my father and me that he would do everything he could, but also suggested we look at alternatives.

Upon returning to the family home later that night, I emailed Owen.

To: cowboy4ever@comcast.net
From: kookygirl33@aol.com
Subject:

Sorry I haven't written or called. It's been a busy few days. We're still trying to make sense of everything. My father is coherent. He seems a little off, but he always does. I haven't noticed much of a difference, which makes it that much more difficult to believe. I'm trying to stay positive. We saw a doctor at Hopkins who told us about some clinical trials going on at NIH for stage-three brain tumors. We're going to see if we can pull some strings and get him into the program.

Thanks again for helping me out on Wednesday and for taking me to the airport. Don't know when I'll be able to make it back to town. I'm feeling a little overwhelmed right now. Let me know what you need me to do regarding my case. It's not off my radar screen.

I checked my email first thing in the morning. I had not received a response from him, which made me think that Owen had reconsidered his offer. It had been a week since I had arrived. The hospital released Dad so that we could care for him in the comfort of his own home. We set up Wally's room for him, because it received the most sunlight and had a cable hookup. Vicki and I met with the doctor before the release.

"Your father wants to begin chemo in the hope it will extend his life, but in my opinion, this is not the best course," the doctor said. "I don't think it will buy him much time, and it will negatively affect his quality of life since he'll have to deal with all the side effects but ultimately, it's his decision."

"I think he is optimistic about some of the other avenues we're pursuing. There's a clinical trial at NIH, and they are focusing on this exact type of cancer," I said.

"I don't want to dash your hopes, but the statistics aren't in your favor. However, nothing is certain, and it is his decision."

The truth was that Dad had not made the decision alone. We had evaluated all the pros and cons and had made a decision as a family. I did not understand the mentality of someone who would chose not to fight. The statistics for winning the lottery are slim, yet people continue to play, and the reason they do is that there is a chance to win. The hope exists, and the advertisers play on that fact with their campaign: "Somebody's gonna win. Might as well be you."

There had been cases where tumors shrank as a result of chemo. There were even cases where the tumor magically disappeared. It did happen. It could happen. Dad was going to begin his first round of chemo before coming home. The doctor told us that my father would experience nausea and also stressed the importance of maintaining his weight. The doctor suggested we fill the house with the most high-calorie foods possible.

"I don't care what he eats or how he gets it, but he needs to be taking in at least 1500 calories a day, preferably 2000 but he's not going to feel like eating." Dr. Dapoor had warned us.

Vicki went to pick Wally up from the airport, and Mags went to the hospital to sit with Dad in the therapy room. I headed to the Kroger grocery store to buy food that I normally did my best to avoid. I bought cheesecake, ice cream, fried cheese, cheese Danishes, an entire palette of 1200-calorie milk shakes, and a case of coconut milk. Billed as a cancer patient's best friend, one can of coconut milk had as many calories as a day's worth of Jenny Craig meals. When I returned, Mrs. Weitzman was reorganizing the kitchen cabinets.

"I don't know why your mother has it set up this way. It's all wrong. The cabinet for dishes is opposite the dishwasher. It's not very logical, so I'm fixing it."

"I'm not sure she wants it fixed," I suggested.

Mrs. Weitzman dismissed my comment with a wave of her hand. "Oh, Gordon Olstein called while you were shopping. He said you had his number."

"I don't know who that is. Did he say where he was from? Is he with NIH?"

"Didn't say."

Mrs. Weitzman began throwing bottles of spices into the garbage.

"I don't think your mother has cooked with these spices in years. I've never even heard of some them. Marjuro root? Never even heard of it."

I didn't have the patience to fight with Mrs. Weitzman about the need for the kitchen reorganization. I put away the groceries and placed some fresh daisies in Dad's recovery room. Vicki arrived with Wally shortly after. I hardly recognized him. When I had seen him off at the airport the year before, he had been wearing a blue-striped button-down oxford with khaki pants and suede lace-up shoes. His hair color had been undetectable since it was cut so close to his scalp. He had looked organized, uptight, and nerdy. The brother who now stood in the doorway of the kitchen was quite the opposite, and the transformation startled me. His hair had grown to his shoulders, and he sported a shaggy goatee. He was wearing cargo pants and a fisherman's vest. He embraced me, and the fabric of his hemp shirt roughed my cheek.

"Hear you're a jailbird."

I shot a look to Vicki, who shot back, "It's not like he wasn't going to find out."

"And you look like Jesus," I said.

"If Jesus shopped at J. Peterman," Vicki added.

Wally grabbed a beer from the refrigerator.

"A little early for the brewskis, don't you think?"

"It's 8 PM in Tanzania." Wally plopped down at the table and leaned back in his chair, splaying his arms and legs.

"How long do they think he's had it?" he asked, taking a swig.

"They don't know," I answered. "Maybe a year. Maybe ten. They have no way of knowing how long the cancer has been growing."

"Does it matter?" Vicki asked, picking up Wally's beer and taking a drink.

No one answered. Vicki grabbed the keys and her purse, and we followed her out the door and headed to the hospital to meet Mags and Dad, so we could follow the ambulance that would transfer him home. An hour later, we reconvened downstairs after getting Dad organized in his new digs. I placed a schedule on the fridge detailing when he needed to take his medicine, with a column recording what he ate each day. I volunteered to monitor the medicines and food. Vicki volunteered to drive him to his chemo rounds for the next week until she needed to return to work, and Wally took the night shift, so he could remain on Tanzania time. I also took the responsibility of doing research.

That night I got online again and checked email. Again nothing. Not even some spam. It had been ten days since I had heard from Owen. I picked up the phone to call him, but then reconsidered. If he had wanted to talk to me, he would have replied to my email. I was giving Dad his nightly meds when the phone rang.

"Paige! Phone!" Vicki screamed. I kissed Dad, and he fell back to sleep. I gently pulled his door shut and picked up the phone in the hallway.

"Hello?"

"Why haven't you called me?"

"Owen?"

"Yes, Paige. I know you're dealing with a lot right now, but this isn't just going to go away."

"I emailed you a week ago."

"I never got it."

"You're Cowboy4ever at Comcast, right?"

"Yeah. What account did you send it from?"

"From my AOL account—Kookygirl33."

"Damn. I deleted that one. I didn't recognize the name and thought it was spam. I stopped opening random emails, because I kept getting an email soliciting me to buy Teenage Girls Having Sex with Farm Animals Volume I. I thought Kookygirl was sending me a notice about Volume II."

I laughed and sat down on the floor against the wall, twirling the phone cord in one hand.

"Nope. No farm animals. Why didn't you call me on my cell phone?"

"I didn't have your number. So I called Carlita and she said to call your family home because you rarely answer your cell. She also said and I quote, 'Tell that sweet baby girl that I'm praying for her.'"

"She's a great friend. So what's the word?"

"Well, I tried to call you yesterday but, of course, you didn't call back."

"Did you leave a voice mail? 'Cause I didn't get it."

"I left a message with your neighbor. She said you were at the store."

"Oh, God. She told me that some guy named Gordon Olstein called."

"OK, that's not even close. That's bad."

I smiled again. I loved my family, but it was good to talk to someone from the outside. It was a relief to talk about something other than doses of medicine and appointment times and the number of milk shakes consumed. It was only at the tail end of the call that the conversation turned to my harassment charges.

"I've managed to postpone the preliminary hearing, but it's scheduled in two days, and unless you're able to make it, I am going to submit a plea on your behalf. Some states don't allow it, but D.C. does. I just need you to complete a plea submission form, get it notarized, and overnight it to me."

"Email it to Kookygirl33 and also send your mailing address."

We talked a bit more about the preliminary hearing. After which a trial date would be set. He promised to ask the judge to schedule the actual trial for a few months out but could offer no guarantees on how soon the judge would set the date.

"Thanks for everything, Gordon Olstein," I said jokingly before we hung up.

"You're quite welcome, Kookygirl."

He seemed so ideal. But, I quickly thought of the notation in his personnel file, which had yet to be addressed. Owen appeared perfectly capable, knowledgeable, and normal. I decided whatever skeletons were in his closet could stay there.

Chapter 19

Owen emailed me after the preliminary hearing. My trial date was set for November 8, a mere two months away. I spent the next three weeks doing cancer research. I was certain that the researchers and physicians studying the disease had missed something. I had once read about a doctor who had discovered that cells taken from the foot of an aardvark could be synthesized into a topical cream that alleviated a rare, pediatric skin condition. I wondered what had prompted the doctor to look to the aardvark as a source. It seemed completely random and ridiculous, yet it had worked.

The case of the aardvark was ever-present in my mind as an example of what was possible. I believed that if I tried hard enough and looked beyond the norm, I could find a cure. I came upon an article about a Native American tea made from a combination of herbs that was hailed by many Cherokees to shrink tumors. I mailed $75 to a P.O. box in Arizona and made the tea for my father every day for a week, until he refused to drink it because the taste was so repulsive. This was actually happy news for everyone, because the tea smelled about a hundred times worse than it tasted.

The following week I purchased $400 worth of shark cartilage. I found a recipe online for a soup that claimed to be 90 percent effective in curing cancer. In cooking it, I discovered a smell worse than Klavic, the Cherokee tea, and the anal glands of a skunk combined.

A week later, I took my father to a faith healer priest in Maryland at the National Shrine Grotto of Lourdes. By this point, he was too weak to get out of the car. The healer, Father McNally, told my father he must believe in the power of God to heal. My father said he did, but I saw doubt in his eyes. The healer spoke about Moses and the miracles he performed, and how those who doubted his power did not receive the gifts and temporal benefits that the Almighty could offer. Father McNally spoke of the devil's evil spread of disease and the power of the Lord to rebuke sickness and pain. He reminded us of the story of Jesus and the lepers. When the ten lepers called out to Jesus to have mercy on them, Jesus told the lepers to go show themselves to the priest—while they were still lepers—and then they would be healed. Jesus had required them to step out in faith first, and if they did, they would be healed. He told my father that he must fight against the foul spirits in the name of our Savior. "With faith and in Jesus's name, you will be saved," he cried out.

My father had lost over twenty pounds. He sat in the passenger side of the car with his eyes closed. Father McNally kneeled at my father's feet, raising his fists up in the air, praying and chanting for mercy. A faint smile flashed on my father's face. He was amused. He opened his eyes and glanced at me as if to say, "Why am I here?" However, he knew the answer. He wasn't there so much for himself as for me. *I* needed to believe he could be saved. *I* needed to believe he could be cured. *I* was the one who needed the miracle.

When we returned to my father's oncologist the next week, there was no change. By this point, he was even more nauseated, and his overall suffering had accelerated. That evening his breathing became labored. I sat with him watching Moneyline on CNN. For all the years he had spent idolizing and honoring words, he had become suddenly obsessed with numbers. The doctor said that often people with brain tumors focus on things that are concrete and easy to understand. Hence his obsession with clocks, ticker tapes, and the calculator. On numerous occasions during his illness, he would ask me to multiply numbers. I was not sure what they represented. At first I thought he wanted to ensure there was enough money to care for my mother when he died. Other times I sensed that the numbers were completely random. He would calculate the equations in his head, and then I would punch them into my handheld calculator and validate the answer. He seemed relieved when his calculations would match the scientific accuracy of my machine. It was as if this ability to multiply a random combination of numbers contradicted his cancer. How could he successfully divide 2046 by 6 if he had a brain tumor?

We had not spoken about my troubles since the diagnosis. The fact was that I rarely thought about it. Owen and I had been emailing every day, but the content focused mainly on my father's status or Owen's negotiations with MAX TV. I had applied for family medical leave the day after I arrived home. Carlita had arranged it, and I had barely spoken to anyone from H2O since.

"What's happening at work?" my father asked breathlessly, opening his eyes.

"Well, there's going to be a trial." I sat up and positioned myself so that he could see me without having to move. I fingered the crochet loops of the afghan blanket that covered him. "It's scheduled for November."

"I'm pretty sick, Paigey." He struggled for breath, and I held mine, trying to feel what he felt. The cancer had spread to his lungs, and his capacity to breathe was severely diminished. Imagining the suffocation he felt with each breath made it difficult for me to catch my own. "I may not be here next month or next week."

"Shhh, Daddy, don't say that."

"Paige." He looked at me, and it seemed an entire conversation was exchanged in our eyes. Then he said, "Sometimes acceptance is a good thing. You can't always control life."

"I know that," I answered. "But you should have some control, some power over the direction of your life. I feel that I have no control now. None. Zip. It's frustrating."

"I'm not saying that you shouldn't fight for what you want, but sometimes you waste so much time fighting." His eyes lit up. "Ten thousand River Commissions with the mines of the world at their back cannot tame that lawless stream, cannot curb it or confine it ... cannot bar its path with an obstruction which it will not tear down, dance over and laugh at," he recited, all in one breath. He looked surprised at himself—and pleased. "See, I remember. I'm not out of the game yet."

He coughed, and I turned up the oxygen on his machine. I smiled at him and smoothed out some of his hair, which had tangled in the elastic of his oxygen mask.

"Mark Twain," he said. "He was talking about the Mississippi River." He coughed again.

"Shhh, don't try to talk."

He was moved to the hospital the next day and was intubated with a breathing device, which left him unable to speak. He suddenly began pointing to me wildly. I wasn't sure what he was trying to emphasize or tell me. I grabbed his hand and kissed it, and he returned to sleep. That night his breathing became much worse. We sat vigil in his hospital room for the next seventy-two hours.

The doctor told us my father had developed pneumonia. The cancer had weakened his heart as well, but I knew that. In the wee hours of the night, we would whisper, trying to guess how long he had had the tumor, wondering if his increasing general oddness could be attributed to it. Did he have it the time he had gone grocery shopping for Thanksgiving and left $200 worth of groceries in the parking lot? Did he have it the time he bought a painting of a giant iguana at an antique auction, or when he used a tube of Icy Hot to brush his teeth before my mother caught his error ... or even when he dismissed his financial sensibilities and had mom buy me an expensive paisley dress to wear to a homecoming dance?

The nurse administered Mags a valium to help her rest. Curled on the small loveseat beside her husband's bed, she slumbered with her hand resting on his shoulder. While my father slept quieted by the morphine drop, the three of us passed the time whispering about everything and nothing. We even laughed, because dad's behavior was not far removed from what we had known all of our lives. In fact, in the last few weeks, he had seemed even more lucid than he usual.

Wally spoke about how familiar he had become with death. He often saw children die of disease and malnourishment. Recently he had witnessed the death of a volunteer, killed by a hippopotamus during an attempt to rescue a sealed container of vaccines that had floated into a watering hole after a heavy rain.

"Hippos kill more humans than any other animal over there. They have only four teeth. But each tooth is twenty inches long. Snapped the guy like a toothpick. It was awful."

"Can we talk about something else?" I pleaded.

He ignored my request and launched into a detailed discussion of dying at the hands of an animal, asking, "If you had to be killed by an animal, what beast would you pick?"

Vicki selected a guinea pig, which he and I both argued did not qualify as an animal capable of killing a person. Vicki switched her answer to a lion, since it would be quick. Wally chose a cobra, because he had become fascinated with them while in Africa, and little blood would be shed. Although he also believed he could outrun it if challenged.

"What about you?" Wally asked, peering at me through the dimly lit room.

I thought back to the sea creatures attack series. I definitely didn't want to die at the hands of a sea creature. After several minutes pondering his question, I finally chose a boa constrictor stating that I didn't believe they could actually squeeze the life out of someone. Wally contended that he had seen one devouring an antelope once—hooves, antlers, and all.

"Lovely," I responded.

We sat on the floor, digesting this piece of information. Suddenly a huge breath came from my father. We all stood, gathering around him. He looked up at me, his eyes watery and glazed.

"It's okay, Daddy, you can go now," I said. "We're with you."

Mags began to sob. He took one last breath, as if he were about to go underwater for a while, and then was gone. My mother didn't believe he was gone, even after the first doctor pronounced him dead. After the physician left, I grabbed a nurse in the hall and asked her to check him. She confirmed there were no vital signs. Yet still, my mother requested that our doctor be called immediately. Wally left the room to find him.

Vicki and I loitered just inside the door, watching our mother look at him as if she could will him back from the dead. She grabbed his hand, kissed it, and placed it back on his stomach. Then she moved it down to his side. She pulled the oxygen mask off his face and fixed his hair, smoothing it down around his forehead. She looked as if she were posing a mannequin in a store window, trying to position him just right.

Chapter 20

▼

My mother remained in complete and utter shock. For the first few days after Dad died, she drifted through the house aimlessly. When we spoke to her, she seemed startled.

Vicki had been named the executor of Dad's estate and announced during the funeral planning that Dad had requested that my Charlie McCarthy ventriloquist dummy conduct part of his eulogy. Of course I thought she was joking, but she promptly showed me the piece of paper with the request and his signature at the bottom.

Charlie McCarthy had been on my Christmas wish list the year prior to the start of my Barbie obsession. Santa apparently couldn't find him on sale, which to my mother was an absolute requirement. I had wanted him after watching a locally produced puppet show called *Mr. Jugg's Junkyard*. The show featured an old man with four puppets: a junkyard dog, a ratty sneaker, a soda can, and a misanthropic rat. You could usually see the guy's arm underneath the puppets' bodies, and he would frequently get the characters mixed up. The worst part was that their mouths never moved when they were supposed to be talking. It was like watching a dubbed movie, puppet style. I was fairly certain that I could do better than Mr. Jugg and believed that my exceptional ventriloquism skills might prompt an offer to do my own show on PBS.

It was a Charlieless Christmas that year. But a few months later, my mother sidetracked my passionate lobby for a Barbie doll by surprising me with Charlie. She had found him on the $5 table at the annual Women's Club Whale of a Sale Event. "You know, he has a monocle, too! So fun!" she informed me as she handed him to me.

For the remainder of the summer, I studied the manual that came with Charlie and perfected my ability to make the sound of a *P* without pursing my lips. I became quite good—so good that my father would have me perform each time someone stopped by the house.

"Go get Charlie," my father would direct me and then inform our houseguest, "You're in for a treat." What would follow was a five-minute skit, which consisted of Charlie calling me a dummy, to which I would reply, "No, Charlie, you're the dummy." This would be repeated at least five times or until the visitor politely acknowledged my "extraordinary" talent to my father, who would always end with a short history lesson on ventriloquism.

"The name ventriloquist means, belly speaker in Latin. In the sixth century, Christians condemned the practice of ventriloquism, they thought it was a way to communicate with the dead."

My love affair with Charlie ended when Marcy and her bevy of Barbie-doll beauties came into my life, at which point I completely abandoned him.

"Paige! Paige!" my sister blurted, demanding my attention. "I acknowledge that it's weird, but it's what he wanted."

"No way," I said. "It's ridiculous."

Vicki squeezed my hand and said two words: "Paisley dress."

"Vicki, please. It's insane. I mean really. It's not normal."

"And neither was he. Hey maybe you can wear that paisley dress?"

And with those words, I acquiesced. Vicki was referring to an item of clothing that had hung in my closet since high school. A week before the homecoming dance, I went with Mags to the mall to return a blouse that, upon review of the receipt, had not been on sale, as she had believed. While she completed the paperwork for the return, I strolled around the racks—and that's when I saw it. The fabric of the dress was a stylish paisley in burgundy, green, and cream, with an intricate lace collar. It was tight at the top, with dolman sleeves and a fitted waist. The skirt was flowing and cut slightly longer at each side. It reminded me of a dress I had once seen Ginger Rogers wearing in a movie that I had watched with my father.

"Supposedly she loved ice-cream sodas, but it sure doesn't look like it, does it?" my father had commented. He whistled at the television screen. Ginger whirled elegantly around the dance floor, her skirt flowing up and down like rolling waves.

I didn't touch the dress. I stood in front of it, as if I were at a museum admiring a beautiful painting, cocking my head to one side and then to the other.

"That's lovely." Mags interrupted my appreciation.

"What?"

"The dress. It's beautiful. What are you wearing to the dance, anyway?"

"The gray skirt and the yellow sweater," I replied.

"Why don't you try this on?" she said, as she flipped over the tags that dangled off the sleeve until she found the one with the price.

"How much is it?" I asked.

She whistled. "A lot. $150 ... too steep for our budget."

I knowingly nodded and turned to leave.

"Try it on," she said again. "Just for kicks."

"Why?" I asked.

"They don't force you to buy it just because you tried it on. Just for fun. C'mon."

I shrugged and delicately took the dress off the rack. As I strained to slide the last button in place at the back of my neck, I felt both wonderful and terrible. I stood in front of the mirror in surprise. The dress looked as if it was made for me—and for the very first time, I felt like a girl. I felt pretty and feminine and dainty. This feeling lasted for only a few seconds and quickly devolved into frustration and disappointment. We couldn't afford the dress. My mother called from outside the door.

"Well, let's see it."

I walked out and turned, flattening the front of the dress against my hips. She didn't need to say anything. I saw the same surprise in her face.

"It's great. OK?" I blurted despondently. "But it's too expensive. So, let's just go." Part of me hoped that playing the martyr might manipulate the minuscule spontaneous bone in my mother's body, prodding her into purchasing the dress for me, but this did not happen. I retreated to the fitting room, placed the dress back upon its hanger, and went to place it with the rest of the clothes that people had decided against, because they didn't fit or were the wrong color. I stopped before reaching the rack and instead carried the dress out with me to return it to the display.

"Paige, I'm sorry," my mother said. "That gray skirt does look darling on you, and I have always said that you are absolutely radiant in yellow! It's your best color."

The hours leading up to the homecoming dance were full of dread, not only because the gray skirt was as drab as its color but because my date was Chris Flack.

The truth was that I hadn't originally known that I was saying yes to Chris Flack. When he had telephoned me, he said, "This is Chris," and I had assumed it was Chris Brock, quarterback and love of my life. I already had admitted that I didn't have a date by the time I realized who it really was. I tried my best to tactfully wriggle out of the commitment. That was when he gave me the big guilt trip. He claimed that I owed him, because his father had saved my mother's life. Chris's father was a pulmonary specialist at the local hospital. One night, after combining some over-the-counter cold medicine with the use of her asthma inhaler, Mags had experienced a massive asthma attack. Chris's father administered the breathing treatment. It wasn't a life-or-death situation, but it was traumatic for the family. It was the one time that my father stopped emitting facts and figures.

Chris was overweight, had braces, and sometimes wore ascots with his oxford shirts to school. I finally agreed to the date, and he promised me that the "Flack Attack" would be a good time.

At 5 PM, Mags knocked on my bedroom door.

"Paigey, it's 5 PM, sweetie. You better get ready."

I finished the last chapter of *To Kill a Mockingbird*, the required reading for my advanced English class, and began preparing myself for the Flack Attack.

"Has anyone seen my skirt?" I yelled from my bedroom.

"What's it look like?" my mother returned fire.

"The gray one," I screamed. "It was hanging in my closet, and it's gone."

I was panicked. I wasn't concerned about looking good on the fleshy arms of Chris. I was just being a typical teenage girl.

"Ask your father if he's seen it."

"Daddy won't know!" I shrieked. "He doesn't even know where *he* is."

"Just go ask him."

I barreled down the stairs to the first floor and down the second flight of stairs to the basement. My father sat at his desk, reading.

"Mom says to ask you about my skirt."

"Hmmm?" he replied, without lifting his eyes from the book in his hands.

"It's gray tweed. Mom had it dry-cleaned, and it was hanging in my closet, and now I can't find it anywhere." My voice squeaked at a pitch that caused my father to wince. He looked at me blankly.

"Dad? Helllooooo? Have you seen it?" I asked indignantly.

Without answering, he returned to his book. I rounded the banister of the stairs and had mounted the first step when he said, "Check the linen closet."

I turned in a huff. "Why would it be in the linen closet?"

"Why wouldn't it be?" he countered. I rolled my eyes and stampeded up the steps. I blew past my mother, who was standing in the kitchen, and back up the stairs to the linen closet. She followed quickly behind me. I opened the louvered door … and there it was, the paisley dress, my dress.

I turned to Mags for an explanation.

"I told Daddy how beautiful it was on you, and he told me that his little Paigebug should have it."

"But it's too expensive." I still searched for an explanation.

My mother simply smiled. "Well, hurry up and put it on. You're going to be late."

I waltzed back down to the basement, trailing one leg slightly behind me like a ballerina. My father continued to read. I came from behind him and wrapped my arms around his shoulders. He patted my forearm.

"Thank you. Thank you. Thank you."

He replied, "You're welcome," and put his book down. He then grabbed my face between his hands and spoke to me, not to the air, not some imaginary person, but to me directly.

"Masquerading as a normal person every day can be exhausting. You should know this." He returned to his book. I waited for more, but that was all. Before I left home to pick up Chris, as he did not drive, my father called after me, "Kindness, nobler ever than revenge. Shakespeare."

In preparation for my father's eulogy, I unearthed a trunk from the attic crammed with mementos from my youth. Mags had packed most of my toys away, and I could only hope that Charlie had not been discarded. I rummaged through the musty contents, removing a few stuffed animals, a couple of academic ribbons, my tenth-grade yearbook, and a small lump of coal. Sandwiched between a shoebox full of cassette tapes and a box of photographs was Charlie, looking as debonair as ever. He even had the old book of ventriloquism routines with him.

I sat in the middle of the floor, encircled by the keepsakes of my childhood. My hands grazed each reminder. I picked up the yearbook and turned to the index at the back. My finger trailed the names until I found my own. "Sheehan, Paige. Pg. 6, 18, 30, and 41." I was in the background in every picture. I returned to the index and found Marcy's listing. "Roberts, Marcy. Pg. 1, 3, 5, 6, 12, 15, 18, 20, 22, 26, 30, 31, 33, 36, 40, and 41." I began reviewing the yearbook's account of Marcy, but stopped after the fifth reference. I felt deep despair. For whatever reason, I expected the yearbook to have changed as miraculously as I had, memorializing me as someone who was in the foreground, not the background. A quotation came to mind: "Past performance is the best indicator of future performance." That phrase was the footer on every slide of the annual performance review training for managers. Had I changed? Yes, but I still desired almost everything I had wanted back in tenth grade.

Systematically I returned the contents of the trunk, so it was just as I found it. I grabbed the last piece, an oversized, stuffed kangaroo, and noticed a plastic arm jutting out from its pouch. Smiling, I pulled out the Skipper doll which I had taken from Marcy's house the last time I had been there. Aside from the kangaroo fuzz that spotted her hair, Skipper looked the same as I remembered. She still wore the bathing suit I had fashioned out of medical gauze, and remained plain and simple, her main feature being bendable legs. I closed the trunk and brought Charlie, Skipper, and the piece of coal to their rightful place—my bedroom.

The night before the service, I practiced with Charlie. I was a bit rusty, but most of the technique came back to me. Wally passed my bedroom as I was rehearsing and said, "Just like riding a bike."

"Shut up," I replied.

He appeared in my doorway, as he had many times during my youth, and I braced myself for his oncoming taunt.

"I'm just kidding. I think it's great that you're doing this."

"I don't even care what people think. I want to do it."

He nodded and dug his hands into one of the various cargo pockets sewn into the clothing he wore. "What's with the Barbie doll?" he inquired, gesturing toward Skipper, who sat against my vanity mirror.

"That's not Barbie. That's Skipper," I informed him. "She's wearing haute couture."

"What's with all the bandages? Is she supposed to be like a burn victim or something?" he asked with a smirk.

"Shut up," I replied again.

In addition to an unusual eulogy, my father had requested to be cremated. He had always thought it was a waste of earth to bury bodies. "Some of the best land is in cemeteries," he would say, "and land should be for the living." I spent the four days after he died preparing for the memorial service while Mags coordinated his cremation. The memorial service was scheduled at 2 PM on Saturday. I did not realize until that morning that I had nothing to wear. I had been so focused on the logistics that I had not had time to think about anything else. During the eleven weeks leading up to my father's death, I had worn jeans and sweatshirts and a few T-shirts of Wally's. Nothing I had was appropriate attire to wear to my father's service, which was scheduled to begin in two hours. I ran into the kitchen, where Vicki was working on her opening remarks for the service. Mrs. Weitzman was there, rearranging the refrigerator.

"Vic, do you have an extra skirt or something? I just realized that I have nothing to wear."

"No, I just have the one dress. Doesn't Mom have something?"

"I can't wear something of Mom's." Mags was six inches shorter than I and several pounds heavier. In addition, her style was completely different. She wore a lot of scarves and bows and pearls and bouclé suits. Mrs. Weitzman's head popped up over the refrigerator.

"Oh, I have something perfect. Sarah left a few things behind when she moved out. You can borrow something of hers. Just let me finish this up, and I'll bring it over. She has some darling things."

I barely remembered Mrs. Weitzman's daughter, Sarah. She had been my neighbor, but she was fifteen years older. When I was selling my high-priced lemonade, she was already in college. I had met her once, years ago, when I had come home for Christmas, but I couldn't remember anything about her except that I once saw her making out with a boy behind the Weitzmans' gardening shed.

Vicki continued to write, and without looking up from her pad said, "That should work. She was about your size."

I felt guilty for being so curt with Mrs. Weitzman. She had been very helpful during the entire ordeal, bringing over food, cleaning, answering phones, and running errands. Mags felt truly indebted, and suddenly I did too.

Wally loaded the many flower arrangements we had received into the back of the car to take to the church. I gathered my notes, cleaned Charlie's face, and finished my makeup as I waited for Mrs. Weitzman.

"Paige, we need to leave in about two minutes. Hurry up and get dressed." Mags appeared in the bathroom doorway, looking beautiful in a black bouclé suit, pearls, and a heart-shaped pin.

"You look wonderful, Mom. I don't have anything here to wear, so Mrs. Weitzman is bringing something over of Sarah's."

My mother touched her hand to her chest. "The woman is a saint, isn't she? She should be canonized. Well, not that Jews can be saints, but you know what I mean. We're pressed for time, so I'll run over and get it."

Moments later my mother appeared with Mrs. Weitzman in tow. In her hand were two items: an orange-colored chiffon jumpsuit with a sailor collar, and a shirtdress featuring large colorful bananas and pineapples.

"Oh, my!" I said, staring at the clothes and then at my mother.

Vicki stood behind them, mouthing "Aw-ful."

"I wish I could fit into them, because they're so darling," Mrs. Weitzman informed me, taking the jumpsuit and placing it in front of herself. "What I wouldn't give to be a size eight again."

"I don't know. Aren't you supposed to wear dark colors to funerals?"

"Oh, nonsense," Mrs. Weitzman said. "Those rules have changed."

I looked to Mags for help, but she looked at me pleadingly, giving me a look that only mothers know how to give. Her eyes said, "You must wear one."

"Paige, I know it's difficult to choose, but we've got thirty minutes before the service starts." She paused. "I have always loved you in orange. It's so fresh and bright!"

"I have shoes to match that one too!" Mrs. Weitzman added.

"Oh, great!" I replied, with as much fake enthusiasm as I could muster.

I changed into the orange, nautical nightmare and met my family, who eagerly awaited my one-woman fashion show at the foot of the stairs. Mrs. Weitzman had returned to the house to get the shoes.

"What the hell are you wearing? Don't tell me. It's haute couture," Wally said, as I descended the stairs.

Vicki laughed heartily, and Mags quieted her.

"Ask Mom," I replied. "She's making me wear it, because she doesn't want to upset crazy Mrs. Weitzman."

"It's not going to kill you," my mother replied.

"Mom, are you looking at this?" I questioned.

Vicki added, "It looks like what the inmates wear at County."

"Maybe this is just practice for when they throw you in the slammer," Wally added.

"That's not funny." I glared at him.

"It isn't funny, Wallace," Mags remarked, and Wally pretended to cower. I did a catwalk turn, so the horror could be seen from all angles, and stopped in front of Mags. She eyed me from head to toe.

"It *is* hideous," she said.

"Where does one buy something like that?" Wally asked.

"Didn't Cyndi Lauper wear that in the 'She Bop' video?" Vicki chirped. I shot her a look.

"Maybe the bananas and pineapples would be better. Should I change?" I looked to all of them and grabbed the head of the banister to begin my ascent to retrieve the lesser of two evils.

Mags looked at me sympathetically. "Paige, it's fine. Besides, the church will be packed, and we'll want to be able to find you in the crowd."

Wally grabbed Mags around the shoulder with one arm and jostled her. "That's the spirit! Mags made a joke." I looked at her, and she was smiling and laughing. It was the first time in days that I had seen animation in her face.

The doorbell rang, and Mrs. Weitzman pushed open the door with the dyed-to-match shoes in hand. She gasped when she saw me. "Looks like it was made for you. I'm so happy I could help. I know you want to look your best for your dad."

I smiled politely and grabbed a long raincoat from the closet, and we headed to the church. Wally took the simple, mahogany box, imprinted with a small Celtic cross that contained Dad's ashes, and promised to meet us at the church. He was responsible for picking up the group of extended family staying at the local Holiday Inn across town.

Chapter 21

Ten minutes before the service, Father Joe instructed us to place Dad's remains on the white, marble podium that stood before the altar.

"I'll allow some time at the beginning of the service for the congregation to pay their respects, since you didn't host a wake."

"Where in the world is your brother?" Mags asked anxiously.

Garbed in my raincoat, I ran to the back of the church to find Wally rushing in with extended family in tow.

"What took you so long?" I snapped.

"We couldn't all fit in my car, so we switched to Aunt Judy's rental."

Realizing that Wally was no longer carrying the mahogany box, I gasped, "Where's Dad?" Wally patted himself once, as if he were looking for a misplaced wallet.

"Shit! Shit! I must have left him at the hotel."

"What?"

"I went in to help Judy with her bags, 'cause she's headed back to Jersey today, and didn't want to leave him in the car."

Mags and Vicki suddenly appeared.

"What's going on? Where's your father?" Mags cried.

Wally stared at me blankly, unable to explain his mistake.

"Wally left him at the Holiday Inn," I responded, exasperated.

"Oh, good Lord. We have to put something up there. What will people think?" Mags instructed Vicki and Wally to find something to place on the podium in Dad's absence. I called the Holiday Inn and was informed that Aunt

Judy's room had already been cleaned. I was also advised to contact housekeeping about forgotten items.

With the church filled, Wally dramatically entered from the back of the church, carrying a black, vinyl case the size of a shoebox, which he placed upon the marble pedestal. The organist began the prelude, and Wally eased in beside me.

"What is it?" I whispered, and both Mags and Vicki leaned in to hear his answer.

"It's the roadside emergency kit from Mom's car," he quietly answered. "The one from Lorne's Travel Agency. I turned it over, so you can't see the logo."

We all sat in horror as townspeople, students, family, and friends patted, kissed, and prayed over the roadside emergency kit. Father Joe even blessed it with holy water. We later learned that the logo on the roadside emergency kit included the phrase "to get you safely to your next destination." *How appropriate*, I thought.

I kept the raincoat on during most of the service until just minutes before I was to speak. My mother leaned into me and whispered, "You cannot wear the raincoat up there."

"I know," I whispered. "I'm going to take it off."

Finally my time at the podium arrived. I peeled off the raincoat, walked to the lectern and hoped it would shield the congregation from my glow-in-the-dark frock, and began. "I have the distinct pleasure today to tell you about a wonderful man: my father. Not many people really understood my father. Many found him peculiar, but as I reflected upon the reasons why he was so peculiar, I realized that the answer is simple. What my father cherished and regarded was different from most. He did not care about fashion. My mother usually selected his daily attire, but that was more for her benefit than his. He did not care about celebrity. To him, the name Madonna evoked images of the Blessed Virgin. He didn't care about money, except about having enough to feed and school his children. He did not long for material possessions. All he needed was a good book and a comfortable chair and his beloved wife nearby. When I was a child, I became quite proficient as a ventriloquist … so much so that my father would ask me to entertain anyone who walked within a hundred yards of our house. I never quite understood why he loved my routine so much. I eventually asked him one day, 'Why do you find it so funny?' He said that he thought it was a great representation of how the world works. 'The world is full of talking heads, Paigebug,' he said. 'So many of us say what we are supposed to say and do what we are supposed to do, because there is someone behind us, pushing a button.' He then looked at me intently to emphasize his message. 'It's easy to become someone's dummy,' he warned me.

"My father requested that good ol' Charlie be a part of his eulogy, so please indulge me and his wishes."

I grabbed the doll from underneath the lectern, propped him on top of the podium, and began slightly moving my lips in precision with Charlie's mouth, "I would like to ask that everyone stand and applaud Paige's father, John Sheehan, for speaking freely and living simply and loving easily and prompting us today to ask ourselves, 'What is so peculiar about that?' Thank you." Then I did my best to update some of Charlie's old routines to a contemporary funeral setting. This was no small feat, considering the joke guide that came with Charlie was scripted during the Eisenhower administration and had to do with his lascivious quest to find a Mrs. McCarthy.

Whatever I did, it seemed to work. As I looked out into the congregation, there was not a dry eye in the house, nor was there a frown. Afterward, Vicki hugged me tighter than she had ever done before.

"You're a good person. You're a really great person," she said, as if she were experiencing some grand epiphany.

As the church was clearing, I saw Owen standing in back. He had come. I had emailed him the information about the service but had not expected him to make the trip. I thought he had only asked for it so he could send flowers or a card, but there he was.

He extended his arms to me, and I fell into them.

"I'm so sorry," he said.

"Me too. It hasn't truly sunk in yet," I pulled away from him. "I can't believe you're here. When did you get here?"

"Today. I drove. You're very colorful today."

"You mean my prison suit? It's not mine. I am wearing it for comic relief."

"It's fetching." He beamed, and I mirrored him.

"What's the latest on MAX?" I asked him. "Do you have a contract in place?"

"Yes and no. We're still in talks. But first things first. When are you coming back? The preliminary hearing is next week, and we need to prep."

I furrowed my brow. "I don't know. We still have some things to sort out with my father's estate, and we have to find a place for his ashes. He said he wanted them to be spread over campus, but our priest says that's a no-go."

"Why?"

"Supposedly, the body has to be completely buried in one place. You can't scatter him."

"Why not?"

"Something about the resurrection. In order for it to count as a Christian burial, all the ashes—his whole body—must be in one place. He can't be spread out. I guess the Church doesn't want his arm resurrecting by Jenkins Hall and his head popping up by itself over by the dorms. Who knows?"

"That would be kind of creepy."

"And anyway, the campus says that we can't scatter him or bury him. It's against policy."

"Do they even have a policy on that?"

"Apparently. The dean said that burying a body, albeit a cremated body, on campus might cause uneasiness among some students."

"I can see that. There'd be all the stories about the ghost of Professor Sheehan."

I looked at him, and my eyes widened. "Oh, my God, you're brilliant."

"What?"

"It's brilliant! True genius! He would have loved that. Vicki will freak over the idea."

"What idea?" he questioned.

"First things first. Can you take me to the Holiday Inn?"

After explaining how my father's ashes had been misplaced, I told Owen about Dad's love of folktales and ghost stories—and his most certain thrill at becoming one. Owen agreed that burying my father on campus, although illegal, would certainly honor his memory and his passion.

The search-and-rescue effort to retrieve the ashes was unsuccessful. The head housekeeper responsible for the lost and found room was gone for the day, and no one else had a key to the room. The front-desk manager informed us that the matter would have to wait until 8 AM the next morning.

The reception was in full swing when we returned to the house. I hadn't cried since my father's death, four days earlier. Planning the service, calling the funeral home, and scheduling his cremation had distracted me.

I left Owen talking with Vicki to find more toothpicks for the cheese platter. The toothpicks were not where we typically kept them, as crazy Mrs. Weitzman had reorganized everything. My search brought me to a cupboard packed with empty mason jars and miscellaneous items. As I rummaged through it, one of the jars crashed to the floor, shattering into large, aquamarine pieces. I knelt down to pick up a lid with jagged holes poked through the top and collected the glass onto a paper towel. Masking tape covered one of the shards, which faintly said Paige's Bugs in my father's handwriting. It had been years since I had seen the jar, and I was surprised it hadn't been discarded years before. As I collected the glass, I was suddenly struck with an intense feeling of loss. I stood up and brushed past Vicki, who had come to find the source of the noise.

People filled every corner of the house. I retreated to the dark closet underneath the stairs and wept intensely, muffling my cries by pressing my father's winter coat against my mouth.

Chapter 22

Owen volunteered to meet me in front of the lobby of the Holiday Inn at 8 AM the next morning. I had promised my mother we'd track down dad's ashes. We navigated our way to the lost and found closet, located in the bowels of the hotel's basement.

"Thanks for meeting me," I said, as we waited outside the door. "I know this is kind of bizarre."

"I don't mind. I'm all for helping a friend in need," he chuckled.

I smiled. "I can't quite make sense of you, Owen Holden."

"What do you mean?" He thrust his hands deep into the pockets of his khaki pants.

"You're not very consistent. I've asked for your help before, you know, and you said, 'I don't have time right now. I'm sorry.' I did my best imitation of his slight Texas twang.

He looked at me indignantly. "What are you talking about? When?"

"Remember that record-low day last February, when we got all that snow?" He nodded. "Well, I had dropped my keys in a grate in the parking lot. You came out of the elevators, and I called out to you, and you said you wouldn't help me."

He looked down at his feet. "You're crazy. I always help people with car trouble. I would have never said that."

"I'm not crazy. You said it. You didn't even look at me. Oh … and then you said, 'I can't be everything to everybody.' Real nice."

I squinted to read his expression, illuminated by the bare bulb that hung from the ceiling. He shuffled his feet, turning around in a circle, and suddenly his head shot up defiantly. "I wasn't talking to *you*. I know exactly what day you are talking about … and I was talking on my cell phone to my former coach. He had called to ask if I would fly to Dallas that night to cover some event for a benefactor of the stadium. I knew because of the snow that it would be next to impossible to get a flight out, and basically, I just didn't want to go. I was on my cell phone, using an earpiece." He laughed heartily. "I was not talking to you."

"You weren't?" I squeaked.

"No! Lord, no wonder I was always getting the cold shoulder from you. I honestly didn't see or hear you when you called out to me. Classic!" He roared with laughter.

I checked my watch. It was fifteen minutes after eight. I jiggled the handle of the door to verify it was locked.

"I can pick it," he offered, inspecting the lock.

"I don't know." I looked around nervously and checked my watch again. "Let's wait five more minutes."

At precisely 8:20 AM, Owen pulled a keychain from his pocket, from which dangled a miniature Swiss Army knife. In less than thirty seconds, he managed to unlock the door.

The closet was the size of a bathroom, and poorly lit. Floor-to-ceiling shelves overflowing with forgotten treasures of past travelers lined three walls. There were items that understandably had been left behind: belts, sunglasses, toiletry bags. However, there were also items I could not believe had been forgotten, let alone never retrieved: several vibrators, an infant car seat, a cello, a wedding dress, and even a pacemaker.

After twenty minutes of scouring the lengths of each section, I began to give up hope when I heard Owen shout excitedly.

"I think I see it," he said, pointing to the top shelf. Stuffed between an ice chest and a toilet-training seat was my father. Owen carefully pulled the box down and placed him in my arm. I gripped the box tightly and closed my eyes. Owen tenderly placed one hand on my shoulder.

"You're tall!" I blurted nervously, as if just noticing. He peered down at me, highly amused. "How tall are you, anyway?" I asked.

"And you have a glob of cobwebs on your head." He reached for it, as did I, patting wildly to find it.

"Where are you from?" he asked, grinning, brushing down the hair that had been tangled in the web.

"What do you mean? I'm from Fairville." I nervously backed away from him, only to be stopped an inch later by the perimeter of the small space.

"Don't," I said.

"Don't what?" He took a step back while I glared at him.

"Don't what?" he asked again.

"Don't …" I began. "I thought you were going in for a kiss or something."

"Yeah, this is how I seduce all my female clients. I help them search for the misplaced ashes of one of their parents, and then I move in for the big, wet one," he said. "Why? Would kissing me be such an awful thing? You know, I was voted one of *People* magazine's Top 50 Bachelors in 2000."

"Which is exactly why I don't want to kiss you," I responded. "People like me do not get involved with people like you. I'm not your type, believe me."

"Who are *your* people, and what's *my* type?" he asked.

"Can we just not do this? OK?" I picked up my father and walked out, with Owen trailing behind. Back in the well-lit, people-filled lobby, I felt comfortable again.

"I'll be back in town by five tomorrow night," I said distantly. "I'll give you a call."

I waited for him to respond, but he didn't.

"OK, well, thanks for this," I said, raising the box slightly in the air.

"Sure. What are friends for?" he replied sarcastically. I watched him as he walked into the elevator to return to his room. His anger was purposefully obvious. I knew that I had hurt his pride, but I also knew that he had pride to spare. My rebuff would be a mere scratch on his ego, whereas I believed I had just saved myself from great harm.

At 3 AM the next morning, Vicki, Wally, Mags, and I drove in hushed silence to campus under the cover of night. We selected a patch of ground near a concrete bench where my father sometimes had sat reading in between classes. For reasons that I now believe were purely dramatic, we dressed in head-to-toe black. Wally even donned a ski mask, claiming he had yearned for an occasion to wear one. After digging the hole, I opened the box, and each of us placed something atop his ashes, which were conveniently contained in a plastic bag. Vicki kissed a photograph of herself with Mr. Fatboy and tucked it inside. Mags included a love letter. A giraffe's tooth was Wally's contribution, and I added Charlie McCarthy's monocle. Each of us moved piles of dirt by hand to cover the simple wood box, smoothing the dirt evenly until it was level with the ground. Holding hands, we prayed silently and said good-bye.

Chapter 23

I welcomed the drive home to D.C. It had been weeks since I had been alone with my own thoughts. I always enjoyed the drive to and from West Virginia so I rented a car for my return. The bulk of the drive was spent passing picturesque farmhouses perched atop rolling hills. The morning fog was thick, and it lingered well beyond its normal departure time, which seemed somewhat fitting, since I was living in an emotional fog. The past three months had been a blur of doctors, pills, and tears.

I was relieved it was behind me, although some part of me felt I had failed my father and my family. I had not been able to save him. I wondered if the outcome would have been different if I had done more research or pushed harder to get him admitted into the clinical trial at NIH.

After the memorial service, our family priest, Father Joe, came to the house to check on the family. He had known me since my birth and had always been very close to our family. He served as the Catholic chaplain on campus, and the students called him Papa J. He was cool, usually dressed in jeans and Birkenstocks. Besides saying mass on Sundays, Father Joe's primary job was to counsel students. He was called upon when students were in crisis or pain. Over the years, he had dealt with some horrible situations: a freshman who awoke to the blast of her roommate shooting herself in the head, a senior whose parents were killed by a drunk driver on their way home from parents' weekend, a junior who was brutally raped by a janitor. I only learned of these stories through my father. After Dad told me about the rape and Father Joe's counsel to the victim, I had commented, "That has got to be the worst job. How can you continue to believe in God when confronted with such things? It's awful."

"Well," my father said, "better a priest, I guess. He should have some faith to spare."

When he visited after my father's death, Father Joe sat down with a cup of coffee at our oversized oak farm table, which sat just beyond the kitchen. I was busy finding room for all the food that family and friends had delivered to the house and also trying to avoid Mrs. Weitzman, who was dashing in and out of rooms draping all our mirrors with black cloth.

I whispered to Father Joe, "I'm on the verge of killing her. Hello? We're not Jewish."

"She's just trying to be helpful, Paige," the good father noted.

At that moment, Mrs. Weitzman dashed into the kitchen and began to cover the small mirror that was part of our combination key hook/chalkboard that hung upon the door leading to the garage. A list of groceries in my father's writing was still scribbled on the chalkboard: *milk, eggs, Icy Hot, cream soda.*

"Don't cover that," I snapped. Mrs. Weitzman seemed completely unaware of the tone of my request and continued to tuck the cloth around the corners.

"Dear, we need to cover all the mirrors, even the small ones," she answered dismissively.

Father Joe interrupted, realizing I was mere seconds away from taking the black cloth from the mirror and choking Mrs. Weitzman with it.

"Paige, sit down." He patted the chair beside him. Mrs. Weitzman dashed out of the kitchen, scarves of black cloth draped over her arm as if she were a French waiter. I sat down next to Father Joe, and he took my hands in his and simply asked, "And how are you?"

"I'm fine. I'm fine, really ..." my voice trailed off, and I swallowed whatever was welling inside of me.

"That didn't sound so fine."

"I'm just feeling sorry for myself, that's all. I don't understand why God had to take my father. Why not some deadbeat dad or some father who abused or neglected his children?"

"Fair questions," he said, "but God has a master plan for all of us."

"Screw the master plan," I said. "The plan was for my father to be here. He was to walk me down the aisle and hold my firstborn child in his hands and take care of my mother and grow old with her. The master plan did not involve this." I moved my hands from his and folded them underneath my arms.

Father Joe raised his eyebrows. My reaction had surprised him, and his surprise only irritated me. I had been a happy child and, for the most part, had grown to be a happy adolescent, and then a happy adult. My positive attitude was frequently cited on performance reviews. Over time I discovered that people looked to me as some sort of energy source, with eternal optimism flowing and silver linings to spare. I was Paige, happy-go-lucky Paige. I loved that I was perceived as this high-on-life kind of girl. I prided myself on being the go-to girl when skies were gray, for turning a frown upside down. The Skippers of the world were good at this.

The high-school cheerleading moderator was correct: I had an undeniable spirit. The problem with being cast in this role was that the slightest deviation from Pollyannaville caught those who knew me off guard. I was not allowed to have a bad day or be irritable. If I did exhibit behaviors that weren't aligned with my happy-go-lucky label, people were disappointed, which made me even more irritable. I expected Father Joe to ignore my bad behavior, as I had seen others do, excusing whatever had escaped from my mouth the way one does when bumping into a stranger in a crowded store. You bump. You assume it was unintentional, barely acknowledge it, and you move on. But Papa J stopped to investigate.

"I see. I got it. Screw the master plan. What the hell, right?" He pulled his white collar off from his neck and rolled it between his fingers. "It's perfectly understandable that you are angry. I'm angry too."

"Do they teach you to say these things at the seminary?"

"What do you want me to say, Paige? That God messed up? That you're right, and God is wrong? That no one good should ever die? I'm a priest. My whole life is based on faith. Wonderful people die. Innocent babies and beautiful, smiling children die ... and magnificent fathers. You can waste hours questioning, but you will never get an answer ... not on this earth."

"I know. I just ..." I sighed, taking the collar out of his hands. It was not made of a starched fabric, as I had expected, but of plastic. I handed it back to him. "Where is he, anyway? Is there a heaven? Is he flying around with wings, wearing billowing, white vestments? I mean, that's crazy, right?"

"I believe that death is a state. I don't think it's a tangible presence. Your father is wherever he wants to be, but I don't think it's up in the sky on a cloud. That's just an image we create, because we need images. Truthfully, I think that everlasting life is an existence that is intangible. Peace, that is what Jesus promised ... but what does peace look like? It's different for everyone. I don't think your father is in a place, per se. He is in an existence."

Father Joe's comments did not provide me with much consolation. I actually wanted him to say, "Yes, Paige. Your dad is sitting on a big, fluffy cloud right now, eating apple pie, and drinking good Scotch in his underwear while watching the Miss Marple miniseries on BBC. Tonight he is going to bore some of the angels with random facts about the gaseous makeup of clouds."

That would be my father's heaven, I decided, and I desperately wanted that image. I needed it, because it provided me with hope that my father was still doing the things I knew him to do—and if that were true, then nothing would have changed except his location.

I arrived in D.C. at noon and spent a good hour sorting through mail and unpacking. I had received a certified letter from the courthouse with my preliminary hearing date. It was set for Tuesday, and I was not prepared. I dreaded calling Owen. I had thought about our recent conversation and felt guilty for being so distant. He had driven all the way to West Virginia for my father's funeral, had helped find his ashes, and was graciously representing me free of charge. I decided that an apology was in order. I called him at 2 PM.

"Hey," I said, "It's me. Just got back. What time did you get in?"

"At 5 PM last night. I decided to just hit the road after our little scavenger hunt."

"Oh. Wow, you must be exhausted."

"I'm OK." He replied curtly.

"Listen, I wanted to thank you again for all your help. It really means a lot to me, and I'm sorry I was being such a bitch yesterday morning. It's just a weird time for me right now, and I was tired … and I'm just sorry, OK? I owe you, and I promise to be the best client you've ever had." I waited for a few seconds for a reply. "Are you still there?" I asked.

"Yes. Still here. And I accept your apology. And given your offer, I expect you to be at my place tonight at 6 PM to begin planning our strategy for this week."

"Six o'clock it is," I replied.

Chapter 24

Owen's apartment was not what I expected. I knew he had garnered a hefty sum of money from his advertising gigs, and his father was a very prominent attorney in Texas. I expected it to be similar to Ken's apartment—clean and orderly; espresso-stained furniture; brown leather chairs; a state-of-the-art entertainment center; and a bed that was all about "business." To my surprise, it was just the opposite. Owen had a poster of a whale in his living room and a cartoon cell of Homer Simpson. There was only one couch, a dreadful Goodwill contender in a ragged green leather. Nothing quite matched, and as for the get-down bed, it was nonexistent. Instead he had a futon. It was the apartment of a twenty-six-year-old graduate student, not a thirty-six-year-old attorney. I went into the bathroom to freshen up.

"Sorry it's a little messy," he said, as I nosily walked around.

This proved to be inaccurate. It wasn't messy, as in "used boxer shorts on the floor." It was *dirty*. There was toothpaste cemented to the sink, and the mirror had flecks of water all over it. I had seen this type of bathroom maintenance in college. (Again, not what I was expecting.) Even in the haze of the water-flecked mirror, I looked like a hag. I did my best to fix my hair. I did not realize there was no toilet paper until I had already *tinkled*. I thought about yelling out to him, but I then I thought, *How awkward ... it's not exactly like he can pass it through the door while I sit sexily on the can.* I grabbed my purse and sifted through it until I found a tissue in the vortex.

When I reentered the living room, Owen met me with a glass of wine. On the coffee table was a Christmas candle with its flame flickering.

"Do you have any music?" I asked.

He smiled. "Well, your choices are 'She Blinded Me with Science' or 'She Blinded Me with Science.'"

I arched an eyebrow.

"The open/close thing on my CD player is jammed, and I can't get it open. It's stuck on the same CD ... *80's Rock*."

"Let's hear it," I said.

Owen walked over to the stereo and pushed Play. "Doesn't exactly set the mood unless you were a Chemistry Teacher."

I grinned coyly. Obviously he would not say such a thing if wasn't trying to set a romantic mood. The music began, and he lowered the volume. I sat down on the couch, and he followed.

"I hated you when I first met you," I said.

"Why?" he asked, shocked.

"Because you laughed all the way through the orientation, and it was the first time I had ever conducted it."

"And you don't know why I was laughing?" He gulped down his wine.

"Apparently not," I said, tugging my V-neck shirt down nonchalantly.

He shook his head from side to side, smiling.

"Was I babbling the whole time?"

He smiled and looked at my lips. I nervously bit my bottom lip and brought the glass to my mouth. It was what I believed to be a *moment*.

"Your fly was kind of unzipped," he told me. My eyes widened.

"What do you mean, kind of?" I asked, mortified.

"Not something you often see on a woman. It was"—he smiled—"memorable. Moman was not the first to see the green-shamrock underwear."

I tried to remember my outfit that day and believed it was Vicki's split-zippered pantsuit.

"It must have been Vicki's. She's not the best about clothes maintenance."

Owen plopped down beside me on the leather couch. It creaked. I felt my face warming as he looked at me.

He whispered, "You have a kind face."

"Well, I was born on a Monday," I said nervously. "And you know what they say: Monday's child is fair of face."

He cocked his head and put his wine glass on the coffee table.

"I like you, Paige. You're different. I can't put my finger on it. Amusing, I guess, is the word ... and nice. Good. Wholesome." He placed his hand on his knee and turned toward me, positioning himself. I reached for the coffee-table book on the side table.

"Oooh. Frank Lloyd Wright," I announced excitedly, holding the book up. "I went to Taliesin West a few years ago. It's great. Have you been?"

"No."

I began leafing through the book. "So, what's the first course of action in planning for next week?"

"First, I want to finish this conversation."

"OK, and what conversation would that be?"

"Stop fidgeting. You seem so nervous all of a sudden. Do I make you nervous?"

For a split second, I hated him. The fact that he had teasingly asked such a question bothered me, because he knew the answer. He was fishing, but I took the bait.

"Yes, you do make me a little nervous. It's not that I'm afraid of you, but …"

"But what?"

"Well, you have a bit of a reputation, you know?"

"What reputation?"

"Oh, come on," I begged, putting the book down. "You're a player and … well, you're a little bit of a mystery."

"Me? I'm the guy next door," he declared, exasperated. "An open book."

"I don't know. I sense you're hiding something from me." I eyed him, curiously watching his reaction.

"No, this is it. What you see is what you get," his voice softened.

I decided not to push any further and took two long sips of wine, returning my glass to the side table. When I turned to look at him, he kissed me.

Although I hadn't had many boyfriends, I had indeed kissed my fair share of men. During the years following college, I was somewhat of a kissing bandit at bars. Owen beat them all, hands down. He moved his hand up to my head and threaded his fingers through my hair as he pulled me closer into him. I melted. I was slightly buzzed, exhausted—and as a result felt as if I were experiencing some altered state.

Despite this my mind still was able to separate itself from the deliciousness of the moment. As he eased me farther down on the couch, all I was thinking was, *This is wrong. This is bad. You should stop. Not good. Not smart.* I could smell his cologne and feel him against me. He whispered, "I can taste the red wine on your lips," at which point my thinking changed to, *This is right. This is great. Go for it. So what if he's crazy? End of discussion.*

We continued to kiss and tried our best to lie comfortably together on his couch. After several attempts to share the small space he finally said, "Why don't we go into the bedroom?"

I crab-crawled my way backward onto his futon, and he followed. As expected, he unhooked my bra with dexterity, and he slithered out of his shirt like a snake molting its skin. I had never been one to care for muscles, but what emerged was fabulous. For me physical attraction was always rooted in intellectual and emotional attraction. I didn't understand some women's reactions to Chippendale calendars or the way women swooned over oily, shaved chests. He hovered above me, and I anchored my arms to his, which felt like two posts. In an instant, I understood the appeal of a physically strong man. I wiggled out of my jeans, and his tongue trailed my stomach as he pulled my Category A undies off. Suddenly a reverberating sound escaped my mouth, accompanied by a violent lurch. He stopped, mumbling something underneath the sheet.

Hiccups. I held my breath, but the next hiccup proved more forceful and earsplitting than its predecessor. Owen shifted and crawled on his elbows until his face met mine. He rubbed his nose.

"Good thing it's already broken," he said, laughing uncontrollably.

I stood up, clutching the sheet around me, and bent over as if touching my toes as another bout of hiccups ensued.

"What are you doing?" he asked.

"Sometimes if I hold my breath upside-down, they stop." I counted to thirty before standing upright. "I don't get them often … but when I do, they're intense."

"Dangerous, even," he quipped.

"Is your nose okay?" I asked, concerned.

"I'll live."

It was not exactly a mood-enhancing moment. I was mortified, and there was no going back. The moment was gone. Owen lay on the bed with his arms outstretched behind his head, until he moved his left hand and motioned toward the empty side of his bed.

"Don't go … stay awhile."

I tucked the sheet tightly around me, cocooning myself inside it, and moped over to the mattress. I lay beside him, and he brought his arm down and tucked it under my head.

I sighed heavily.

"What did you mean the other day," Owen asked, "when you said that people like you don't get involved with people like me?"

"I'd like to plead (hiccup) the fifth on that."

"Come on, you owe me," he said. "I'm going to be working very hard for you in the next few weeks, and if people like me shouldn't be mixing with people like you, I think I should be told the reason why."

I propped myself up on my elbow, and he turned into me. He sleepily repositioned himself and folded his pillow underneath his head.

"OK." I swallowed and tried to think of a way to explain myself.

"I'm waiting," he teased.

There were so many examples that I could give him, including the fact that I had just inadvertently injured him with my crotch. Moments that were amusing individually—but, strung together, were proof positive that I wasn't his type.

"(hiccup) Barbie," I said.

"Is that a friend of yours?"

"No, Barbie, as in the doll."

"Aha."

"The world of Barbie dolls essentially boils down to three characters. (hiccup) Barbie, of course," I began.

"Ken?" he offered proudly.

"Yes, Ken. And Skipper (hiccup. hiccup)."

"Are you trying to tell me that 'your people' are into threesomes?"

"No!" I covered his mouth with my other hand. "Let me finish. Do you know who Skipper is?"

"Oh, wait, I think you tried to tell me about this the night you sang Sister Sledge, but you were a little fuzzy. Please tell me." He sat up and picked up a pillow that had fallen to the floor, shoving it forcibly behind him.

"Skipper was Barbie's little sister. She was the less glamorous one. Kind of a tomboy, flat chested and nondescript, but perky and fun. Mattel had it all mapped out for Barbie ... she had a house, a car, a boyfriend ... everything. But they hadn't done the same for Skipper. She was kind of out on her own, fending for herself."

"And you think you are ... a Skipper?"

"Yeah, and you're a Ken, which is why we could never be together."

"And based on your theory, I should be with ..." he paused, his tone questioning.

"Someone like Blair ... someone flawless. Last week, I watched her eat spaghetti, and not one speck of marinara got away from her," I recounted, still amazed.

He slid back down again, tugging the covers around his chest, and kissed me on the nose. "I see. You're right about being perky, and you are funny. Totally funny."

My message seemed to be lost on Owen. Five minutes passed in silence. I turned onto my back and watched the ceiling fan as it appeared to jump with each rotation. I blinked quickly, so I could determine the number of blades.

"Funny as in ha-ha, or funny as in weird?" I asked finally.

"Funny only has one connotation."

"That's not true," I said, pulling the sheet more tightly against me.

"Whatever. I meant funny as in a good thing," he answered. "Sounds like your hiccups are finally gone." We lay there quietly for about twenty minutes, then I blurted out a question that had long been on my mind.

"Why are you so nice to me?"

He didn't answer. I turned onto my side and looked at him. His eyes were closed, and his bare chest was rising and falling with an even rhythm.

Chapter 25

The bed was empty when I awoke. I borrowed some mouthwash and wiped the mascara bruising my eyes. Sometimes I felt that my face looked like a painting that had yet to be colored in, with prominent lip lines and cheeks and eyes that longed to be brought to life. My Irish heritage had blessed me with a cool and pale complexion that needed blusher like tonic needed gin. I wasn't much without some key ingredients, which in my case were lipstick, mascara, and blush.

I didn't spend too much time salvaging my face, since Owen was gone. I walked the length of his apartment. On his kitchen table was a bowl of Cocoa Puffs and a glass of water with a small packet of sugar. On a napkin, he had written, "In case the hiccups possess you again. I do have breakables in the apartment."

I ate the Cocoa Puffs and casually snooped around his apartment. It looked very different in the daylight. It was minimally furnished and felt cold and empty. A collage of pictures meticulously arranged on the wall above his desk was its most charming feature. He had pictures of himself as a child with his brother, pictures of himself at graduation, and a picture of himself at the NFL draft party. One half of the wall was devoted to his time as a Dallas Cowboy. He looked younger, and his expression in the pictures bore no hint of the proud, arrogant, Cheshire grin that I had seen. Instead he looked enthusiastic and eager, like a boy who didn't know yet that he was a man—and a handsome one at that. I imagined the number of women who had spoiled him, throwing themselves at him, teaching him that manipulation was easy with good looks and power. My imagination kicked into high gear as my eyes arrived at a parade of pictures featuring the heaving bosoms of the Dallas Cowboys cheerleaders. Most of them looked like publicity shots, but there were some candids. Among the décolletage, I saw a face that looked vaguely familiar. I moved closer to inspect it, and my eyes widened.

"Oh, my God … you've got to be kidding me."

Dressed in a silver, metallic bikini and the trademark white cowboy boots was an older and even more beautiful Marcy Roberts. She was crouched forward, holding a football between her legs, as if to hike it to Owen, who was positioned behind her. The photo was artfully posed so that it was unclear whether Owen was staring at her ass or the ball.

"Oh, my God," I muttered again.

The last time I had seen Marcy was at Bonfire Night, the traditional after-party following our high-school graduation. Almost as soon as I arrived, I was tapped on my shoulder. I turned around, but no one was there. When I turned back to center, Chris Brock, the dreamy high school quarterback stood in front of me.

"Hey there. Made you look," he said, smiling. "Gotcha, Sheehan."

I blushed. "Hey there, Chris."

Chris dug his hands in his pockets. "Just wanted to tell you good luck next year. I hear you're going to Maryland."

"Yep. Thanks. You here with Marcy?" I asked. We both glanced in the direction of Marcy, who appeared to be passed out against one of the bales of hay.

"Shit," Chris exclaimed. "I told her not to have so much beer. Goddamn that girl!"

"What's wrong?" I asked.

"Sammy's parents are out of town, and Marcy is s'posed to drive us over there. Sammy is having one of her famous parties."

My heart was pounding at Mach speed. I was certain Chris would see it throbbing through my sweater. I stood in anticipation. He began speaking: "Hey, why don't you run Marcy up and …" The fire crackled behind him, and I missed part of his sentence. I nodded, too embarrassed and nervous to ask him to repeat himself, but I definitely heard the words "drive to Sammy's" and "would be really great" and "I'll come get ya when we're ready to go."

Chris walked back to the other side, where the Barbies and Kens stood. I could not determine if it was the heat from the fire or the nervous knots in my stomach that made me feel so flushed. After thirty long minutes, the signal came. He motioned for me to follow, which I did, floating.

"Where's your car?" he asked as he dragged a very intoxicated Marcy Roberts.

I pointed to the good ol' Chevy Citation that sat amid a parking lot of shiny, new trucks and muscle cars. I opened the driver's door and leaned over to open the passenger door. Seeing this, the beautiful Chris Roland said, "I'm just going to put her in the back."

He laid Marcy down on the backseat and slammed the door. Instead of jumping in the passenger side, I watched him walk around the front of my car, toward me. I rolled down the window.

"Thanks, Paigeturner." He winked. "Just make sure her mom doesn't see her like this, or she'll go fucking nuts. I'll bring her car back early tomorrow."

"Oh," I said, puzzled. "I ... um ... we're not going to Sammy's party?"

Chris's expression changed, and I knew the answer before he gave it. His face wore an expression cocktail consisting of ½ speechlessness and ½ pity with a splash of guffaw. The bottom line was that I was not going to Sammy's party. Chris double-tapped the top of my car with his hand to christen my voyage with Marcy.

As we neared the neighborhood, I slowed the Chevy and asked my inebriated passenger, "Are you OK to go inside?" There was no answer. Concerned, I put the car in park, turned around in my seat, and gently shook her. "Marcy? Marcy?"

She mumbled incoherently. I turned back and stared straight ahead, wondering where I could take her to sober up. I couldn't take her home with me. Mags would be hysterical, and when Marcy sobered up, the risk of my father expounding on something like the drinking habits of the East African Wobie Tribe was too great. I couldn't drop her off at her home either. Then, in an instant, I knew.

The key to the room above the garage was still hidden in the mouth of the verdigris garden frog. With one arm balancing Marcy, I managed to open the door. I decided not to turn on the light for fear it might alert Mrs. Roberts, and the streetlights and moonlight provided just enough light to see. It had been five years since I had been there; the Barbie Dream House was turned on its back and was stuffed like a box in a corner. It was like a big, Barbie coffin. Leaning up against it was a ten-speed bike. The room looked as if it had been turned into an office, with a small drafting desk and minifridge. However, the blue velvet recliner remained. I moved Marcy toward it, and she willingly fell onto it.

"You don't haf to be doin' this, Saaaamy," she slurred. "I nees sa wahta."

I didn't bother to inform Marcy that it was not her best friend, Samantha, who was caring for her. I didn't see the value in wasting my breath, as she lay spread-eagle across the velvet fabric.

I opened the minifridge and found a can of generic cherry soda and sat down beside her, which caused the recliner to rock slightly.

"Stop ff-fucking moving," she whimpered.

"Sorry," I whispered. "Drink some of this."

I lifted her head slightly and did my best to funnel the drink into her mouth. Most of the syrupy drink dribbled down her chin. She swallowed and fell back in place. Even though she was wasted, I still thought she looked fantastic—clearly not as good as she had earlier, but still better than I had ever looked in my life. She was curled on her side, and her blond hair fanned out around her.

"Saamay," she cried again, "didcha see those jeanzsh Paul Revere was swearing?" She snorted.

"Who?" I whispered.

"Paige Revere, da muskateer," she sang, her eyes still closed.

I panicked. I wanted to run, but I thought that maybe I had misunderstood.

"Paige Sheehan?" I asked.

She nodded, her eyes still shut. "Those jeans swere fucking knockoffs." She hiccupped, then continued. "She is such a saddie. She doesn't even know it." Marcy snorted heartily, which caused the recliner to rock again. I stood up quickly, ready to run … but not before the movement of the recliner got the better of Marcy, and she vomited all over my Joe-Dash jeans. Marcy spit the remnants from her mouth and returned to the conversation.

She snorted again. I stood frozen. I was down for the count—and then, with one figurative kick, Marcy finished me.

"Chris sayz that somebody's should suffocate her with her beret or shoot her with her musket and put her out of her misery."

I don't remember how long I stood there. I wanted to cry but couldn't. I was beyond crying. I walked over to the Barbie coffin and pushed it over spilling its contents onto the floor. Barbie and Ken were there, on top of a mountain of clothes. Buried underneath was Skipper, scantily clad in her makeshift swimsuit. I smiled sadly, stuffed her in the outside pocket of my jacket, and snuck away, hoping never to see Marcy again.

The discovery of Marcy's picture on Owen's wall prompted a *Where's Waldo*-type exercise. I searched for her in other pictures and indeed found her, again and again and again. There were several candids of them together, both in and out of their uniforms. There was even what looked like a recent photo of them in San Francisco. *She must have been his girlfriend*, I thought—*or still is his girlfriend.*

I felt my stomach sink. It was as if I were the subject of an absurd movie by a German film student, morphed into Skipper at that moment: I could almost feel the texture of her denim gaucho pants on my legs. There was Barbie, with her heaving bosoms and her perfect hair, pressing her pom-poms into Owen in every photo. I caught a glimpse of my face in Owen's living-room mirror. My hasty makeup job included applying mascara to my cheek. I grabbed Owen's phone and nosily scrolled through his caller-ID history. Calls number 9, 22, and 35 read "Roberts, M.P." Marcy Priscilla Roberts. My stomach sank further. I decided not to conduct any additional snooping since no more evidence was needed. I dressed quickly and returned home.

There was a voicemail from Vicki. "I think there's something wrong with Mr. Fatboy. I took a personal day from court. Could you come over and look at him? Maybe I'm just crazy."

I quickly returned her call, promising that I would come over within the hour. I changed, donned a baseball cap, and headed cross-town. When I arrived, Vicki led me to her loft, which had become guinea-pig central. Mr. Fatboy sat in one corner of his cage, his breathing labored, and there was an audible wheezing when I listened closely. I turned to Vicki. "I don't know, Vic. He doesn't sound good. I'd take him in just in case."

"Really? Are you sure? You know he's been diagnosed with diabetes."

"If it were me, I'd take him in."

I drove Vicki to the Vet Trauma Center. She cradled Mr. Fatboy in a flannel shirt on her lap. The nurse took him immediately, and several staff followed her. We waited at the front desk for further direction. After only five minutes, the nurse reappeared with a solemn look upon her face. "I'm so sorry, Ms. Sheehan, but Mr. Fatboy didn't make it."

Vicki fell dramatically to her knees in the middle of the waiting area and sobbed. I went to her and tried to wrestle her to a standing position, but she sank further to the floor, pounding her fist on the vinyl floor

The people in the waiting room who had initially shown sympathy now were beginning to look slightly uncomfortable. One of them leaned forward from her chair and inquired, "Was it her dog?"

"No," I whispered, "her guinea pig."

"Oh," she said, surprised.

Most understood the devastation of losing man's best friend but could not comprehend Vicki's relationship with her guinea pigs. But I had come to appreciate how these furry little creatures could squeak their way into one's heart. The nurse escorted us to the examining room, where Mr. Fatboy lay swaddled in the flannel shirt. Vicki sat down and held him, then requested some time alone with him to say good-bye. I waited outside the door until several minutes passed, and she tearfully peeked open the door and asked, "Do you want some time with him?" There was really only one answer I could give. I entered the room and sat down, and she handed him to me as if she were handing over a new baby. I didn't quite know what to do as she watched thoughtfully. I closed my eyes and appeared to pray while stroking his little body, which had already begun to succumb to rigor mortis. I looked up toward Vicki, who seemed to be waiting for more.

I returned my attention to the body and mustered a "Sweet little Mr. Fatboy. You were such a good little piggy. I will miss you." I kissed his little stiff body and, for reasons unknown to me still, burst into tears.

Vicki seemed genuinely touched. "I didn't realize how much you loved him," she said afterward.

That afternoon we placed his body in a clear plastic shoebox that had formerly contained my sewing kit. Vicki lined the coffin with some purple velvet she had leftover from a Halloween costume. We pretended to have a midafternoon picnic in the park, even though it was the beginning of December. Because it was illegal to bury an animal in the park, we smuggled his coffin and some garden tools in a large wicker basket. It was my second illegal burial in three days. I sang the prayer of St. Francis, and Vicki recited the Irish Blessing. It took us a while to dig his grave, as the small shovel and triple-forked hoe were not the best gravediggers, and the ground was pretty frozen. We eventually managed to create a space large enough and deep enough to contain him. We covered up the hole with the extracted dirt, and Vicki threw an orange Gerbera daisy on top of the mound.

We decided to toast the life and times of Mr. Fatboy by having a few drinks at Flannigan's bar. I was also anxious to get Vicki's perspective on the Marcy Roberts quasi-shrine in Owen's living room.

We ordered a pitcher of beer, and I recounted the previous evening's events, even divulging the harm my hiccups had caused.

"That is so awful," she said, smiling.

"Well, at least it put a smile on your face."

She nodded. "You should just ask him about Marcy Roberts. Don't tell him that you were scrolling through his caller ID, though."

"I'm not stupid."

"You do need to ask him."

"But it's not like he's my boyfriend. I mean, I don't know what we are. So, I'm not really in a position to ask."

"You've got a perfect opportunity simply by mentioning that you know the girl in the picture."

"I guess."

"It's either that or you drive yourself crazy wondering."

Vicki knew me too well. While I was pretending to pray over a very dead Mr. Fatboy, in reality I was wondering about Owen's past and present involvement with Marcy.

As we waited for the change from the waitress, I called my voice mail and had three messages: one from Owen, a call from Carlita, and, surprisingly, a message from Ken. Vicki and I said our good-byes, and I rushed home, so I could call Ken. I was somewhat comforted that he had called. The blow of our breakup had been softened by the prospect of a budding romance with Owen. However, I was concerned that whatever was brewing with Owen was just a casual thing for him, and that Marcy was indeed his girlfriend. Instead of calling Ken on his cell phone, I played his game and left a message on his voice mail at work, knowing full well that he was probably not there at 8 PM. I didn't want to seem too eager and was not ready to engage in a drawn-out, heavy talk.

Chapter 26

I called Owen. "Thanks for the Cocoa Puffs."

"Were you cuckoo over them?" he joked.

"I'm always cuckoo, and I did not break anything. I was hiccup-free all morning."

"Good to hear. Why don't you come over?"

"At 9 PM? Sorry, but I saw that movie!"

"What movie?"

"*Booty Call.*"

"This is not a booty call. I want to see you, and I thought that we could go over the notes for tomorrow's meeting. As you know, we kind of got sidetracked last night, and I need to finalize some points with you before tomorrow. Come over."

I pondered his invitation until he pushed, "C'mon."

Although I was beat and ready for bed, I really wanted to ask him about Marcy and preferred not to make inquiries over the phone. I drove over to Georgetown. After twenty minutes searching for a parking space, I finally found a spot, which was questionably less than the required six feet from the fire hydrant.

Owen was wearing a forest green turtleneck sweater and sable brown corduroy pants. His hair was tousled. I could smell and feel the mist from his shower as I walked past his bathroom and into his small office. He kissed me on the forehead.

"You look ... nice. That color looks good on you," he said, adjusting the collar on his turtleneck.

"Thanks." I glanced down to take note of what I was wearing, since he had never remarked on my appearance before. I was outfitted in a pair of dark jeans and a mauve-colored long-sleeved T-shirt emblazoned with the letters GMAGPR. It was an outfit that neither Barbie nor Marcy would have been caught dead in—pure Skipper attire.

"What's Gimagaper?"

"Huh?"

He pointed to the shirt.

"Greater Metro Area Guinea Pig Rescue. We lost Mr. Fatboy today and buried him in Banning Park."

"You're kidding."

"Unfortunately, I'm not. It was actually very sad. I cried."

"Maybe you weren't crying over Mr. Fatboy."

"What do you mean?"

"I mean, maybe you were crying over something else. You know, I didn't see you shed a tear during your father's service, and your mother said you were a brave little soldier through the whole thing."

"When were you talking to my mom?"

"When you disappeared at the reception. She came over to thank me for helping you. She asked that I watch out for you."

"Oh, is that what you're doing?" I responded, annoyed. I was unnerved that my mother had gone to Owen and wondered what else she had shared with him.

Owen grabbed my hand and squeezed it. "You're entitled to grieve, Paige. It's not healthy to just keep going, to charge through it. It's like running a marathon. It's about pace. You can't run it fast and get it over with. It doesn't work that way."

I nodded, knowing he was right, but also hoping to move the discussion to the topic du jour: preparing for the preliminary hearing. Before beginning, though, I was going to ask about the pictures. I stood up and casually walked over to them, pretending to notice them for the first time.

"You've got a great collection of pictures."

"Thanks. My mom took most of them. Most are from my Cowboys days."

I stopped scanning in front of the picture and produced a dramatic, "Hah! Oh my God."

"What?" he looked up from the stack of files he was poring over.

I pointed to Marcy. "I think I know her. She looks familiar. Who is she?"

Owen glanced up quickly and walked behind me, putting his head beside mine to see my finger pointing directly at a picture of a cowboy-hatted Ms. Roberts in a blue-fringed half shirt. Her mouth was seductively poised over a pistol, as if she were blowing smoke. I hoped it was another publicity shot and not from Owen's private collection.

"She's a friend," he said, walking back toward the paperwork.

I paused and assessed the situation in my head. If I pressed him with more questions, I might appear overly eager, and a girl should never appear eager or jealous, especially when the relationship is not categorized.

"What's her name?" I asked innocently, plopping down in the big La-Z-Boy chair next to his desk.

"Ho-How How do you think you know her?" he asked, scratching his head. I watched him. He seemed nervous and awkward. It was the first time I had ever seen him depart from his usual "goldenness."

"I'm just curious. She looks familiar." I popped the side lever of the La-Z-Boy and reclined, trying to appear easy.

"Her name's Marcy," he said, watching me.

"Marcy Roberts?" I inquired.

"How do you know?" he shot back.

"She's from my hometown."

He slapped the papers he was shuffling around down on the table.

"Sh sh she is?" He stuttered again.

"We grew up together. Small town. Small world." I told Owen a happier version of our childhood friendship. He sat, astounded.

"I'm shocked."

"Why?"

"Because you're so ... well ..." He motioned toward me, his hand waving back and forth over my body. "You're so completely different from her."

I hated the word "different." I wanted it stricken from the English language altogether. During my childhood, it carried the connotation of something positive. "Dare to be different." It seemed to mean unique and special, something good. In the last ten years, I had noticed that the word's positive flavor had waned. Now it was used as a euphemism, like when I told Carlita my idea for a children's television show featuring guinea pigs. "Well ... that's, uh, different." Or when I decided to be a hair model for a Vidal Sassoon hair show to get a free $150 cut, and everyone remarked that my new cut was "so different ... so really, really different ... and interesting." The word "interesting" was also on the cusp of becoming a euphemism, but hadn't quite crossed over to the dark side. Owen thought I was different. Funny and amusing and different. These were terms that I felt should be used to describe a circus act or a new amusement-park ride.

For the remainder of the evening, the conversation was stilted. We talked mostly about the trial. Owen questioned me and prepped me until he seemed satisfied that I was sufficiently brainwashed to provide the right answer, verbatim, every time. I peeled myself off the leather La-Z-Boy chair, and he followed me to the door.

"It's after midnight," he said, "You should go."

"I could stay," I replied

"You'll be fine tomorrow. Nothing to worry about," he said ignoring my offer.

I waited halfway between the open door and the hallway leading out of his apartment. I scanned his face, looking for some sign that he was about to kiss me. I was hoping that the weirdness between us that afternoon was just my paranoia, but after fifteen seconds, his gaze left my face and went to his shoes, which he tapped against the baseboard of the door.

"Well, see you tomorrow," I said in a higher-than-normal pitch. "Thanks for all your help. I really appreciate what a good friend you've been." I thought maybe dropping the friend bomb would also stir something inside of him that I could easily detect, but there was nothing.

"No problem. Be careful getting home."

He closed the door, and I waited for the elevator, glancing back at his door and hoping it would open again. As I watched the numbers change and the elevator ascended, I heard him deadbolt and chain the door.

Chapter 27

▼

The day of the preliminary hearing was bitterly cold. More than five inches of snow had fallen during the night, and I awoke to a winter wonderland. My mother called at the crack of dawn to wish me good luck and suggested that I dress as if I were going to church.

"Just ask yourself, 'Would the Virgin Mary wear this?' Always a good guideline."

"Mom, the Virgin Mary would not wear anything that I own. She was from Israel. She wore sandals and burka-looking things. She did not own any business suits."

"I know, but just imagine if she were living here today. It's just a suggestion."

"OK. I'll keep that in mind."

My mother did bring up a good point. I needed to consider that my dress could affect how I'd be perceived. I was extracting every single outfit from my closet in hopes of unearthing something that said "I am not a sexual harasser," while at the same time saying "Owen, I would like to be sexually harassed." This was quite a difficult combination to pull off. I settled on a navy blue suit that was on the short side, but which I decided the Virgin Mary would wear if she were attracted to her legal counsel. I was dabbing some pink nail polish on a run in my stocking when my cell phone began spazzing on the corner of my kitchen counter. It was Carlita.

"Have you seen it?"

"No, I have not seen his penis yet, but I'll try to get you a picture when I do."

"No, not that, baby girl ... have you seen the news?"

"Why?"

"Turn on Channel 4."

"Why? What happened?"

"Girl, just do it."

I had canceled my cable over the summer, because I felt that my television watching had become a problem. I would find myself viewing one of those *Funniest Home Videos* shows, which always seemed to be the antithesis of funny, as the videos normally featured someone flying off a horse or getting hit in the crotch with a baseball. I had also begun watching too many animal-adventure shows, which had resulted in my relaying random trivia the same way my father used to do. "You know, the komodo dragon's bite causes almost instantaneous gangrene."

Channel 4 was one of the few channels I received. The picture was still forming when I heard a female announcer remark, "They say that life imitates art, and a local Silver Spring man is involved in a legal battle that would be fodder for any made-for-television movie.

"Mr. Ishmahed, thank you for speaking with us today. Am I pronouncing your name correctly?"

"Yes, thank you. I happy to talk to you. I big fan of Channel 4. It is best news station for weather."

Moman was standing in front of the downtown courthouse, holding his finger to his ear to listen to the audio feed. On the screen, he was framed like a photograph in a bright blue box with a caption that read, "Moman Ishmahed, Alleged Victim in H2O Sexual-Assault Case." I slumped, dumbfounded, on the couch, dropping the remote as I settled into the lumpy impression of my green chenille couch. I still held the phone to my ear, but had forgotten about Carlita. Her voice startled me.

"Can you fucking believe it? Money-hungry fuck! I've got some boys that could fucking windmill his ass."

I did not respond to Carlita. I wanted to hear every word that escaped from my television.

"Well, thank you, Mr. Ishmahed. You have charged that a young woman at H2O ... who is, in fact, responsible for handling employee complaints just like this ... has assaulted you. As you know, most sexual-assault cases involve a woman charging a man, not the other way around. What response have you gotten from friends and family on this matter as to the nature of the charge?" Gwen Weizel, D.C.'s top morning anchor, leaned forward into the camera and smiled. The picture returned to Moman.

"Family and friends are supporting me in this. They are very supportive and know that America will serve me justice."

The phone was no longer pressed to my ear; my hand had slid down to my shoulder. I could faintly hear Carlita's voice cursing: "Goddamn, money-hungry son of a bitch."

The interview was brief. I think Gwen was a little disappointed that Moman was not providing juicy responses to her questions. He seemed robotic and gave her the answer, "My lawyer advised me to not say about that." However, in the end it was clear that Moman was positioning himself as a victim of a sex-crazed, mentally unstable criminal, and the media were happy to chew on that notion. I switched off the small television that sat atop my kitchen counter and thought I saw my father's face shadowed in the screen before the picture withdrew into a small, white dot. I glanced at the clock. It was 8 AM. The preliminary hearing was to begin in two hours. I ran into my room and bent down to pull my boots out from the corner of my closet. Crammed between a stuffed bunny and my yoga bands was the Skipper doll which I had smuggled home from West Virginia. I rubbed some dirt off her plastic chin and sat down upon my bed, holding her in one hand and my boots in another. Her arms were raised above her head as if she had just made a touchdown. She looked victorious. I stuffed her in my briefcase and headed out the door as the phone began to ring.

The Metro was packed. I weaseled myself onto the train and was sandwiched between a man quite shorter than I (which meant he was now positioned directly across from my breasts) and a young girl wearing a GW sweatshirt. It had always bothered me that people rarely spoke on the train. I started to think about how the city had changed me since I moved to D.C. In the town where I grew up, you said hello to strangers. You struck up conversations with people while in line at the bank. Here everyone was about keeping to themselves, so intent on maintaining anonymity. I had read a story the week before about a street vendor in Baltimore who had been robbed and beaten the past summer after an Orioles game. The article had estimated that hundreds of people had walked past the incident while it was occurring, and no one made an attempt to help.

Just then, the doors of the train opened, and the operator called out the name of the stop, although one could rarely make out what the operators were saying.

"Farragut West. Next stop, McPherson Square." A woman brushed past me to exit, at which point I noticed a beautiful, silk pashmina fall to the floor. I knew how expensive they were; Ken had purchased one for me the year before. I had taken it back after several attempts at tying it, draping it, and bundling it, only to look as if I were one of those people in a Red Cross commercial, swaddled in the emergency blanket after some natural disaster. I took it back to Nordstrom, and they credited me $425. I was in shock at the cost, and that Ken had spent so much on me. It was, after all, just a piece of fabric. I picked up the pashmina and caught another man about to exit.

"Excuse me. The woman in the blue coat just dropped this."

"Which way did she go?" he asked, taking it from me.

"She went left, toward 14th Street." I pointed to the left. He waved and gallantly saluted me just before the doors closed.

As the train carried us to the next stop, I was feeling rather proud for not becoming indifferent to someone in need. I noticed a woman standing diagonally to me, patting herself around her neck. She then turned her attention to the floor. I smiled at the man still looking at my breasts.

"Excuse me," she said. "I seem to have dropped my scarf. It's blue ... do you see it anywhere?"

I pretended to look around me and debated whether to fess up. The pashmina was by now either on the shoulders of the woman in the blue coat or happily tucked away in my accomplice's briefcase as a surprise gift to be given to his mother or wife. I decided that telling the truth would do neither of us any good. I continued to look, and to my surprise, one of the normally uninvolved, keep-to-themselves Metro riders volunteered, "She just gave it to someone at the last stop," pointing to me. The woman turned to me, confused.

I did my best to explain. "I'm so sorry. I was going to say something. I thought someone else had dropped it."

Her mouth formed a tight lock, and she angrily grimaced. "It was a birthday gift from my husband."

"I'm so sorry. I ..." I realized that the best thing to do was to exit the train, even though it wasn't my stop. I squeezed out the door just as it was closing and waited on the platform until the next train came.

I walked the two blocks to Circuit Court and saw two television trucks and three reporters standing outside. Surely they were not for me. I continued walking up the steps when they descended on me. I said nothing and fought my way to the front door, where a guard waved them off. I found Owen waiting for me behind the security station. He was not alone. He was talking with Blair. I couldn't hear their conversation and could not get over to him fast enough. It took me several times to get through the metal detector. After four attempts, I was still beeping. I had taken off my shoes, jacket, hair clip, earrings, watch, and rings. Owen watched as I stood, arms out, legs spread like the famous Da Vinci drawing, as the guard brushed the wand across my body.

"Open your bags, ma'am," one of the guards said. I unzipped my purse, and he grimaced when he saw the amount of junk he would have to sift through.

"Sorry," I sang.

He handed it back to me, "Briefcase, please."

I handed my leather attaché to him, and he briefly looked inside. "What's this?" he said, pulling Skipper out.

"It's a doll," I said.

"Why's she all taped up?"

"It's a long story."

"Well, it's going through the scanner," he told me decisively.

"My doll is going through the scanner?"

He raised his eyebrows. "Last week I had a woman bring in a box cutter inside of Elmo. This is criminal court, you know."

I stood to the side and watched Skipper move down the conveyor belt. Her hands were still raised high. I took it as a good omen. When I was finally cleared, Blair was gone, and Owen looked angry.

"We're late," he said impatiently.

"I'm sorry. I got hung up on the train … and then, of course, my doll had to be scanned."

"Your doll? Never mind. Let's go"

Suddenly the magnitude of the trial hit me, and I began to sweat profusely. I stuck Skipper back in my briefcase. We walked up the marble steps inside the courthouse. My heels clacked, echoing off the walls. We walked to a wood door with a frosted-glass pane, like the door of an old-fashioned detective agency. In black letters outlined in gold, it read, Public Waiting. The door opened, and we walked into an office that reminded me of a picture of a typing pool I once saw. Several desks were lined up against one wall, and behind them sat several women busily typing away.

"Can I help you?" a woman asked. The voice had come from the second desk in the group. At first glance, I thought the woman was standing. However, she rose from her seat and walked toward us. She was the tallest woman I had ever seen up close. Over the years, I used Wally as my height reference for most everyone. He was six foot three, and when standing barefoot, I was level with the top of his shoulder. Using this as my guide, I deduced that the woman was easily six foot five.

"We're here for a preliminary hearing with Judge Walker," Owen said, looking up at her.

"Courtroom 3," she said quickly. "Down the hall to your left ... but they're doing some remodeling, so you have to go to the other side of the building to the west elevators. Give me five minutes, and I'll walk you over there." She motioned to a set of two red leatherette chairs across from the counter. I pulled my skirt down and tucked it around the sides of my legs to keep it from rising. Owen glanced down toward my legs.

"Nice gams."

"What?"

"I said nice gams."

"What's that?"

"Your legs. Gams are legs."

"Oh. Thanks." I crossed my legs, causing the skirt to rise slightly. I leaned toward him and whispered, "You know who's got some big gams."

"I know. She's got to be at least six five. That must be hard for a woman."

"She's like *Guinness Book of World Records* material," I commented, smirking.

"Don't say that. She's somebody's daughter."

"I'm just saying she's a little freaky."

"Look who's talking." I stared at him, hoping to catch his eyes to show my hurt. Something had definitely changed. Owen glanced at his watch. I picked up a *National Geographic* magazine from the side table and began reading an article about the migration of the Konuska frog from Latin America. The frosted-glass door opened, and someone walked past me to the counter. I continued to read about amphibian mating rituals but looked up when I heard the voice.

"Has the Sheehan hearing started yet?"

Although his back was turned to me as he leaned forward on the counter, questioning Somebody's Daughter, I knew the voice, the stance, and the cashmere jacket.

"What are you doing here?"

Ken turned around from the counter, smiled, and exhaled. It was the same sigh I had seen seven months earlier, when my period was a week late, and I had taken a pregnancy test. Although I was also relieved that it was negative, Ken's dramatic reaction combined with, "Whew. Thank God. Thank God. That would have been awful," didn't make me feel warm and fuzzy.

"I got your message last night and called you this morning, but got your voice mail," Ken said. He paused and looked at Owen briefly, and then back to me and continued. "You must not have gotten it. I'm going to participate in the pretrial just as an observer. This is my sweet spot ..."

"It's just the preliminary," Owen interrupted. "I think I can handle it." Owen stood up, and Ken thrust his hand toward him.

"Kenneth Marxen—Norton, Totton, and Dinnhaupt."

"Owen Holden," he said firmly, taking Ken's hand, "We met a few months back at the Bridesmaid Ball. We had that nice chat in the men's room."

Ken's expression changed as he appeared to register their meeting. It was clear that something had occurred between the two of them. I looked down at my shoes to the run in my pantyhose. The run had now fanned out around the glob of pink nail polish in search of fresh stretches of panty hose to destroy. I stood up and gritted my teeth. "Ken, why don't we talk in the hall?"

"Baby? What is it?"

I motioned to the door when another door opened from the back of the office. I glanced to the door and did a double take. Gathering a black robe off a stand in the corner was the woman from the train.

"Oh, that's just great," I mumbled.

Owen stood and said something in the direction of the woman. She motioned for us to follow her, like a police officer directing traffic.

"What?" Ken asked.

"I had a run-in with the judge on the Metro this morning. She dropped an expensive scarf, and I gave it to someone else by mistake."

"Well there's nothing you can do about it now. Is it all right if I attend?" Ken politely inquired. I was not sure if he was asking me or Owen for permission.

"You're not her primary counsel," Owen barked.

Ken countered. "I think it would be to Paige's benefit if I were in the meeting. You're not exactly an experienced trial attorney."

Owen ran his hand through his hair, and it rested at the back of his neck. He held it there, then quickly withdrew it, like a sword from its sheath. For a moment I thought Owen was going to strike him, but he stopped short and patted the top of his right arm.

"Knock yourself out."

Somebody's Daughter appeared and motioned for us to follow. Owen took me by the elbow and steered me down the hallway. He looked over his shoulder to see Ken following closely behind.

Luckily the judge did not seem to recognize me without my winter hat and scarf. Owen had warned me that the purpose of a pretrial was to demonstrate to the court that there was reason to believe a crime was committed, and that I, as the defendant, was indeed the person who committed the crime. Ken sat quietly at our table, furiously taking notes. Every time he began a new page, Owen looked over at him, annoyed. Both Blair and Moman testified, and although Owen's questioning highlighted many discrepancies, the judge agreed that there was satisfactory evidence to schedule a trial. The date was set for December 11, a month away.

"How long do you think it will last?" I asked Owen.

"What?"

"The trial."

Ken answered, "Probably a week, maybe two. It all depends."

Owen cleared his throat and chimed in, "No more than a week, I'm sure."

"There are two charges, Owen," Ken advised.

"I am aware what the charges are." Owen looked pissed.

I attempted to change the subject. "Lunch, anyone?" I knew that Ken never ate lunch. He said stopping for lunch in the middle of the day added up to at least six less hours billed a week. I had frequently asked him to meet me for lunch, and he never agreed. To my surprise, he replied, "How about McCormick's?"

"Oh. Uh," I searched Owen's face, but his gaze was directed at Ken.

"Sounds good."

I would rather stab myself in the eye with a pencil ten times than relive that lunch. It was beyond awkward. However, there were brief moments that I relished. For example, when Ken ordered the eight-ounce, blue-cheese burger, Owen then ordered a twelve-ounce burger, which prompted Ken to change his order to a twelve-ounce. When the check came, there was a minute-long scuffle over who would pay. Ken grabbed the leather holder saying, "Please, let me. Ten minutes of my time would pay for this, and both of you are unemployed, right?"

Owen grabbed it back saying, "I got it. Endorsement money."

Ken retrieved it and said, "I insist. I just made partner."

"You made partner!" I exclaimed, "Ken, that's great. Congratulations!"

While Ken was distracted by my comment, Owen grabbed it back and swiftly handed the check and his credit card to the waiter.

"Yes, congratulations," Owen said. "By the way, how are you and Blair doing?"

Ken was rattled by the question, and I was most eager to hear his response. All he offered was a spiteful grin in Owen's direction, and that concluded lunch.

Chapter 28

The weeks leading up to the trial were long. The economy was strong, the terror alert normal, and all seemed well with the world. This was great news for most of Washington, but bad news for a sexual-harassment defendant facing trial there. The only other story that seemed to share my spot on the nightly news was the progression of Christmas retail sales.

The attention increased when word got out that Golden Boy Holden was trying the case. The camera loved him, and every talk show in town was trying to secure an interview. However, he got called to LA shortly after the flurry began. MAX was obviously responding to the attention and suddenly seemed anxious to get a contract in place. Their plan, according to Owen, was to launch *Touchdown* in conjunction with the Super Bowl. Part of me wondered if Ken's sudden interest was prompted by all the media attention, but I was afraid to question him since I wanted to keep him around in case his expertise was needed. Owen seemed distracted. I felt that while America's interest in the case increased, his interest and commitment were fading. He had assured me that he was all set for the case, but I questioned his preparedness. I drove him to the airport, and he kissed me on the cheek.

"Good luck," I said sweetly. "I'll keep my fingers crossed."

"I'll call you to check in later this week." He grabbed his luggage out of the trunk and reappeared in the window.

"Do you need me to do anything with the case while you're gone?" I asked.

"Not to worry." He winked and waved good-bye.

On the way home from the airport, I called Carlita at work. I had been keeping her posted through email but had not talked to her in quite some time.

"Hey, baby girl."

"I need a dose of Carlita. Not working with you every day is like missing therapy."

"Oh, shut up. Let me close my doors, 'cause I got something for you." I could hear her chair roll across the floor to the door.

"OK, I'm back. Your ears must have been burning, 'cause I got some 411 for you on Miss Thing."

"No thank you. I'd rather hear about your latest sexual feat."

"Girl, let me tell you, I was getting licked so good last night that I thought I was a human Tootsie Pop, and he couldn't wait to get to the center if you know what I mean."

I smiled. Carlita said things that were crude and inappropriate, and that a good Catholic girl like myself should find completely repulsive and unrefined, but I never did. Instead I found her remarks honest and funny and welcome.

"Lovely," I said. "And what flavor were you?"

"Chocolate, of course ... but you need to hear this little bit of info."

"If you insist."

"So I was talking to Mike Hanley today. He's divorcing Witchypoo."

"Good for him."

"And guess who he took out for drinks last night?"

I waited for the answer.

"Miss An-droid," Carlita crooned.

"You're kidding. And she went?"

"Oh, she went, all right ... and apparently got blitzo. She called in sick today."

"And this piece of information does what for me?" I asked sarcastically.

"Oh baby girl, I got the goods for you."

According to Carlita, Blair had invited Mike Hanley out for drinks, and he enthusiastically agreed. They split a bottle of wine, and after three glasses, she proceeded to share her sordid love story of meeting Ken at last year's H2O Christmas party and falling for him. She pursued him, and they dated on and off for six months behind my back, until Ken abruptly ended the relationship last week, claiming he was still in love with me, and that the two of us were reconciling.

"That's insane. It's 100 percent not true!" I exclaimed. "We are not getting back together. He's helping out with the case, but that's politically motivated, I'm sure."

"Girl, I'm just telling you the word. And one more thing ... apparently they did the nasty in the men's bathroom while you were being crowned at the Bridesmaid Ball."

"What?" I was incensed.

I spent the rest of the evening digesting this new information. Ken had made no obvious attempt to reconnect with me and certainly had not professed his love. Moreover I was enraged to find out about his interlude with Blair at the ball. After mulling it over, I finally said aloud, "Enough, I'm calling him." For a change, he answered.

"Hey, it's me," I began.

"I was just thinking of you."

"You were?"

"I'm still at the office, and I was thinking of dropping by."

"For what?"

"Can't I just drop by?"

"What is going on with you? We are not friends, Ken. I don't know what you think we are."

"Paige, I don't want to have this conversation on the phone."

I ignored his remark.

"You cheat on me, abandon me professionally, and all of a sudden, you're my best friend again? I'm afraid not."

"Paige, you have every right to be angry."

"Every right to be angry? My father died, you ass, and you didn't even send a goddamn card. Forget the fact that we weren't together. Jesus, Ken."

"I'm coming by."

Before I could say otherwise, he hung up. He arrived twenty minutes later with a bouquet of wildflowers. I wanted my pain and fury to incinerate him, but instead I found myself opening the door and fixing him a glass of Scotch and water, his favorite. I wanted to face him one last time. He looked like a Ralph Lauren ad, all charm and ease and elegance. He grabbed a vase from above the sink and put the flowers in water. Starting over with someone new seemed like a daunting prospect. Ken and I had a history. He knew me. He knew my life. He knew where I kept my vases. He knew I didn't like Chinese food. He knew I loved wildflowers. He placed the flowers on the table in my foyer and sat at the edge of the upholstered ottoman, sipping his Scotch.

"You look great."

"I've been doing yoga and running. I gained some weight when Dad was sick and wanted to get it off."

"You've succeeded and then some."

He looked around my place as if he were searching for something. His eyes moved to the entrance of my bedroom, and he leaned forward to increase his vantage point.

"Nobody's here," I said.

"Oh, no, I know." He smiled. His expression changed when he saw a Stanford Law sweatshirt on the arm of the sofa. I had borrowed it from Owen the night we were preparing for the preliminary hearing and had forgotten to return it. I sat down opposite Ken on the sofa, using the sweatshirt as my backdrop. He took off his tie and took another sip from his glass.

"I miss you," he said softly.

I waited for more. I wanted him to acknowledge his great loss and fall to his knees and beg for my forgiveness, but he didn't. He merely sat waiting for my reply. The phone rang, and thankful for the reprieve, I answered it.

"Hey, what are you doing? I just landed and wanted to remind you to arrange for a car service for the trial next week. It would be better, I think, because sometimes the reporters stake out the parking lot."

"OK. Will do." I answered curtly.

"What's wrong?"

"Can I call you later? I have company." There was a long pause. I added, "Ken just stopped by."

"Sure, whatever." And he hung up.

I returned to the chair, and Ken blurted, "I want you back."

When I asked him why, he seemed surprised. I sensed that he had not expected me to challenge him. I sensed that he thought I would jump into his arms, so grateful for wanting me.

"Why should we get back together?" I asked again.

"What's with all the questions?" He stood up and walked to the window, taking off his jacket.

"It's just one question."

"I want you back. Isn't that enough?" He turned around and walked toward me, stopping a few feet away. He took off his sweater and repeated his answer: "I want you, Paige. Blair and I are over."

"Run out of bathroom stalls?" I seethed. He stared at me blankly. "Don't you remember the Bridesmaid Ball ... or are all the times you screwed her behind my back running together?"

He came toward me and nuzzled my neck from behind. I did not return his affection. Again I waited for more from him, but that was it. He had made his plea. I realized at that moment that I had mistakenly interpreted his knowledge of where I kept a vase and how I liked my coffee and what movies made me cry as an indication of his love for me.

When I was in high school, I won the West Virginia Golden Horseshoe competition, which tested students on their knowledge of West Virginia history. I had memorized the name of our state flower, countless facts about winning our independence from the state of Virginia, the chemical makeup and burn rate of coal, and dates of battles won and lost within state lines. I learned them because they were easy to learn, and not because I had a great passion for my home state. The questions I could not answer were about why battles were fought, why the state had sought independence, and why coal was the primary resource for energy. I had succeeded in memorizing statistics and locations but failed to seek out or understand the stories behind them. My knowledge of the subject was superficial and I now realized Ken's grasp of me was no better.

Ken poured himself another drink and sat down next to me upon the couch as I processed. He nuzzled my neck, as I sat staring unresponsively. I had always thought that the more he knew about what I liked and how I lived, the more he must love me. However, he never did seem to understand my story and never knew what I needed or wanted most.

I had often wondered if I would experience a defining moment in my life. I had heard people talk about them, about when they realized or accomplished something great—and how, at that moment, their lives were forever changed. I had always expected my moment to be grand, with bands playing and flags waving, but it was quite the opposite.

"Bewildered" would be the word that I would use to describe Ken's behavior after I informed him that I did not feel the same, and that I did not believe we were compatible. He left my apartment and returned twice after forgetting his keys and his jacket. When he finally was gone, I poured a glass of wine and raised it in the air.

Chapter 29

The courtroom was old and, in my opinion, looked more like a small Baptist church than a courtroom. I sat at a large wood table that smelled as if it had just been cleaned that morning but looked as if hadn't been cleaned in years. A white, painted radiator sat just two feet from my chair and hissed and seethed. I was nervous, and Owen seemed more nervous, which fueled my fears. Beads of sweat formed above his brows, and he repeatedly licked his lips, muttering the beginning sentence of his opening remarks. I looked up at the carved, plastered ceiling and felt like a schoolgirl sitting outside the principal's office. My heart pounded and my stomach churned.

Moman came in shortly thereafter. I had not seen him since the Friday of the incident, and I tried to catch his eye. He would not look in my direction. Owen was studying the notes on his yellow pad intently. I wanted Owen to talk to me. I needed a distraction. I looked over at Moman again, and this time his eyes met mine, and he quickly looked down at the floor.

Vicki had taken a personal day to attend the trial. She gave me the thumbs-up sign when I turned around. She mouthed, "It's going to be fine." Behind her sat every member of the HR team. According to Owen, each and every member would be questioned and cross-examined to establish my character, past and previous.

Carlita had mailed Owen a card to give me just before the start of the session. It was a note card from her Successories collection featuring a photograph of an iceberg with a caption about how people mistakenly only see the tip of the iceberg, which is only a fraction of its mass. "They're going to see the rest of you today," she wrote. "No worries." The absurdity of the situation and the charges had seemed so silly that part of me had believed that it would all work itself out. The fact that I was sitting in a courtroom about to defend myself against sexual harassment allegations was surreal. The bailiff announced the judge, and everyone stood as requested. He settled himself and untangled his reading glasses from an access badge that hung around his neck. He sighed heavily, leaning forward in his chair to read the papers before him. He looked like a man who no longer enjoyed his job and didn't seem to care if anyone noticed. I said a silent prayer as he directed Owen to begin his opening remarks.

"Hostile. The word is derived from the Latin word *hostilis*, meaning 'opposing.' Sexual harassment is a serious charge. A work environment should be a place where one feels comfortable to successfully do his or her job … to do it without distractions … and, most important, without any *opposing* element. Ms. Sheehan's career is focused on creating an atmosphere where all are treated fairly, where all are comfortable, and where any and all opposing elements are eliminated. The victim in this case is Ms. Sheehan. She will be the first to admit that the events that occurred on the afternoon of September 14 did involve a lapse of judgment, but they were not purposeful, and certainly not hostile. Today, you will meet a young woman who is anything but. A woman who is, at her core, good. And her goodness is not just at her core, it's all around her. This woman fell victim to the very trait that defines her: trust. Ms. Sheehan was only asking for one thing that day, and it wasn't sex. She was asking for the same thing that is asked of her day in and day out … help. She asked for help. She did make a mistake that day. She made the mistake of trusting someone to respond to her in the same way she responds to everyone: to give a helping hand, without judgment, without reason. And who here hasn't asked for that from time to time? If that creates a hostile environment … well, then we're all in trouble, aren't we?"

Owen straightened his tie and returned to the seat by my side. His whole body slumped as if he had just completed the most physically exhausting task. Relieved, he mumbled under his breath, "One down. One down."

I was overcome by sheer happiness. Vicki had once told me that happiness could not be a constant presence in one's life. At the time, we were guarding a parking space for Mr. Chelby, our ancient neighbor. He wanted to go to the grocery store one winter and was afraid that if he left his spot, he would not find another, because so much of the street parking had fallen victim to the snowplows. We promised to guard his spot in exchange for a bag of potato chips and a case of beer. We grabbed some beach chairs and sat in his spot for forty-five minutes, and Vicki announced that this experience would become a "happy memory." When I questioned her about the statement, she said that people who claimed they were happy were basing their entire state on a few moments in life.

"It's inconceivable to be blissfully happy all the time. Completely unrealistic," she had said. The state of happiness boiled down to a mere smattering of happy moments. "It's like placing a drop of red ink in a glass of water. The entire glass of water appears rosy afterward. That one drop colors everything." She used the summer in Martha's Vineyard as an example. "That was a happy summer, right?"

"The best," I said. I thought back to that summer and certain memories stood out—flying kites with Wally on the beach, collecting tiny shells from the shore, winning a lobster dinner for the whole family when my hermit crab won the annual crab-crawl race on the boardwalk. "That was the best summer," I said.

"See, my point exactly."

"What do you mean? It was awesome."

"No, it wasn't. You have forgotten all the shit times." Vicki proceeded to recite a long list of not-so-happy events that occurred that summer. "For starters, there was that weekend that we all got food poisoning from Darryl's Fish Shack, and we were all fighting to get into the one bathroom. Wally was unable to wait and threw up in the kitchen sink, then tried to rinse it down the sink, but it got clogged."

I winced at the memory. The superintendent was having his first child that weekend, and the vomit-clogged sink sat for two days until he was available to repair it. I smiled and chimed in with my own memory: "And Mom got into that argument with the caricaturist, because he had drawn a picture of me as a rabbit, because I had such severe buck teeth, and she said it was 'ridiculously cruel to make fun of a child.'"

Vicki roared, "That's right! That *was* cruel. He was obviously making fun of you."

"Remember, she threw all his colored pencils into the street."

"Awful," she said. Vicki continued to laugh, and I joined her, although I wasn't sure what she had remembered that was so funny.

She continued, "and Mom hardly packed any clothes for you, because she was trying to pack light, and forced you to wear all of Wally's stuff."

"Well, I do remember that. It was completely humiliating. I didn't even have a pair of shorts. I just had those Evel Knievel pants and a terrycloth sundress." We laughed until the cold air caused us to cough. We were silent until Mr. Chelby returned, honoring our agreement.

"That's why you have to hang onto the good moments. They can color an entire season," she had said as we carried our beach chairs back into the apartment building.

We sat silently in the courtroom for several moments, and I remembered yet another aspect of that summer. It many ways, Vicki was right. It was in some respects a dreadful summer: dread of running into the Izod clan, dread of a season of 2-for-specials, and dread that morphed into genuine fear. The fear was the direct result of my father's eagerness to share the ghost stories and legends that he was researching. The most horrifying tale was that of the ghost of young Edgar DuBois. According to my father, Edgar, a young boy, had been tied to a large rock and thrown into the sea by a crazy uncle. He had drowned, and legend had it that he roamed the water's bottom, looking for someone to drag down with him, so he would not be so alone. This story kept me in no more than two feet of water the entire summer. Then one night, as I badgered Wally and Vicki to play Connect Four with me, my father burst through the front door of our apartment, claiming that he had seen his dead father sitting on our station wagon outside.

"Stop scaring them, John. Go to the store. We need some milk," my mother directed.

My father asked if I wanted to go with him, and I reluctantly agreed. I wasn't too thrilled that Grandpa Sheehan was hanging out on the hood of our car. As we drove to the store, I was afraid to look out toward the hood and instead followed the moon above me as we drove.

"Do you see him now?" I asked my father.

"No," he replied. "Do you?" I straightened in the front seat and cautiously leaned forward, peering out toward the hood.

"No."

I nervously brushed the velour of the seat back and forth, making it lighter and darker, depending on the direction my hand moved.

"What does he want?" I asked.

My father paused as he parked the car. "The last time I saw him, he told me he wanted a meatball sandwich."

"I don't want to talk to him," I answered. I looked at my father, the fear apparent in my eyes.

His hands cupped my head. "Are you scared, Paigebug?"

I nodded.

"Don't be," he said, opening the car door. "Although you don't remember him, he loved you. Thought you were the bee's knees. He wouldn't do anything to hurt you. He wants you to be happy."

Recalling that night somehow made me feel safe. Although I was sitting in a courtroom defending a serious charge against my character, at that moment, I experienced what Vicki had described that winter day—a pure moment of happiness. Owen scribbled a note to me on his notepad: "It's looking good. Chin up."

Hearing Owen speak of my goodness, having him by my side and seeing the corners of his mouth turn up when I acknowledged the note he had scribbled, was blissful. I could have died at that precise moment ... but, as Vicki predicted, moments such as these were short-lived. Ken pulled the sleeve of my blazer and whispered from behind me, "He should have said something about Moman. Big mistake. This is not looking in your favor."

The prosecutor presented the most horrid and desperate picture of me. I was thankful that Mags had not flown down to be in the courtroom as she once offered. Moman's attorney was Kate Bennett from the U.S. Attorney's office. My dear sister did share with me the fact the other attorneys referred to her as Crazy Ho. The name was coined by one of the inmates after he tried to make a move on Ms. Bennett in a hearing interview. She responded by taking a stapler and stapling him three times in his face—twice in a cheek and once on his nose.

"You wouldn't think it was possible, I mean, the staples didn't exactly stay in but they left a mark," Vicki had said, "I saw the pictures on the director's desk. She went crazy on his ass, as they say."

Crazy Ho had been temporarily suspended after the incident but was reinstated after an investigation. It was apparent that she felt very strongly about unwelcome sexual advances. Crazy Ho and Owen were up at the bench, talking to the judge. She was almost as tall as Owen, and I decided that if this were an episode of Survivor and I had to pick someone for my team, I would pick Kate. She looked as if she could catch a wild boar with her bare hands and till a field just by wearing heavy shoes.

The entire HR staff of H2O was questioned and cross-examined. For the most part, their testimony was credible, and benign—except for Brian's, which for some reason included the fact that I sometimes took his office supplies and did not return them. Both Carlita and Mike Hanley sang my praises, sharing stories about my integrity and kindness. Even Perry came to my aid. He presented a flipchart with a list of all of the H2O staff whom I had assisted during my stay as the employee relations specialist. He stated that he had received countless calls and emails from staff offering to testify on my behalf. Perry returned to the stand after his flipchart presentation and added, "When I excused her that day, I did so more because Mr. Houston demanded it. This entire situation has spun out of control, and I feel, in part, responsible. Paige and I have not always seen eye-to-eye, but I should have handled this internally. Quite frankly, I believe Blair Davis planted a seed that should never have been watered."

The last two days of the trial were very tense. Several H2O staffers attended, some whom I knew, and some whom I had only seen in the halls. Klavic was there but appeared overly distraught when I talked to him at the recess about his luxury lifestyle at the CorpRate Suites.

"Oh, yes, it is very well. There is room for my whole family. They come next month. Caroline said she found permanent place for me in Cleveland Park, which will be available to me in January. It was so helpful and kind. You are very thanked. I am apology that you are in this trouble."

I assured him that I would be fine, and that justice would prevail, but I was beginning to worry. The sentence for the harassment alone could be six months in jail and up to a $15,000 fine. The intent-to-harm charge carried a much stiffer penalty of twelve months and a $25,000 fine.

After lunch, Moman and Blair took the stand, and it was difficult to sit silently as they shared lies and exaggerations. Moman was wearing a Scottish plaid shirt and a purple sweater vest. He looked small and deflated.

"She after me for many days. I kept telling her, Ms. Paige, I marry man, but she tell me that I take her, or she take Moman's job, and there would be trouble."

As he recounted tales of my advances and threats, I turned to the jury to watch their reaction. I half expected them to be chuckling to themselves at the absurdity of it all, but they were not. Instead they looked concerned and sympathetic. I grabbed Owen's hand underneath the table.

"That Friday she took the weapon and press my neck and told me to rip her pants or she hurt me. I so scared, as she big girl and strong. She seem crazy."

I buried my head in my hands. Owen reprimanded me, whispering in my ear, "Don't do that ... it makes you look like you're remorseful, which makes you look guilty. Keep your head up."

I followed his advice and bore my eyes into Moman, willing him to look in my direction—but he never did. He had been coached well and never took his eyes off the jury.

The trial adjourned at 6 PM that Thursday night. The judge requested a recess for Friday, so he could attend a funeral service out of town. Jury instructions and closing arguments were scheduled to begin on Monday, and Owen speculated that the jury would deliver a verdict on Tuesday morning.

"What do you think?" I asked him as I walked to the Metro station.

"Should be fi-fine," he stumbled. I took note of the doubt in his voice.

"I'm sure your final performance will be stellar," I assured him, stopping in front of the station's entrance. His gaze reflected a mixture of emotions that I could not decode.

"What?" I asked.

"I don't know." He looked frantic and uneasy. "Maybe you should call Ken."

"No way. We're done."

"Blair said you were getting back together. She told me the day of the preliminary hearing. That's why you asked him to co-co-come?"

"Um, hello? And you believe Blair? Who claims that I was attempting to rape Moman with a letter opener? The woman is a pathological liar."

"But he was at your p-p-place last week."

"Where he was getting the boot. You saw them, didn't you? That night at the Bridesmaid Ball? You knew."

He nodded sheepishly. "Ken and I had some words that night. I should have told y-y-you."

"This cold weather is really catching your tongue," I observed, "It doesn't matter now. Like I said before, Skippers and Kens don't mix. Don't worry about the case. I have every confidence that we'll win this."

He bear-hugged me, holding me for a period of time that became awkward. I pulled away.

"What's up with you?" I asked, puzzled. "You've been kind of acting strangely these past few days."

He rubbed his eyes and drew his hand to his chin. "I have to tell you something. I should have told you before, but ..."

I sensed he was struggling. "What? Tell me."

He sighed. "When I was a kid, I had a severe stutter. The kids called me Santa Claus, because I would stutter over my last name. Ho-Ho-Holden."

"Tsk, tsk," I uttered with a hint of sarcasm. "You poor thing. But honestly, I can think of worse names than old Saint Nick." I squeezed his hand lovingly, showing sympathy for his childhood woes and said, "Well, you sound perfect now."

"That's the thing," he replied. "It's ba-ba-back."

At first I thought he was joking, but his face showed no sign of it. He proceeded to explain that he had finally overcome the problem in high school, after years of speech therapy. The problem had presented itself again after the blow he had received in the Super Bowl. At first Owen's doctors believed the injury had caused a lesion on his brain, leading to a condition known as acquired stuttering.

However, no lesion could be detected, which left his doctors to conclude that it was psychological.

Since then, he had undergone treatment on numerous occasions, including a recent stint paid for through H2O's Employee Assistance Program. On a day-to-day basis, he was able to function normally. However, the disorder presented itself in stressful social situations and had recently become progressively worse. During the high-profile case Owen tried in San Francisco, he stuttered on the introductory sentence of his closing argument. Experiencing a panic attack, he waived his right to closing remarks, a practice that is permissible, but rarely—if ever—exercised. As a result, the client filed a grievance with the state bar association, and H2O reassigned him to research work.

Now, just days before the trial's close, and as pressure mounted, he was concerned it would happen again.

When he completed his account, I stood shivering and speechless. I hopped slightly to promote blood flow to my feet, which tingled. In midhop, he kissed me, his soft lips warm and urgent.

"I'm sorry. I should have told you. You deserve more, but I di-di-di-didn't know what to say." He pressed his forehead to mine and kissed me again upon the cheek. I said nothing.

"Be careful getting home. The si-si-sidewalks are icy," he advised, and walked away.

Chapter 30

Upon returning home, I Googled the term "stuttering," which produced 770,000 matches. Interestingly, I discovered the disorder was four times more likely to occur in males than females. Stuttering was often compounded by a social anxiety. The pressure to speak in public or to quickly respond to a question usually increased one's incidence of the problem. Symptoms included breathlessness, excessive sweating, nausea, dry mouth, shaking, heart palpitations, inability to speak or think clearly, a sensation of detachment from reality, and—if all that weren't enough—fainting.

Searching for Owen's name produced 275,000 sites. Combining the word "stuttering" with Owen's name produced no hits, but when I coupled his name with the words "public speaking," two articles appeared. Both Web sites dealt with a reported breach of contract between Owen and Ziploc three years prior. Ziploc stated that Mr. Holden was unable to continue his duties as spokesperson for the Snack Sack, citing an undisclosed medical reason.

I suddenly felt guilty for being so disillusioned and disbelieving. The news of Owen's problem was rather surprising but it made me feel closer to him. He and I weren't so different. The desire to be flawless consumed both of us.

Owen stuttered, and I stumbled—both actions spasmodic, halting, and ultimately rooted in fear. Our anxieties were laid out before us like a series of never-ending speed bumps, tripping us up and slowing us down on our daily drive, preventing us from living free and easy days. And our inability to forgive these imperfections prevented us from overcoming them.

Owen said he was eight when first diagnosed; ironically the same age I had been when my Barbie fixation began. Like Owen, I was afraid I'd never feel comfortable with who I had become. Every day I questioned myself: Were my clothes right? Were my words clever enough? Were my breasts adequate? In the beginning, I was anxious to measure up to the Barbie image that preoccupied my world and worried that I would never be seen as ideal to anyone. Now it was no longer about how others viewed me, but how I saw myself. In the darkness of my bedroom, I dialed his number.

"It's me," I spoke gently. "Why don't you come over tomorrow afternoon."

"Why?"

"Just be here, OK? Say, 2 PM?" I responded, hoping he would be encouraged by the upbeat cadence of my voice.

He huffed curiously. "OK. Whatever you say."

I contemplated doing more research on stuttering but ultimately believed the activity would be time wasted. As his doctors confirmed, Owen's problem was in his head. And I felt empowered. Managing fear was one thing that I knew well. Although I had yet to overcome fear, years of embarrassment and humiliation had forced me to develop a tool kit of coping skills. Like a phoenix from the ashes, I had risen time and time again, shaking the dust free and starting anew. That was what Skippers did best.

Later that afternoon, Owen arrived. I directed him to my sofa and handed him a yellow legal pad.

"What is this?" he asked.

"It's a list of famous stutterers." A bulleted list filled the page and included Winston Churchill, Marilyn Monroe, Carly Simon, James Earl Jones, Lewis Carroll, and Bill Walton, a NBA All-Star and sports commentator.

He tossed the pad of paper onto my coffee table. "I don't think too many people cared what came out of Marilyn's mouth."

"True." I nodded. "But I wanted you to see that you were in good company."

"You mean co-co-co-company," he purposefully stuttered in a self-deprecating tone.

"I can help you," I announced emphatically.

"Really? And what can *you* do that four specialists, one neurologist, two psychiatrists, and numerous speech therapists couldn't do?"

"I know you."

"You know me?" he questioned.

"Yes. I know what you feel."

"And what is that?"

"Ashamed, awkward, anxious. Like at any moment you'll be found out. You look in the mirror, and despite your successes, fame, and the man you've become, you still see that eight-year-old boy who's afraid to utter his last name."

"Is that what you think?" he asked.

"It's not what I think. It's what I know."

He settled into the couch and unfolded his arms. "I don't know how to fix it."

"You're not broken. You know, my father used to say, 'A diamond is merely a lump of coal that made good under pressure.' It's simple."

"It's simple?"

"Yes. A simple question. What are you going to do with your lump of coal?"

Owen did not necessarily reply to my question, but over two hours, he talked about his fears and his struggle to overcome his problem. During this he answered many questions I had pondered since hearing his news. He had been given an exemption for his mock trial class at Stanford. He had assisted on a number of trial cases, but had never been the primary attorney—until the fateful case in San Francisco. He had practiced with perfection in his living room, but practice did not make perfect. He stuttered only when nervous or thinking carefully about his words. The sample tape he sent MAX TV for his initial interview was flawless, although he claimed it had taken him forty-two takes. With the trial and his anxiety over the looming MAX deal mounting, he felt panicked, which was like starter fuel to his stuttering fire.

"It's in your head," I said gingerly, as I positioned myself across from him on the floor.

"I know," he replied, "but I can't seem to get it out."

I handed him the nugget of coal that I had retrieved from my jewelry box, where it had sat since I returned from West Virginia. Fairville had been the host to the annual Coal Festival for forty years. Every spring the town celebrated its rich mining history and its most valuable resource. Coal sculptures were erected. Children rode coal-cart replicas on haphazardly constructed tracks. A full-fledged parade featuring the Coal Court Princesses, dressed in black gowns and wearing quintessential lighted miner's hats, culminated the four-day-long festival. Mags had gotten roped into serving on the festival's planning committee during my junior year of high school. Wally and Vicki were away at college, so my father and I grudgingly attended to show our support. One of the displays was a giant wall of coal that had been cut and extracted from one of the mines. For $2, festivalgoers could purchase a small pick and mine a piece of "black gold." After successfully chipping off a nugget, my father placed it in my hand.

"Here," he said, closing my fingers over it.

"I don't want it," I replied, brushing off the soot that had fallen from it.

"It's a good reminder," he replied, walking away.

"A good reminder of what?" I responded, offering him back the jagged nugget.

"That ordinary things can be extraordinary. A diamond, you know, is just a lump of coal that made good under pressure."

My father continued walking, but I stood there fingering the piece and wondering if it had diamond potential. I carried it in my purse as a good-luck charm for many years, blackening every lining with its soot. When I felt anxious, I would roll it between my fingers, and over time, the jagged edges had worn smooth and shiny.

Owen sighed when I concluded the story of my lucky charm. He bounced it in his hand.

"And you think this is going to help me?"

"No," I replied. "You are going to help yourself. You aren't Santa Claus. You're Owen Holden! NFL star, Good Samaritan, top-notch attorney, and future commentator for MAX TV. Be the diamond!"

"Be the diamond?" he asked, laughing, the tension seemingly fleeing from his eyes.

"Yes!" I screamed enthusiastically, jumping to my feet to make some coffee.

We spent the remainder of the day in the most lazy fashion. *Superman II* was conveniently playing on HBO, which I found quite serendipitous, as despite being weakened by kryptonite, the hero prevails. A better movie for the occasion could not have been playing.

Afterward Owen read the newspaper, and I read hilarious stories from the *World Reporter* tabloid, which featured the recent marriage between Bigfoot and Sarah Ferguson. I felt compelled to share one of the *World Reporter* articles about a ninety-three-year-old woman who had recently delivered a set of triplets.

"Most surprising was the fact that Ms. Swanson didn't even know she was pregnant when her labor began at Clayton's Nursing Home in September," I read, without a note of frivolity.

"Paige?" he whispered, but I read on.

"Nursing home officials believe eighty-nine-year-old Leroy Samuels, the resident Casanova, to be the father."

"Paige?" he called again.

I looked at him, and he slowly took the newspaper from my grasp.

"Thank you," he exhaled.

"For what?" I knew the answer. It was noted in his face and posture. He appeared relaxed and easy.

"I may not be as debonair as the eighty-nine-year-old Casanova, but why don't we move into your room? I'll show you how thankful I am."

Chapter 31

When I arrived at the courthouse on Monday morning, Owen was all smiles as he displayed the piece of coal in his palm.

"Luck be a lady, I think," he sang. I searched for clarification. "There has been a development," he informed me. Standing next to him was Klavic, dressed in a beautiful charcoal gray suit.

"Klavic, you look fantastic!" I said admiringly.

"Owen let me borrow suit. So Mr. GQ, yes?"

"Very GQ," I said. I was trying to appear upbeat and breezy, but the reality was that I had spent over an hour in my bathroom waiting for my nervous stomach to stop producing.

"I am here to help tell truth and nothing but truth." I looked at him, confused, and then to Owen for an explanation, which he happily provided. On the Friday that Moman and I were in the bathroom, Klavic was in the women's bathroom, using its shower.

"Cause you said it had door, remember?" he asked.

I nodded. He had thought everyone had left for the day and had hidden when Moman and I came in together. He did not reveal himself since he was naked and fearful of getting into trouble for being in the women's room. He had witnessed the entire episode from start to finish.

"I so sorry, Ms. Sheehan, I should have come to tell truth, but I was afraid, as my family is coming to America, and I need to keep job. I did not know how much trouble you had until last night, when I called Mr. Owen to teach me what could happen to you. I did not know you could lose job and monies and be prisoned."

"He's going to testify," Owen chimed. "You're going to get off."

"But it's too late," I said. "Closing arguments are today."

"It's not a problem. I have submitted a request to enter new testimony, which means that the state will request a couple days to prepare for the cross-examination of Klavic's testimony. Judge Walker will most likely recess early and ask that we reconvene on Wednesday."

I sighed and sat down—and watched Owen's predictions come true. The judge ordered that Klavic's testimony be presented on Thursday, with closing arguments to follow on Monday. That night I took Owen to dinner at the Lebanese Taverna. It was crowded, and they sat us side by side at a corner table that butted up against the kitchen door. For the first twenty minutes, we hardly spoke. We just ate and drank and sat watching waiters go in and out of the kitchen like a pendulum.

"It's like summer camp," Owen tried to yell over the noise.

"What?"

"The trial has seemed like summer camp. Did you go to camp?"

"Yes, Camp Tygart." I launched into a fast rendition of the camp theme song, "When you wake up in the morning where the pretty flowers grow and the sun comes peepin' into where you're sleeping and the songbirds say hello. Then you know you're in Camp Tygart, the finest camp I know. Tygart. Tygart. Tygart. Go. Go. Go. Go. Go. Yeah."

"Wow, you remember the song and everything. Impressive." He dipped his pita bread into the yogurt sauce on my plate.

"What do you mean, though? What's like summer camp?"

"The trial. It's concentrated, and the days are long, and you really don't want to do the day stuff, like make macaroni necklaces. The class part sucks. It's all the other stuff that's great. My favorite night was the last night before the end."

"Did you do a talent show?" I asked. "We did a talent show."

"What was your talent?"

"Ventriloquism, of course."

He gestured dramatically with his hands. "Ah, but of course."

"And what about you?" I took a bite of my couscous and playfully dangled the spoon in my mouth.

"Break dancing," he responded quietly.

"Well, you've seen my talent, so I deserve to see yours."

"And so you shall." He swallowed his wine and added, "I just need two more of these," pointing to his glass.

We returned to his apartment after he believed he had the adequate "juice" in his system to get his "boogie on." I had not been back to his apartment since we began preparing for the preliminary hearing. I noticed instantly that all the photographs had been taken down from his wall.

"I got my CD player fixed," he announced, as he searched the titles of his extensive collection and popped a disc into the player. I settled onto the couch for the show. Michael Jackson's "Thriller" began to play, and Owen took position.

It was at that moment that I knew I loved him. I could not stop smiling as he entertained me for the duration of the song. To my surprise, he was quite good. Panting, he collapsed onto the couch. He pulled off his sweater, and in the process, his undershirt rose up, revealing his taut stomach. He threw the sweater behind the couch and pulled his T-shirt back down.

"That performance stays in this room," he said. His head rolled against mine, and without a thought, I grabbed his face and kissed him with fervor. He kissed back, and we found our way into the bedroom.

"I take it that you found my performance satisfactory?" he asked. I replied by crawling on top of him. Afterward I curled myself around him, thinking how excited Carlita would be to hear of my recent conquest.

"Paige?" he whispered softly.

"Yes?" I answered in the darkness.

"I'm not going to be a lump of coal."

"I know," I replied, and we both fell asleep.

Chapter 32

The rest of the weekend was more than merry. It was December 21, and I had been filled with the Christmas spirit—as well as with Owen Holden. Dad had left each of us a small inheritance that supplemented the reduced salary I was receiving during my leave of absence. It also provided me with Christmas cash, which I exhausted with ease. I prided myself on being a fabulous gift giver. Much time was spent thinking and searching for the perfect gift. Normally my shopping would have been complete before the Christmas season began, but my father's passing and the trial had prevented me from my normal routine.

I thought back to the previous Christmas. Ken had given me bath soaps and a scarf. I later found out that his assistant had bought them, which explained why the scarf was a duplicate of one I already owned.

I spent most of Saturday and Sunday playing Christmas catch-up. I contracted a carpenter to build a guinea pig mansion for Vicki's recently adopted guinea pigs. Wally was receiving what he had requested: a donation to the Peace Corps. And for Mags, I found a jewelry maker at Pentagon City Mall who was molding my father's wedding band into a heart, so it could be worn on a chain. I swung by the mall to pick it up.

Streamers of white lights dangled from the ceilings, and oversized, glitter-encrusted icicles clung to the pillars that separated each section. Santa's Toy Shop encircled the entire quad on the main floor. A line of parents with their children in tow waited for a picture-perfect moment on Santa's lap. I slowed to watch the excitement and commercial splendor of the Christmas season. Shoppers raced past me, struggling to carry the many bags in their grasp. "Walking in a Winter Wonderland" rang out over the loudspeaker, and a voice squeaked behind me, "Merry Christmas." I turned to find a life-size gingerbread man holding a basket of candy canes. He handed one to me. Attached to it was a small tag that read, "Presence for Christmas Campaign: Make the holiday a little brighter for a local child by sponsoring a Hansel or Gretel this year. See the Gingerbread House outside of Santa's Toy Shop."

I walked over to the gingerbread house covered with multicolored gumdrop-shaped slips of paper. I chose one from the roof and opened it. "Sharon, seven years old. Needs winter coat, size 6. (Toy optional.)" Finding a coat was easier than I had thought. Macy's had an entire rack on sale. I selected a fuchsia-colored peacoat with flower-shaped button covers and a detachable hood. Although the toy was optional, I could not bear the thought of a child waking up on Christmas morning without a single toy.

KB Toys was one floor down. I was not prepared for the chaos. The entrance was guarded by an electronic barking dog and a pig that spun in circles. A pair of children, sans parents, raced up and down, spilling toys over into the aisles. A very frustrated teenage boy followed closely behind them, restocking the shelves.

"Excuse me," I said to him. "I need a toy for an seven-year-old girl."

"Aisle 3," he answered curtly and returned to cleaning up after the little monsters.

As I turned the corner from Aisle 4, I was almost blinded by the amount of pink that seemed to glow from the shelves of Aisle 3.

Beauty boxes, dress-up clothes, paintable ceramics, and make-your-own jewelry kits lined the first section. The second portion of the aisle was dedicated to the one and only Barbie. She had not changed much, although there were multiple new versions, and her clothing selection had almost doubled. She was more popular than ever, judging from the significant increase in Barbie-related paraphernalia. An entire wall was devoted to Barbie notebooks, jewelry, hair accessories, nail polish, and even glue. I made a note to remember to buy stock in Mattel.

I found Skipper on the bottom shelf. There was only one version of her. Skipper had changed slightly. She had finally been designed with an open-mouthed smile that made her look happy instead of expressionless, like the Skipper of my youth.

I contemplated buying Sharon the Millennium Edition of Barbie. She was dressed in a silver, chiffon gown with a white, faux fur wrap, and her small feet were punctuated by metallic, strappy sandals. I grabbed the box and examined its contents. *This is what I would have selected when I was seven*, I thought. I stepped back from the shelf and glanced at all the selections to ensure I had not missed anything.

"You know, she was modeled after a prostitute," whispered a woman about my mother's age, who was pushing a cart full of stuffed animals and jigsaw puzzles.

"I'm sorry?" I responded, seeking some clarification from the stranger.

"It's true. She was based on a prostitute from a German comic strip, named Lili. Way back when, she was sold in adult stores only. That's why I refuse to buy one for my granddaughter. Hardly a role model."

I nodded politely, assuming that this fierce opposition to Barbie was a generational thing. After all, the woman's sentiments mirrored those of my mother. However, her comment did pique my interest. At the last minute, I decided to purchase a jewelry-making kit and a Nancy Drew mystery novel. The information desk at the mall offered free holiday gift wrap and decorated my package in blue and white, snowflake-dotted paper. I placed my gifts in the gingerbread house as instructed and headed home.

Thirty minutes later, I was online in an attempt to either qualify or disprove the information I had been given on the genesis of Barbie. To my shock, it was reported to be true. Barbie was in fact created by Jack Ryan, an inventor and consultant for Mattel. In 1958, Mattel bought the rights to the German Lili and used her as the basis for the Barbie doll.

During my search, I also discovered some staggering facts about Barbie's anatomical structure. A student at MIT had conducted a statistical analysis of Barbie's measurements. According to his study, if Barbie were a real woman, she would stand seven foot two inches tall. Although technically, the student reported, she would not be able to stand upright and would be forced to walk on all fours. Her top-heavy proportions of 40-22-36 would result in an inability to balance herself on her long legs and tiptoes. He further stated that her narrow body would only have room for half a liver and a few inches of intestines instead of the usual two feet. This would condemn her to a life of chronic diarrhea and eventual death from an inability to absorb nutrients.

I grimaced at this fate and was pleased that I had not contributed to a young girl's unrealistic concept of the perfect woman. Was I slowly becoming my mother? Regardless, the image of Barbie crawling on her hands and knees while continuously popping Pepto Bismol tablets only enhanced my Christmas cheer.

The family had decided that we would host Christmas in D.C. We felt the need to do something different, so my father's absence wouldn't feel like a void.

"New traditions," Vicki had suggested. "We will begin new traditions."

Christmas was four days away, and that New Year's Eve was soon to follow did not escape me. On Sunday night, I called Owen to ask him if he wanted to attend Carlita's annual New Year's bash with me.

"I would love to, but I already have plans that night, back in Dallas."

I was disappointed but did my best to appear unfazed. "No problem. No biggie."

"I had a great time on Monday," he offered, and I wondered if his sudden sweetness was in response to my poorly disguised disappointment.

"Me too."

"I'll be at the courthouse by eight tomorrow. Meet you in the coffee shop?"

"I'll be there," I replied.

The trial reconvened at 8 AM sharp. Klavic's testimony was flawless. He recalled the scene better than I had. His story of why he was in the women's bathroom garnered sympathy, and his testimony was credible. He also shared how I had helped him find a new home. And Owen's closing remarks, while brief, were compelling—and not only to the jury. He was silver-tongued throughout. The Golden Boy was back.

"Why would an attractive, intelligent, and charming thirty-year-old woman sexually harass Moman Ishmahed? The answer is clear: She wouldn't. She didn't. An eyewitness has testified that no crime was committed. This case is the result of two misguided motivations. Paige Sheehan was motivated to approach Moman that day by need and by trust. Her intent was innocent and pure. These charges were solely motivated by greed. His intent is self-promotion and monetary gain. What motivation do you choose to reward this day? What is your intent? If it's justice, then you will find my client not guilty. Thank you."

The jury only took one hour to deliberate—and, as expected, the verdict was "Not Guilty." Afterward, Perry apologized and directed me to enjoy the Christmas holidays and New Year. "I'll see you on January 2."

"Can you send me a Post-it on that?" I asked jokingly.

"Absolutely," he replied.

Before leaving the courthouse, I stopped in the ladies' room. Blair was washing her hands when she saw me.

"Oh, hi!" she said nervously, backing up defensively.

I had envisioned a moment such as this, an opportunity to speak my mind and tell Blair what I thought of her. I would assume the role of lobbyist, representing all women who had been affected by her disregard. When it played out in my mind, I would say truthful but hurtful things. I would devastate her with my vicious diatribe. This fantasy battle would culminate with Blair sobbing and begging forgiveness.

I approached her and prepared to deliver the first line of my monologue. Her eyes widened with fear. As I opened my mouth, I saw a black smudge on the collar of her crisp white shirt, and on her pants leg, on her face, and all over the sink behind her.

"Please," she pleaded.

I responded with, "What is that?" which was not part of the brilliant attack I had planned.

"Please," she shrieked again. "It's all over me! It's in my hair, on my clothes … and I can't get it off." She was crying now, rubbing frantically at her collar with a wet paper towel.

"What is it?" I inquired again.

She whimpered pathetically, showing me her hands, which were covered with the black, chalky substance.

"It's from Owen," she wailed. "I had just put Chanel moisturizer on my hands when Owen threw me his good luck rock. He said that I could use some luck … and it's like, leaking!" She choked back tears. Fragments of paper towel dotted her blouse and pants.

All the anger and envy I had carried suddenly receded. It was replaced with a surge of emotion that left me speechless. Owen had had given her the coal, knowing it would rub off all over her. I turned on my heels and left Blair alone with her dark devastation.

Chapter 33

Owen decided to take fly out that night instead of the following morning to avoid the rush of holiday travelers. I offered to take him to the airport, and he accepted. I sat waiting for him to finish packing and carefully asked him about the photographs.

"Why'd you take all the photographs down?"

He came out of his bedroom with a handful of ties and stood in front of the couch, where I sat again leafing through his Frank Lloyd Wright coffee-table book.

"My contract came through with MAX," he said gingerly.

"Oh, my God. When?"

"Last week, but I didn't get the formal paperwork until today. And didn't accept until this afternoon. I already started doing some packing ... just some pictures and books."

"Oh."

"The show will be taped in LA. They want me to move out there right after the holidays. The first show is going to be a review of the past twenty years of Super Bowls leading up to this year's game. Pretty cool stuff."

"Uh-huh." I was stunned. I feigned interest while I internally managed my shock. "Who's playing this year?"

"Don't know yet. Philly looks like a strong contender. They're playing the Cowboys in a week or so. MAX may want me to begin shooting some footage there. Talk about some crazy fans. Philly games are extreme."

"Wow. Congratulations. That's great." I closed the book, returning it to its place on the table, and mustered a weak smile.

He pursed his lips and tossed the ties on the arm of the sofa, moving his hand on top of mine. "You don't seem happy."

"I am. Why wouldn't I be? It's wonderful." I was crumbling inside.

He tossed his toiletry bag onto the stack of travel gear accumulating near the front door. "I wouldn't have accepted the job if it weren't for you. You got me over my mental hurdle." He kissed my forehead and returned to his bedroom to finish packing. I casually strolled around his apartment. One of his bags was already packed and sat at the entrance of his foyer. I took advantage of his being in another room—I ran to my tote bag and took out a colorfully wrapped gift. I tiptoed to his suitcase and unzipped it, coughing loudly to disguise the sound, and placed the gift under a stack of clothes.

"You want some water?" he yelled. "There's some bottles in the fridge."

"No, I'm fine." I zipped the bag closed not a moment before he reappeared, carrying a garment bag over his shoulder. He grabbed his wallet and asked, "Shall we?"

I turned on the engine of the Fox to warm it as Owen loaded the bags in the trunk of my car. I felt nauseated.

"Shit, I forgot something. I'll be right back." He threw his wallet and some other stuff onto the passenger-side seat. I was swimming in my own despair when I was jolted by a high-pitched version of "Camptown Races" emanating from Owen's little, silver phone. Highlighted by a blue neon light was "Marcy calling …"

Just as it stopped ringing, Owen came jogging out from the entrance of his apartment building. He jumped in, fastened his seat belt, and stuffed the phone and his wallet into his backpack. "Sorry about that. I always forget something at the last minute."

The heater was blowing full blast, and I adjusted its intensity so that he would hear me when I spoke.

"You missed a call," I began. "It was Marcy." The tone of my voice said it all.

"Paige, it's not what you think."

His words were the exact copy of what Ken had uttered months before. Owen glanced at his watch. "My plane leaves in less than an hour, and I really don't want to get into this now."

"So, you're still seeing her?"

"No, I'm not seeing her but it's not something I want to get into right now when we're rushing to get to the airport." He was irritated.

"Fine," I said, putting the car in gear. "I don't really care."

We did not speak until we were five minutes from the airport.

"What are you flying?" I asked curtly.

"Delta," he replied.

"Why did you say all those wonderful things about me? I'm not like the other girls you've dated. I'm not plastic. Things don't bounce off of me."

"Again with the Barbie versus Skipper stuff."

"It's true," I responded.

"You're not eight years old anymore, Paige. Practice what you preach. Everyone's life is not better than yours."

I navigated through the normal parade of police cars that sat outside Reagan National. Since the terrorist attacks, the process for dropping off or picking up passengers was closely monitored. Loitering was not allowed, and if your "good-bye" or "hello" lasted longer than five seconds, you would hear two quick, guttural, synthesized honks to notify you that you had extended your stay. It was entertaining to watch the veterans of this process. They catapulted out of cars, and their loved ones wasted not a moment before pulling away. I popped the trunk, and Owen pushed open his door and wrestled his luggage out of the trunk, slamming its door closed. I was about to get out to apologize for my behavior when a police car buzzed behind me. An amplified voice called out, "Do not occupy the middle lane. Vehicles must pull over to the far-right lane. Right lane only." I moved the Fox as directed and hopped out, expecting Owen to be waiting for me at the curb. He was nowhere in sight.

Chapter 34

I picked up Mags at the airport the next day, Christmas Eve, making sure to pull over to the far-right lane. Vicki was busy running a Santa Claws Guinea Pig Adoption Day at a downtown pet store, so Mags and I headed out to get a tree. I didn't think we needed a tree, but when I had informed Vicki that I hadn't gotten one yet, she freaked.

"Of course we need a tree!" she yelled. "It's Christmas, Paige. How could you not get a tree? Christ!" Mags and I scoured the stands, but all the trees were sold out.

"Do you want a boxwood? I have some boxwoods," the man at Brock's Hardware store offered.

"Is that a tree?" I asked.

"It's more like a shrub, but people put lights on them in front of their houses, and some of them are shaped like trees."

"Oh, we need a real tree," Mags said, opening up her purse. "What if I throw in an extra $10?"

"Ma'am, we just don't have any. You could try Frank's Nursery in Gaithersburg."

"Too far," I said. "Let's see the boxwoods."

The man led us to an area shielded by a bright red tarp.

"Damn," he cried. "Darryl must have sold a bunch of them today." I looked around, and only two plants remained, held in large terra-cotta containers.

"Maybe we should go to Gaithersburg," Mags said, folding the $10 bill back into her pocket.

"It's supposed to start snowing, and I don't want to get stuck out there." I looked to the man and pulled a $20 from my wallet.

"We'll take that one. The rounder of the two."

"That one there is $100," he replied, "but I'll give it to you for $75."

The boxwood was far pricier than I had expected, but we had no choice. Seventy-five dollars later, we were back on the road with the boxwood teetering on the backseat. On the drive home, Mags and I sang renditions of holiday songs, substituting the word "bush" for "tree." *O Christmas Bush, O Christmas Bush. How lovely is your bushiness.*

December 25 was being celebrated at my condo because international calls, which required dialing a 1, could not be made from Vicki's phone. Wally promised to be at the camp office in Africa at 5 AM the next morning to receive our Christmas Day call. Mags and I picked up some vegetarian-friendly meals from Sutton Place and placed one string of lights on the boxwood. Vicki arrived beaming—she had managed to place seven of the eleven guinea pigs available for adoption. "Even Chessie got adopted, and he only has one eye."

Mags never had shown interest in my sister's passion and feigned happiness by saying, "Poor little ferrets."

"They're not ferrets, Mom. They're guinea pigs."

"Oh, I'm sorry. It's so easy to get them confused."

"How can you confuse them? They're nothing like each other." Vicki glared.

"All right, all right," I interrupted. "It's Christmas Eve. I think it would be nice if we postpone the arguing until at least the twenty-sixth." This seemed to silence them. I opened a bottle of wine while Vicki used my computer to print out some materials for our new tradition. It was certain to be a difficult evening, since we were without my father's annual performance. Every Christmas Eve, Dad would direct us to gather around the tree, at which point he read the last section of *A Christmas Carol*. It was, he believed, the premiere ghost story, having not only one but three spirits. He had even done his thesis on the symbolism of the ghosts, traveling to London so he could review notes from Dickens' diary at the British Library. After the reading, Vicki would top the tree with an angel, and we would all retreat to bed. It had been the same routine for as long as I could remember.

Vicki appeared with wine in one hand and several pieces of paper in the other. I opened the containers from Sutton Place and placed them on the coffee table.

"Where do you want us?" I asked.

"Where's the tree?" Vicki answered.

I pointed to the boxwood on the floor.

"That's a bush," she said.

"It's a Christmas bush," Mags clarified as she moved into position on the couch.

Vicki stood staring at the bush, and I waited for a tirade. She had been so specific, insisting that we get a Douglas fir. Instead she shrugged and sat on the floor, shuffling papers into piles and handing a set to each of us.

"Each of you has a part to read, and I've highlighted your parts. Mags, you're pink. Paige, you read yellow and I read green." She opened up a CD and placed it into my boom box.

"The only Christmas CD I have is Neil Diamond."

"I think it's great the Jews sing about Christmas," Mags said. "Barbra Streisand put one out a few years ago, and it's fabulous."

Vicki adjusted the volume on my CD player so that it provided just enough background music for the reading.

"What is this?" Mags asked, reviewing her part.

"*The Gift of the Magi.* Don't read ahead."

Vicki took her glass and raised it. "To Daddy." We joined her and drank up. And Vicki began as Neil Diamond accompanied her, "One dollar and eighty-seven cents. That was all …"

One bottle of wine later, we had finished the reading, and Vicki asked Mags to fetch the old angel she had brought from the stash of Christmas decorations back home. She handed it to me; I balanced it atop the bush, and we all admired it.

Christmas Day began with a call to Wally. The connection was beyond poor and made it next to impossible to hear him. Because of a delay in the sound over the phone line, we seemed to be talking at the same time. The conversation bordered on the ridiculous.

"Merry Christmas. Did you get my presents?" Wally shouted.

"How are you?" we shouted, crowded around the speaker phone in my tiny office. "We miss you."

"Can you hear me?"

"They're under the tree. Can't wait to open them. Did you get our donations?" I asked.

"I miss you guys too. Wish I were there to eat some of Mom's famous mashed potatoes from a box."

"Yes, we can hear you, what are you doing for Christmas Day?" Mags asked as he answered, "The mail isn't here yet."

"We don't have a tree. We have a Christmas bush." I yelled.

"Is Paige wearing her beautiful orange outfit to Christmas Mass?" Wally chuckled.

"How often does the mail come? I sent my card over a month ago," Mags added.

"We're having a big dinner at camp headquarters. And I'm told we're even getting a turkey."

"I don't make them from a box," Mags replied.

"No, it's at the cleaners," I joked.

"What?" Vicki asked.

"What's a Christmas bush?"

"The orange one."

"It usually takes a month."

"Your bush is orange?"

The conversation was cut short when Wally explained that there was a line of volunteers waiting for calls from their families in the States and the UK. Mags and I went back to bed for a few hours, and Vicki went to her apartment to feed the pigs. She met us at St. Matthew's for the 10 AM Mass. I prayed for Wally, families in need, and Owen. I wasn't necessarily praying for him as in "give him strength" or "bless him with good health." Rather, I prayed for the want of him: "Please God, make him love me." It was selfish, but I felt entitled to a Christmas wish, and that was all I really wanted. We spent the rest of Christmas Day watching movies and alternating between eating and sleeping.

Mags was scheduled to fly back on the thirtieth. She had hooked up with a group of widows and divorcees, and they were hosting a New Year's Bash at a local restaurant. I was proud of Mags. Although I saw her tear up when we toasted Dad and knew that her heart was broken, she was creating a new life for herself. When I noted her attitude, she simply answered, "Well, the options are be sad or be happy, and I'm tired of being sad."

On the morning of her departure, I could not seem to locate the glass that held my contacts. I had lost my contact case a few weeks before, when I had forgotten it at The Farren Center. Yogi Mushtaq requested that those who wore contacts or glasses remove them during meditation. He believed that having anything artificial on your body interfered with the release of energy. After the class, I popped my contacts in and was gathering my stuff when I felt someone's hand upon my lower back. I turned to find the woman who often stood behind me in class sniffing me.

"I think I know you from a past life," she said, taking in my scent and moving her hand up my back. I basically ran, leaving my contact case and my insulated water bottle behind. I had since been keeping my contacts in a small shot glass with saline solution in my medicine cabinet. I left the bathroom and searched the bedroom, thinking I had perhaps taken it out that morning.

"Mags, have you seen a small shot glass?"

She was folding her clothes, carefully packing and repacking to accommodate Vicki's Christmas present, a foot massager.

"Um, I used it to take my asthma pills this morning. It's over there on the vanity."

"What?" The glass was empty.

"What did you do with the stuff that was in it?" I asked, fearing the worst.

"Well, there was just water in it. I drank it."

"*What*? You drank it? My contacts were in there!"

My mother stopped packing and placed her hand upon her stomach.

"I drank your contacts? Oh, my, what does that mean? Do you think I'll get sick?"

"That means that I have to wear my glasses!"

"I'm so sorry, Paige, but I always thought that you looked so adorable in glasses!"

Truth be told, Mags had not seen me in glasses since eighth grade, when I switched to contacts. I was practically legally blind and only parted with my contacts at night. When my prescription changed the last time, I refused to pay the $200 for the Ralph Lauren frames I wanted and instead opted for a discontinued frame on the 50% Off rack. I had inherited my mother's affinity for sales. The frames were made of thick, olive-colored plastic, and were too large for my face. I figured that since they would only be worn during the first ten minutes of each day, it did not matter what they looked like.

I called my optometrist, but the office recording stated that the offices would not reopen until January 2. I was left with no choice. Vicki had asked that I pick her up on the way to the airport, so we could see Mags off together.

"What's with the glasses? You look like Mrs. Weitzman."

"Mom drank my contacts."

"You did?" Vicki asked, alarmed.

Mags was on her cell phone, checking the status of her flight, and did not reply.

"Actually, I think you look more like Alan Ginsberg."

"Shut up."

Mags' departure was uneventful, and I returned home afterward to find my message light blinking. Owen had called.

"Hey, it's me. Sorry I didn't get a chance to call you yesterday ... it was hectic. Belated Merry Christmas. I discovered your little present last night. I love it. Listen, I apologize for snapping at you at the airport. Let's talk when I get back into town. I'll try you again tomorrow."

Chapter 35

Carlita's annual New Year's Eve party seemed in direct conflict with her personality. It was extremely formal and a bit high society. The first year I attended, I had just met her and was expecting loud hip-hop music, some chips and dip, and a lot of bumping and grinding on the dance floor. Instead she had a small string quartet, butlered hors d'oeuvres, and couples waltzing.

This year I arrived at 10 PM, immediately removed my Weitzmanesque glasses, and positioned myself in a corner. For three straight years, I had rung in the New Year at Carlita's house. Ken had accompanied me to her last two parties, and in thinking about him, I suddenly felt awkward and lonely. I didn't mind being alone, but I did mind the pity I could imagine in people's faces. My nearsightedness kept me from actually seeing the pity at Carlita's party, but I knew somewhere in the room, someone was looking at me and thinking, "That poor girl, all alone on New Year's Eve." Carlita was busy making the rounds, so I pretended to be enthralled by one of her coffee-table books, entitled *Mississippi Moose*. The large block letters of its title were all I could read. I leafed through it, feigning great interest.

"Peculiar reading for New Year's." I could vaguely make out a man standing in front of me, wearing dark clothing.

"Just browsing," I answered. "I love animals."

"Excuse me?" he asked.

"Animals. I'm a big animal lover, but I didn't realize that they were in Mississippi. I hear they can be pretty violent." The man did not reply right away, and any facial expression was wasted on me.

"I didn't think Carlita knew any bigots. Nice chatting with you," he said, in a rather severe tone. He walked away into an area where my visual ability was reduced to blobs of color. I held the book close to my face, and my jaw dropped when I reread the title:

The Mississippi Noose: How the Black Man was Freed.

Carlita eventually found her way to me. By this point in the night, I had almost eaten a handful of potpourri, and apparently word about the bigot in the corner had made its way around the room. No one had said a word to me.

"Come on in the kitchen with me, baby girl," she commanded. "I gotta make some coffee, or I won't make it 'til the countdown."

It had been months since I sat down with Carlita. She busily made coffee and prepared a tray of petit fours while I rattled on about my father, the trial, Ken, and Owen. A tall, dark man breezed into the kitchen and kissed Carlita on the neck.

"Need anything, baby?" he asked.

"You *know* what I need. You're looking so good tonight. At 12:01, I'm tossing these people out the door and dragging you into the bedroom." She cackled, and he kissed her again and apologized for interrupting.

"Who is that?" I asked.

"That is my man. Two solid months, baby girl. He's it. I know it. I knew it the first time we did it."

"How ... practical," I said.

Carlita poured me a cup of coffee and headed out the door to deliver the dessert tray. I grabbed some creamer from the container in the fridge and doctored my coffee. Carlita returned, along with a woman who searched frantically for something in the fridge.

"Carlita?" she asked. "Did you see my breast milk? I pumped some earlier tonight and put it in here."

I figured that was my cue to leave and said my good-byes to Carlita. She protested that midnight was only minutes away, but the thought of having no one to kiss when the clock struck twelve was too depressing. I was waiting for one of her waitstaff to grab my coat when my phone began to ring. I sifted through my purse but missed the call. I felt certain it was Owen. The butler hired for the evening finally arrived with my coat just as the bells and whistles were blowing. I scurried out the door, donned my glasses, and headed for my car. Once safely inside, I scrolled through my "missed calls" and dialed the number that had just called.

"Hello?" I asked.

A woman's voice cheerfully chirped into the phone, "Owen Holden's phone. Ha-ppy Hap-py New Year!"

"Who is this?" I asked.

"This is Marcy. Owen's in the bathroom. Who is this?"

I hung up.

Chapter 36

I hardly slept that night. I felt sick and angry and stupid. Had I once again been misled? The call to my cell phone had been placed at 12 AM. Owen had also called my home phone and left a message at 12:01 AM.

"Happy New Year. Wish you were here. Hope you had a good night. See you soon."

My morning was spent running errands, including a trip to the optometrist to pick up my new pair of contacts. Owen had mentioned that his plane was to get into D.C. that afternoon. I had rehearsed what I was going to say to him and believed I was prepared. At noon he called.

"Hey, how are you? I've missed you."

"Really?"

"How was your night?"

"It was fine. How was yours?"

"It was all right. There was a big Cowboys reunion at the Sheraton downtown, so I got to see a lot of guys I haven't seen in a while."

"Uh-huh."

"What's wrong?"

"Where are you?"

"I'm still in Dallas. There's been a change in plans. They don't want me to wait until the Super Bowl to start the program. They want me to begin filming at the game on Sunday in Philly, so I'm flying there tonight. MAX is hosting a big after party at some bar called Goliath's."

"Oh."

"I'm really sorry. I was really looking forward to seeing you. I've missed you."

"Really? I thought you had Marcy to keep you company."

"What are you talking about?"

"I called you last night, and she answered."

"It was a Cowboys reunion. All the cheerleaders were there, but nothing is going on between us."

"Which explains why she calls all the time."

"I went out with her twice. It was months ago, before I moved here. We're just friends now but she hasn't really let go. I've communicated that it's over to her as clearly as I can."

"And she's obviously getting the message."

"Paige, I really don't want to talk about this on the phone."

"Listen, Owen, I just can't be with you. I appreciate all you've done for me, but we're from two different worlds."

"What are you talking about?"

"I'm a Skipper ..." I began.

"Paige, listen to me. You're right. You are a Skipper, but your woe-is-me attitude wears a little thin, because I think you're lucky."

"Lucky? My life is one disaster after the next. How is that lucky?"

"You know when I got hurt as a player, I was thrilled. I never wanted to play professional football. I love the game, but playing it is a different story. I played because I was expected to play, and because it detracted attention from my speech problems. Somewhere along the way, I stopped being really true to what I wanted. I didn't get to choose my path, which is what I'm trying to do now. But you ... you've created your life. You've built it from scratch."

"But I was never extraordinary at anything, so there were no expectations. For Marcy, things just fell in her lap ... or cleavage."

I was sounding like a shrew—not a position of power for a woman. I checked myself and took a breath.

"Let me tell you about Marcy," Owen said. "All she knows about herself is that she's beautiful. She's a twenty-nine-year-old cheerleader. That's all she does. She didn't finish college, because she didn't think she needed to, because people told her that she could model. All expectations for her are based on what she looks like," he exclaimed.

"And she looks fabulous," I responded.

"You're missing my point. Her direction in life was chosen for her. She doesn't even know who she is, Paige. You think that's a better life?" He breathed excitedly into the phone.

"I think it's an easier one."

"When my stuttering came back, Marcy couldn't deal with it. She can't even help herself, so helping me was out of the question. Paige, you are ten times the woman she is. I see it. Why can't you?"

I paused, trying to digest Owen's analysis. What did he know, after all? All he knew was the Paige Sheehan of today. Where was he when I was the only ninth-grade girl at Fairville High with a bald spot? Where was he throughout my childhood of gender-bending misidentification? Where was he when Charlie McCarthy and I were wowing my parents' dinner guests? Probably at some pee-wee football camp, that was where. I had spent most of my entire life feeling that I had gotten the short end of the stick. It was as if my identity were being challenged. I became angry and, without thinking, mumbled, "It just wouldn't work, OK?"

And with that, I hung up and left my phone off the hook. I got away from my apartment so that I would not be tempted to put the phone back on the hook, only to find that he did not call back. I walked around the city. Most of the shops were closed, and there was a light dusting of snow on the ground. I headed to 14th Street, where the display of the state Christmas trees resided. Each state decorated a tree for the holidays. West Virginia's featured small, woodland animals carved out of coal. My favorite was California's, which displayed glass bulbs filled with colored sand and tiny papier-mâché scenes like a boat in a bottle.

I turned on my cell phone as I headed back and had only one message from Vicki. Later that night, I sat at my desk and had a staring contest with Skipper, who teetered on the edge of my desktop computer. She was my constant companion, and even though I knew she was mass manufactured at a plant in China, I detected a new sorrow in her eyes. I returned Vicki's call later that night and cried into the phone. "I think he's with Marcy."

"Did he say he was with Marcy?"

"No. He said that I was ten times the woman she is."

"Can you entertain that he might possibly be telling the truth? He seems like a good guy. I mean, he has come to your rescue again and again."

"I don't know. Damn. What did I do? I screwed up, didn't I?"

"You need to do something grand now. If I were you, I'd go to that game in Philly tomorrow and find him. Show your support for his first day on the job."

"I don't know. I don't know what to do."

"Yes, you do. You know. My clients give me that bullshit all the time about how they didn't know what was right and what was wrong. Bullshit."

The next morning I jumped in the Fox and headed to Philadelphia. The game was sold out, but I managed to find a ticket scalper who sold me a forty-yard-line seat for $200. I had to park what seemed like a mile from the stadium. When I arrived at the gate, a security officer removed my umbrella and the stadium cushion I had brought from my bag, claiming they could be used as weapons.

"Is that really necessary?" I asked.

"You're not allowed to enter the stadium with anything that could be used as a weapon," he said again.

"It's an umbrella."

"Well, I've worked security here for eight years, and once a guy was almost suffocated with one of those giant foam hands. This is a rough bunch of fans."

"Oh, my God," I replied. He offered me the choice of returning the items to my car, but when I looked at the long line behind me and thought of the long trek back to my car, I let them be confiscated. I was anxious to get inside. The seat was very close to the field. As soon as I sat down, I saw him in the distance. He was near the players' lineup and was being fitted for some sound equipment. He was dressed in a suit and looked absolutely dashing.

For the first half of the game, I watched nothing but Owen. He was down on the field, providing commentary and conducting interviews. I'll admit my attention was occasionally disrupted by the team of half naked men behind me, covered in green and white body paint. I had heard them order over six beers each during the first half, and they seemed to feel the need to shout at every call, every point, and every play made. In addition, every other sentence included the words, "Eagles fucking rock!"

At halftime, the announcer conducted a minicommercial for Owen's new show.

"Stay tuned in February for the premiere of *Touchdown: Behind the Ball*, hosted by the Golden Boy of football, Owen Holden."

The camera moved to Owen, and his handsome face appeared on the big screen, and thousands cheered. He waved graciously and behind me, the boys yelled, "Holden's a fucking pansy prick."

I turned around and gave my evil eye, certain that this would shut them up. When I turned back around, one of them yelled, "Holden likes it in the ass. Fucking homo."

Again I turned around, but this time I added, "Is that really necessary? You guys sound like third graders." I turned back around and searched for Owen. I finally spotted him talking to the one and only Marcy. My heart sank. The cheerleaders had just finished their halftime routine. He kept walking away from her, and she followed.

"Hey, bitch?" one of the fans called out to me, slurring his words.

I ignored his lovely greeting and continued to take in the body language between Marcy and Owen. Finally one of the media guys grabbed her by the elbow and led her away.

"Yo, bitch. You got a thing for Homoboy?" another called out, and they all laughed.

I turned around again and said, "Yes, I do. Jerkheads!"

A moment passed, and then suddenly I felt a surge of pain at the back of my head. Then darkness. Then warmth. Then ... I turned around, and the stands were empty. The crowd of fans, including the half-naked Eagles guys, had vanished. I felt myself falling backward. I extended my hands, reaching for someone, something, to hold onto. I saw all of these faces rushing past: Ken, Vicki, Carlita, Bobbi, the beautician, Neil, and even Mrs. Weitzman. Finally, right before I hit the ground, someone grabbed hold of me. I turned.

"Daddy?"

"Paigebug! How about that?"

"What are you doing here?"

"I came to get a ballpark frank," he said, matter-of-factly. "Have you seen a vendor?"

"No ... I mean, what are you doing *here*, as in 'alive'?"

"Oh, that," he said, setting me down on the bleachers. "You're dreaming. I'm still dead."

"Oh."

"Hot dogs were originally called dachshund sausages. That's how they got their name. For a while there, people really thought they were made from dog meat."

"Uh-huh. What happened?"

"One of the Philly fans hit you in the head with a D battery."

"Oh."

He smiled. "You'll have a headache when you wake up, and you'll probably need stitches. Take an aspirin when you go home."

"That's it?" I asked.

Even though it was only a dream, I was kind of hoping for something more from the ghost of my father than his quest for a hot dog.

"Don't you want me to, like, avenge your death or something?" I asked. "That's what Hamlet's father said!"

He paused. "Uh, OK." He looked at me and whispered, "Avenge against whom exactly?"

"I don't know! You're supposed to tell me. You're supposed to be all-knowing or ... or something!"

He smiled and put his hand on my head. "I'm just here to say hello and get a hot dog, kiddo. Sorry to disappoint you."

His hand felt warm and reassuring. It made me feel small, but not in a diminished way. I felt held.

"Remember what I taught you?" he said.

"What?" I asked anxiously.

He didn't respond.

"Dad? Daddy?"

I awoke in the back of an ambulance. "Daddy?" I called out again. A woman appeared from the front cab and leaned over me.

"Hey, how are you feeling?" she said gently.

"What happened?" I asked.

She adjusted something on my head and patted my hand. "Well, from the story we got from one of the witnesses, one of the deranged guys sitting behind you pelted you with a battery. Could have been a lot worse if they had nailed you in the temple."

"Am I OK?"

"Your eyes are dilated but your vitals seem good. We're taking you to Philly General so that one of the docs can check you out."

We arrived at the hospital shortly thereafter, and once again I was at the hospital for an atypical problem. The ER doctor interviewed one of the paramedics and asked me several mundane questions about the day, the month, my name, my address, and why I believed I was in the hospital. I apparently answered all the questions correctly. He checked my eyes and ears and released me, stating that I probably had a minor concussion.

I called Vicki. "I'm in a hospital in Philly."

"You're where? Why?"

"It's a long story. I got hit in the head, and I have a mild concussion, but I'm fine. I did get to see Owen from afar, but then this happened. I don't know ... it seems like the gods are trying to tell me something."

"Screw the gods. What do you want?"

"I don't know. I'm a good person, right? I have a lot to offer someone. I'm smart and funny. I like that I'm flawed."

"Are you sure you only have a mild concussion?"

I ignored her question and continued. "And for the first time, I thought that maybe I was going to grab the brass ring, get what I deserved ... Oh, God. I almost forgot. I saw Dad."

"Oh, Paige. Stop being so dramatic."

"I'm not being dramatic. I saw him."

"Really?" she asked mockingly. "And what did he say?"

"He wanted a ballpark frank," I told her. She laughed.

"That sounds about right," she said. "How'd he look?"

"Pretty good for being dead," I answered. "Better than he looked at the end."

"That's good to hear," she said.

"I thought he would give me some answers, you know? Tell me what to do. He put his hand on top of my head," I sighed and moaned.

"What?" she asked. "Paige, are you all right?"

"Yes. I'm fine. I'm just tired of waiting."

"Waiting for what?"

"To stop feeling this way. Like I'm always waiting for my turn. When is it going to be my turn?"

"Then, take your turn. Stop waiting. Remember what Dad always said. You gotta make your own luck. Turn coal into diamonds."

Chapter 37

I nabbed some extra gauze from the ER nurse and hailed a taxi to Goliath's bar. My cab driver said, "May I ask you something?"

"Sure," I answered.

"Are you ready for eternity?"

My stomach sank. His dark, brooding eyes looked at me in the rearview mirror, and for a split second, I was certain that he was some deranged, suicide-bomber type who was either going to blow us both up or simply drive straight into oncoming traffic, catapulting us both into eternity.

"Uh, what do you mean?"

"Do you have God in your life?"

"Yes, I have."

"That's good. Then, you're ready."

I jumped out of the cab and pushed my way into Goliath's. The bar was packed with very large men, who I assumed were players or former players. Pockets of beautiful women, lavishly dressed, anchored each corner of the bar. I spotted Owen's golden mop of hair and stopped. I watched him for a while. At that moment, I realized how well I knew him. I knew that at any moment, he would twist one of the long, shaggy strands of hair on his forehead and then rest his hand on his hip. I knew that he would rock back and forth on his toes, a move he made when he was deep in contemplation. I had watched him during the trial, learned each and every move, committing them to memory. He was talking to a group of conservative-looking men, who I assumed were with the network.

I was suddenly acutely aware I had no idea what to say or do next.

"You're making a big mistake!" hollered a distinctly familiar voice behind me. I turned to find Marcy in a heated discussion with a much younger version of herself.

"I have been a feature in the Cowboys Cheerleaders calendar for eight years! Eight years!" Marcy screamed defiantly, poking the woman squarely between her exploding breasts.

"It isn't my decision, Marcy," the woman replied. "And to be honest, Pete told me the airbrush was working overtime so you'd look as young as the rest of us."

Marcy's head shot back, as if a bullet had hit her. She swayed back and forth, dazed by this news—or the cocktail in her hand. As she regained her focus, her eyes found me.

"Paige? Paige Revere?" she said. "Is that you?"

"Yep, it's me," I answered.

"Look at you. You're like a real person." Marcy reached toward me, touching the bandage that encircled my head. "A person with a head injury," she added.

"You're extremely observant," I responded sarcastically. Marcy smiled, interpreting my comment as a compliment.

"Does Owen know you're here?" she asked, taking a swig of her drink.

"Owen told you about me?" I asked, shouting over the collection of voices that filled the bar.

"I thought he was joking, at first. Paige Sheehan. Blast from the past. And with my Owen?" Her blonde curls bounced as she cackled at the notion.

"He's not your Owen. He's mine," I proclaimed emphatically. "He's mine." I began to turn back toward the direction where Owen had been standing, but Marcy grabbed my arm, whipping me around.

"It's like this calendar thing. I will not be pushed out," she screamed to no one in particular. "I'm Marcy Roberts!" Her piercing voice had garnered some attention and realizing this, she added, "*the* Cowboy's senior cheerleader."

The bar patrons in the vicinity shook their heads at her pitiful display. Suddenly my head started to ache, and I felt flush and faint. I frantically searched for a wall or something to lean on. I grabbed at what I thought was a wall, and then my world went dark. I awoke about twenty seconds later, flat on the floor, with an enormous African American man crouched over me. For about five seconds, I tried to place him. Certainly I should know any man that I awoke to. Then he sat upright, allowing me to see past him to the circle of people surrounding me.

"Are you all right, girl?"

"What happened?"

"You grabbed my ass, that's what. And apparently it was so fine, you just couldn't take it. Made your head spin so fast you passed out from its fineness."

His teammates around him laughed. The team doctor suddenly appeared and grabbed my wrist. He was taking my blood pressure when I saw Owen's head pop up excitedly, like one of the whack-a-moles at a Chuck E. Cheese's.

"Paige!" he cried. He worked his way through the crowd and suddenly appeared by my side.

"What are you doing here? And what happened to your head?"

I was stunned and unable to speak. A tear slid sideways down my face, stinging the stitches above my temple.

The doctor asked everyone to stand back to make room for the paramedics. The crowd parted in two, making a clean aisle for the gurney. I was being wheeled past the crowd like I was on a parade float. I caught a glimpse of Marcy as we passed. I could hear Owen talking to the doctor behind me.

"Owen, where are you going?" she demanded.

"Marcy, not now," he yelled.

"But I need to talk to you."

"For the last time, there's nothing to talk about."

"Owen? Owen? Owen? *Owen*!" She sounded exasperated.

My stretcher rolled onto the street. The added noise of the city traffic muffled her flinty voice as the doors of the ambulance closed.

Chapter 38

Back at the emergency room, I was greeted yet again by the doctor who had assisted me earlier.

"Back again so soon?" he joked.

"I like it here," I replied sarcastically.

"I'm going to send you for a CAT scan. I should have done it before, and we are going to admit you for the night, just so we can keep an eye on you."

"My neck hurts," I said.

"Well, as I understand it, it could have been a lot worse. One of the wide receivers caught you just as you were about to hit the floor."

After my CAT scan, I was wheeled into a dark, quiet room. It had been too long since I had been quiet or had quiet. The big clock on the wall showed it was 3 AM. I stared at the clock and remembered the last night in the hospital room with my father. I whispered, "Where are you, Daddy?" and drifted to sleep. At 6 AM, a nurse woke me to take my blood pressure and administer some unmarked pills. I swallowed them without protest. I propped myself up and adjusted my hospital bed so that I was upright. There was something about lying down like that and having people tiptoeing around me that made me feel so much sicker than I actually was.

"I'm Alice," came a voice to my right. I had not even noticed that I had a roommate. Alice had a tattoo on her right arm of an eye with a dagger through it. She looked like an aging hippie. I noticed that her left foot was out from the covers, and she was wearing a toe ring.

"I'm Paige."

"I thought you were dying last night. I pushed the call bell to fetch the nurse three times," she informed me, turning on her side and grabbing her long, white hair into a ponytail.

"Why?"

"Because of the floaters over your bed."

"The floaters?" I asked.

She seemed to shrink inside herself and spoke very quickly, as if she were telling me the most secret of secrets.

"I woke up at about 3:15 last night. I pulled the curtains back, 'cause I had to pee, and I saw like this cloud of air floating over you. Looked misty. Scared the shit out of me. I peed right in my bed."

Obviously Alice was in for some psychiatric problems. "No, no, not dying. I just hit my head, that's all. They just wanted to watch me for a night."

"Well, I started to shiver, 'cause I was scared and cold on account of the pee, and then it told me that it was going to be all right."

"The mist was talking to you?" I asked skeptically.

"Well, not really. It was like telling me in my head, you know? Like telepalathic, or whatever it is."

"Telepathic," I offered.

"Yeah that's right. Telepalathic."

I nodded politely and pulled aside the nurse who had come to replace my water.

"What's she here for?" I whispered, nodding in the direction of Alice's bed.

"She has dementia, but that's not why she's here. She fell off a motorcycle and tore a ligament. By the way, there is a young man who has been in the lounge all night waiting for visiting hours to start."

"There is?" I was embarrassed by the extreme hopefulness displayed in my question.

"Visiting hours don't start for another two hours, but I'll see if I can make an exception."

"Can I have a washcloth?" I asked. The nurse smiled and promptly brought me a warm cloth and some mouthwash. I wiped my face and gargled, spitting into a Dixie cup that she took away.

"It's going to be a good time," Alice said.

"Excuse me?"

"That's what he told me. There are good times ahead. Good times ahead."

My mind tried to remember where I had heard those words before, when the door slowly opened, and Owen walked in with a large shoe box with a purple bow.

"Hey there," he said. His clothes were rumpled, and he had a weird line embossed on his forehead. I pointed to his face curiously.

"I believe this is from using my raincoat as a pillow. It's a pretty amazing imprint. You can even see the words, London Fog, from one of the buttons." He pointed to an area just below his mouth and hovered inches from my face so that I could see it. Having him so close made me ache. He placed a box upon the hospital tray table.

"Can I sit?" he asked.

I scooted over on the bed to make room for him.

"I look awful," I said, just wanting to state the obvious.

"You couldn't look awful."

"That's such a line. I look awful, and I'm OK with it."

Alice was still lying on her side, staring straight at our bed. Owen walked to the curtain and pulled it around us.

"Good times," Alice remarked again when she saw him. He sat back down.

"I'm really sorry," he began.

"No, let me talk first."

I turned into him, and he did the same as if we had just awakened on a beautiful Sunday morning.

"I'm a bit of a disaster. I'll be the first one to admit that … but I'm a fabulous disaster." I straightened myself in the bed and adjusted my hospital gown. "And you're right. I am ten times the girl Marcy is, and I think you'd be lucky to have me. I'm a real woman."

He held my gaze. "OK," he said in a noncommittal tone.

I continued, "I don't mean to put you on the spot, but I just have to know where your head is and what you think of me and where you see this going. And if we're just friends, then that's fine. It's great. Really." He stood and faced the window. "That's all I have to say," I added.

"I heard that you were hit in the head with a D battery. And that you got into an argument with one of the fans who called me a homo boy."

"Yes."

"And you got hit in the head for that?"

"Well, I called him a jerkhead."

Owen nodded. "That's what I heard. Nice. I appreciate you standing up for me, so I got you a thank-you gift." He handed me the box. "Open it."

"I don't want to."

"Why not?"

"Because I need a response to my rant. Were you not here during the last three minutes? Please, spare me. I'm in a hospital bed. I don't get you sometimes."

"Paige. Open it," he directed.

I pulled the purple bow, and it unraveled with ease, sliding off the shoebox. I lifted the cover and pulled some tissue paper to the side. There were two items, each individually wrapped. I unwrapped the first to reveal a bright, shiny Owen Holden bobblehead. It was the one I had given him for Christmas to replace the one I had broken. I looked at him, puzzled.

"But I got this for you," I said. He nudged me to continue, which I did, picking up the other item and carefully pulling the paper aside to reveal a 1979 Skipper doll, dressed in a crudely sewn hemp evening gown. I looked at him for an explanation.

"I sewed the dress myself. Turns out Skipper has never been married, but I think she could be one day. But not to a Ken. I think she's better suited for a Bobble."

He took the doll out of my hands and leaned her against the Owen Holden bobblehead sitting on my hospital tray table.

"When did you do this?"

"Last week. I was planning to give it to you as your belated Christmas gift when I came back to D.C. I want you to come to LA with me. I agree with everything you said, Paige. I love you."

I sat staring at the two dolls, side by side. The bobblehead seemed to nod with approval.

"They make a great-looking couple," I said tearfully.

Owen kissed me as Alice called out again, "Good times."

Chapter 39

It took me thirty years to accept that I did not possess a voluptuous body, perfectly coiffed hair, and a designer wardrobe. Frankly I regretted the time and energy I had spent desiring that glamorous life.

The Barbies of the world had little beyond money and what a good plastic surgeon could provide. Neither of these had any intrinsic value. It did appear, however, that Barbies glided through life just a little easier than those of us with mere 34Bs. But looks and material possessions are hardly adequate armor for the blows that life presents.

I, however, belonged to the Skippers of the world—survivors who dealt deftly with reality and find happiness without elaborate accessories and flawless skin. I did not live in a world of vinyl, which could tear and melt under duress. My flaws were blessings and had given me a thicker skin, an ability to cope with almost anything, and a strong sense of who I was and where I wanted to go.

Ironically I chose to be with Owen in LA—land of Barbies and Barbie wannabes—where there was more peroxide sold than milk, and where high heels took precedence over high IQs. Interestingly enough, I made this choice not just because of Owen, although he certainly played a large part in my decision. I moved to the City of Angels because I had finally gotten past my Barbie fixation, and was well aware that the time had come to put my toys away and get on with life.

978-0-595-36937-9
0-595-36937-5

Made in the USA